Prais

"Fast-pace... an enchanting tale. This book i... wonderful love story and a great mystery as well. . . . I couldn't put it down, an absolute must-read! Five stars." —*Affaire de Coeur*

"Ms. Hall weaves a great story of mystery, sabotage, but more than anything a wonderful story of love and how its power can bring gifts untold into each life. . . . Splendid! 4½ Bells!" —*Bell, Book & Candle*

"Sexual tension, a mysterious stalker and nonstop action. Four stars." —*Romantic Times*

Isle of Skye

Constance Hall

JOVE BOOKS, NEW YORK

This is a work of fiction. Names, characters, places, and incidents either
are the product of the author's imagination or are used fictitiously, and
any resemblance to actual persons, living or dead, business
establishments, events, or locales is entirely coincidental.

ISLE OF SKYE

A Jove Book / published by arrangement with
the author

PRINTING HISTORY
Jove edition / July 2002

Visit our website at
www.penguinputnam.com

ISBN: 0-515-13334-5

A JOVE BOOK®
Jove Books are published by The Berkley Publishing Group,
a division of Penguin Putnam Inc.,
375 Hudson Street, New York, New York 10014.
JOVE and the "J" design
are trademarks belonging to Penguin Putnam Inc.

PRINTED IN THE UNITED STATES OF AMERICA

10 9 8 7 6 5 4 3 2 1

To Camelot, friend, writer, and inspiration maker. May all your dreams come true. And to Pam Ahearn, my agent, who never fails me.

Prologue
1

Isle of Skye, 1790

Nightfall on the island brought with it heavy mists that rose from the sea and veiled eons of Celtic secrets, along with those of the present inhabitants as well. The sound of shoveling echoed from within a circle of towering stones. . . .

Shoop-thump. Shoop-thump.

Almost hidden by a thick gray fog, a dark figure stood thigh-deep in a partially dug grave. Muscles strained against a form-fitting black coat as the shovel was lifted again and again. Spadefuls of dirt spilled onto a mound of freshly dug earth in rapid succession.

Several feet away, a body wrapped in a faded brown blanket was also smothered by the grayish haze. Near the edge of the blanket a large bloodstain widened with each passing second.

A hound howled nearby; the dirge resounded from one stone to another. It was intensified by the unnatural acoustics within the circle until the sound boomed through the air.

The person digging started and dropped the shovel, and the handle struck the cadaver's thigh. A lifeless foot dropped and rustled an edge of the blanket.

Frowning at the corpse, the gravedigger snatched up the shovel with trembling hands, and . . .

Shoop-thump, shoop-thump, shoop-thump.

The shoveling grew to a frantic pace.

Yards away, hidden behind one of the massive stones, a teenage boy stood, watching through glazed, tear-filled eyes. His gaze remained transfixed on the shrouded body. He appeared not to notice the tremors shaking his body, the icy wind stirring the raven hair over his eyes, the blood on his hands.

Another howl filled the air.

The young boy flinched and stumbled back a few steps before he regained his balance. With trembling fingers, he pushed the hair out of his eyes, revealing a distinctive white streak at his temple. Then he glanced toward the circle, clamped his hand over his mouth, and ran silently back into the darkness.

chapter 1

Isle of Skye, June 1810

Regan Southworth skulked past a thicket filled with gorse and heather, aware that her father's reputation as well as his life depended upon what she might find in the next few moments.

The wind banged the satchel strung over her shoulder, thumping it against the unlit lantern swaying in her hand. Moonlight beamed through scudding clouds. She had to squint through the darkness to pick her way along the rocky cliff facing the sea.

Below her, the ruins of Dunscaith Castle jutted from a sill out into the bay. Waves thundered on the rocks of its primitive foundation, engulfing the muffled thud of her footsteps. She remembered the legend that a witch had built Dunscaith in a single night. It had been ruled by Sgathach, a champion warrior queen from the second century A.D., after whom the Isle of Skye was named.

On a night such as this one, Regan could almost envision Sgathach standing on this very bluff, sword in hand, her face painted in bright Celtic war colors, her braided hair adorned with a bronze helmet. A mantle of fur would have covered her shoulders. She would have gazed out over the island as untamed and unforgiving as the mistress who ruled it.

Voices drifted on the wind toward Regan. She held her breath and crept up the slope. When she reached the top, she saw two boys crouching near a wall. Hidden behind a rock, she watched them.

"You goin' first?"

"Nay, you."

"Whoever speets farther."

The boys rolled the saliva around in their mouths, made hacking noises in their throats, and finally spit.

"Mine's farthest. You go first."

"Ain't. You canna even see." The smaller boy pointed at the ground. "They're both even."

"I'm oldest and got a bigger fist, so you'll be goin' first." The bully shoved his friend and shook his fist.

Runt looked at the fist in his face, squared his shoulders, and summoned his courage. "A'right," he said. He rose as if his legs were frozen, then peered over the wall. "Maybe this ain't such a good idea."

Regan looked past him at the grounds of Castle Druid-hean. The imposing structure loomed against an overshadowed moon. Its original corner towers and flanking wall had been removed and a circular stone walkway had taken their place. The eerie white vapor that hovered near the fortress's foundation resembled a menacing grin. An overgrowth of rowans and hawthorns filled what had once been the moat; their gnarled boughs lurched outward at the darkness and mist. Several candles flickered in the upper windows, like cat eyes staring out over the darkness.

"Look at that. It's alive."

"You're scared tae go over," Bully said.

"Am not."

"Am."

"You go first."

Bully rose and followed Runt's line of sight. "You think 'tis true that poachers disappear when they go on the Mad MacGregor's land?"

"Heard Mad MacGregor stews them for dinner. That's a fact. Rory told me it."

"You canna be believin' nothin' he's sayin', " Bully said. "He'd lie tae St. Peter."

"He told me that servants dinna last there either. And that's 'Od's truth. My sister knows a lass from the north who worked there. She said the place was so haunted, the lass went blind and all her hair turned white from seein' one of them ghosts."

"More than likely Mad MacGregor looked at her while he was havin' one of his fits. I've heard that if you look the MacGregor straight in his eyes, the hexed white streak in his hair jumps into your scalp and you're as cursed as he is. You'll go as dafty as the MacGregor. That's a fact."

Runt sighed. "My da said the first MacGregor must have been an arrogant clootie tae ha'e built a castle over a haunted place—"

"Och! He was clever tae be doin' it. The MacGregor knew the McAskills and the MacDonalds would never try to take the castle—"

"Aye, but he win't so clever, was he? The ancient ones got him in the end with their curse. Got the whole lot o' the MacGregors."

"Aye," Bully said in awe and disbelief.

Regan frowned and recalled the myth she had found while researching Castle Druidhean. Lord MacGregor supposedly built Castle Druidhean on the Wood of Torkavaig, an ancient grove sacred to the Druids, where they had made sacrifices to their pagan gods. Rumor had it that the wood had been haunted by the spirits of Druid wizards, and for building on their sacred ground, the MacGregor chieftain and his heirs were cursed with madness. The mere thought of meeting the present Mad Lord MacGregor caused her breath to quicken and a tiny chill to run along her neck.

"I dinna feel like havin' a spell put on me just for a

rabbit or twa. I rather be takin' me chances with your fist.
Go ahead . . ." Runt raised his fists and thrust out his jaw.

Bully thought a moment, looked at the castle, then
glanced back at his companion. He was as afraid as his
friend, but he hid it well behind a persuasive bravado.
"'Taint worth a spat. What say you we go down tae the
dock and steal some fish aff the boats when they come in,
in the morn?"

"I'm for it," Runt said, dropping his fists and looking relieved.

They kept low, slithering past the wall until they reached
the path, and then ran down the hill. Regan watched their
forms melt into the night. Runt's words echoed in her mind:
*If you look the MacGregor straight in his eyes, the hexed
white streak in his hair jumps into your scalp and you're as
cursed as he is.*

Sea air gusted past her, stroking her cheeks like tiny icy
feathers. "Curses do not exist," she whispered, shivering.
She forced her legs into motion again.

She stepped out from behind the rock and crept along
the ridge for another two hundred feet. With her nerves on
edge, every unusual sound made her jump. Finally she
glimpsed the circle of stones. The chiseled megaliths resembled frozen sentinels as ancient and timeless as the
Celtic seashore they guarded.

As she stepped closer, each pillar seemed to come alive,
shifting in the shadows. She felt them watching her, warning her away from their sacred place.

Regan shrugged off the feeling, entered the circle, and
set down the lantern and satchel. Using the star Polaris, she
located the northernmost end of the circle and counted
westerly.

She paused at the tenth stone and noticed that the tail of
the constellation Leo just touched the top of the pillar. Her
jaw dropped open. For a moment she could only stare at the
stone in awe. After years of searching, she was about to
make a discovery that would stun the archeological world
and possibly prolong her father's life.

At the thought of her father, her excitement waned. She felt the region over her heart tighten and wished he were with her. They had both toiled for years to locate this one particular circle. He should be able to share in the discovery. . . .

Out of the corner of her eye, she saw something move. She froze.

Not forty feet from her, a man stood on the edge of the cliff, his back to her. He seemed unaware of Regan in the circle. A black coat of the finest cut covered his broad shoulders. The wind whipped his collar-length ebony hair around his neck and billowed the coat's long tails against the cane in his hand. He gazed out at the darkness that enveloped the sea. An almost tangible melancholic air wreathed him. Clothed all in black, his form eerily melted into the night.

Heedless of the two-hundred-foot drop to the jagged rocks below, he slid the toe of his boot to the edge. He leaned forward . . .

"Don't jump!" Regan screamed.

He turned to look at her, lost his foothold, and tumbled over the side.

"Dear God!" she cried as she ran to the cliff's edge.

chapter 2

Regan reached the spot where the man had fallen, but it took all her courage to lean over and gaze down. What if he'd hit the rocks below? Many years ago she'd seen a mason fall from a scaffold while he was repairing the stonework of Westminster Abbey. There had been so much blood everywhere.

Finally she looked down and saw the man hanging from the ledge by his fingertips.

She let herself breathe again.

"Are you going to be standing there staring at me all bloody night?" he growled, his Scottish brogue hardly apparent through his clenched teeth.

Regan flinched at the barbed tone in his voice. "I didn't intend to."

She knelt, gripped his wrists, braced her knees, and pulled. She felt the tendons of his wrist bunched against her fingers and realized that if he slipped, they would both plummet to their deaths.

"Careful," she whispered.

His weight was no longer a burden, and she knew he

was climbing up the cliff without her support. The front of his coat had fallen open. She watched the muscular ridges of his chest undulate beneath the white linen of his shirt. He was lean and sinewy, not an ounce of excess flesh on him.

He cleared the rocky edge and swung his feet up on solid ground.

Regan released her breath and his wrists. "Here, let me help you stand."

He waved her away, grimacing the moment he put weight on his right leg.

At his cold manner, Regan frowned. After all, she had saved his life. "Did you hurt your leg?" she asked, concerned.

He didn't answer her, only swept up his cane where it had fallen near the edge of the cliff and stretched to his full height.

The stranger towered over her, well over six feet tall. She craned her neck to gaze up at him. Shadows covered his face and accentuated the deep hollows beneath his acute cheekbones, his deep-set eyes, and the cleft in his chin. She sensed the ruthlessness emanating from him.

"I—I didn't mean to startle you." She spoke past the sudden dryness in her throat. "I thought you were going to jump."

"I wasn't." He shifted more weight onto his cane.

"But you stepped toward the edge . . ." Her words trailed off as Regan noticed the white streak in his hair, just above his right temple. She recalled what the boys had said about the curse and blurted, "You must be—"

"Mad MacGregor." He nodded slightly, and moonlight glinted in the blackest, most deadpan eyes she'd ever seen.

"I—I'm so s-sorry about all th-this," she stammered.

His eyes narrowed on her. "Trespassers are no' welcome on my land. What are you doing here?"

"I—I . . ." Regan felt the coiled strength in him ready to strike, and she slowly eased back.

One moment he was watching her, the next his arm snaked out.

Regan dipped and lunged.

His fingertips grazed the back of her head and knocked the comb from her hair. Long blond curls tumbled down her back.

He dove for her again.

Regan leaped to his right side, knowing he could not use his right hand while he clutched the cane. The calculated maneuver worked. She darted past him.

"I'll find you!"

His shouted warning grated against every nerve in her body. The frustrated rage in his bellow told her he would not be paying a social call—if he should happen to find her. She kept running until her side ached, her heart couldn't pump any faster, and her lungs could not possibly take in more air. Fate had been kind to her in allowing her to escape Mad MacGregor. Next time, she would not be so lucky.

L*achlan Nail Alden MacGregor, the tenth Laird of* Druidhean, saw the comb gleaming on the ground and scooped it up. He touched the carved elephant design.

The vision of the lass's blond curls bouncing down her back was permanently burned into his memory, as was the feel of her hair brushing his hand, so silken, so tempting to touch. His fingertips pulsated at the recollection.

He recalled her peering down at him from the top of the cliff. He could still feel the smoothness of her soft hands wrapping around his wrists, see her small breasts straining against the bodice of her black dress as she tried to help him. Her courage was admirable. With no thought to her own safety, she had reached down to help him. He'd never met a woman with such pluck.

He brought the comb up and breathed deeply of the lilac essence of her hair, a pleasant feminine fragrance, mesmerizing. It had been six months since he had smelled a woman's scent. *Far too long.*

With a rueful grin, he dropped the comb into his coat

pocket and turned to leave when he noticed a dark mound inside the circle. Leaning heavily upon his cane, he tramped toward the stones. Each step intensified the ache in his right leg. In his fall, he had wounded the same leg he had limped on most of his life. The lass would not have eluded him otherwise.

He entered the circle and headed for the satchel. Somehow the stones muted the din of the waves crashing on the cliff below him, yet heightened the steady thump of his cane until it echoed like the beat of a drum. He had forgotten the astonishing acoustics within the circle and the uneasy feeling that unnerved him whenever he entered its boundaries.

He picked up the satchel and discovered inside a small shovel and pickax. Since the lass was out so late, he had assumed she had been waiting for a lover. Lovers did not use digging tools, unless of course they planned to bury their secrets—or unearth them. He slapped the satchel's leather flap back in place and draped the sack's strap over his shoulder.

He had to find a way to keep her from returning. Instinct told him she would come back. Danger lurked in the circle. The same dark forces that swirled within it had also caused the MacGregor madness that ran in his veins. He frowned at the stones, then gripped his cane and headed toward the castle's stable, the satchel thumping heavily against his left leg.

Regan galloped her mule, *Vespertine*, along the southwest road. In the far northern sky, the Cuillin Hills loomed like the humps of a massive dragon. The Sound of Sleat was to her left. She could just see the horizon where water met sky. Miles away, the lighthouse on the Point of Sleat glowed with the faintness of a firefly.

The sky had given way to more clouds that completely blocked out the stars. Since coming to the island, Regan had grown accustomed to the unpredictable weather. In minutes squalls could blow in from the sea and batter the shores. She could smell the moisture thickening in the air, dampening her cheeks and hair.

The wind whipped her long curls against her back. She remembered Mad MacGregor's fingertips pulling the comb from her hair. A shudder tensed the muscles along her shoulders and back. She forced the memory away and another took its place.

It had been twelve years ago, but seemed like yesterday. She was back in her mother's room. The familiar smell of rosewater permeated the air. The fragrance followed Lady Candance Southworth wherever she went. Her scent lingered long after she'd left a room. To this day, Regan could not inhale the aroma of roses without feeling the pain of loss. This particular afternoon her mother had spent an hour brushing Regan's hair, then styled it like her own, a lady's coiffure. Her mother had smiled at her and said, "Lovely, Reggie. One day you'll be a beautiful young lady."

"You think so, Mama?" Regan was certain her mother was only saying that to be kind. Even at such a young age she knew she was no beauty.

Her mother had bent and kissed Regan's cheek. "Never doubt it. And I'm giving you this comb so that whenever you wear it, you will remember that you are my daughter and a diamond of the first water."

"I shan't forget, Mama."

After Regan had left the room, she had smelled the rose scent on her hair from her mother's hands. It had lingered on the comb, too, but not long enough. Her mother had died a month later.

When Regan wore the comb, she never fantasized about being beautiful. All her childhood illusions had died with her mother. But the comb was one of her most precious links to her mother. She could not lose the keepsake. Sometime in the not too distant future, when she had steeled her courage, Regan would go back and look for it.

Thoughts of going back to Castle Druidhean caused Lord MacGregor's menacing countenance to form in her mind. Again she sensed that bizarre aura of darkness that radiated from him and shivered. His last words tolled in her memory: *I'll find you.* The words had meant so much more than just *I'll find you. I'll punish you. I'll destroy you.*

The sound of hooves pounded the road behind her. Blood drained from her face. Her breath froze in her chest. Lord MacGregor had found her.

chapter 3

Regan *wheeled around and recognized her neighbor* and landlord. The gentleman sat astride his black gelding, the wind whipping his burnished gold hair back from his face. He was close to forty but looked much younger than his age and was strikingly attractive. His stomach was flat, his shoulders square and broad. And his kind smile was a welcome sight.

She began to breathe again. "Mr. McAskill, you scared the vinegar out of me." She nudged Vespertine into a trot.

McAskill followed. "Saw you ridin' up," he said in a thick brogue. "Wondered if somethin' was wrong with your da."

Since they had moved to the island, Mr. McAskill had been nothing but kindness. He always called on her father and asked after his health. He was one of the few residents on the island who had made them feel welcome. "Not at all," Regan said. "I was out for a ride, sir."

"Alone? At midnight?"

"I couldn't sleep."

"Same with me. Perhaps the same wee fairy kept us both

awake just so I could have the pleasure of seein' you," he said, with a charming smile. "And I think we're knowin' each other well enough to be dispensing with the 'sir.' Call me Eth."

"Very well"—Regan hesitated over his Christian name—"Eth." It felt a little too intimate to address a gentleman she'd known only a month by his first name. She decided to veer away from any personal discussion so she asked, "Are you acquainted with Lord MacGregor?"

He wrinkled his brow at her. "What has brought on the interest?"

"I rode out past Castle Druidhean the other day." Regan kept her voice untouched by the whisker she was telling.

"Stay well away from there." His frown deepened. "'Tis dangerous."

Regan remembered MacGregor reaching for her, felt his hand brush her arm again. Goose bumps broke out on her skin. "Your warning sounds ominous, sir," she said, unable to keep her voice even.

"Just stay away from Mad MacGregor." He grew silent, his expression pensive.

Regan sensed the tension in Mr. McAskill. Had she known him better, she would have pressed the subject. Instead she remained silent, feeling the first sticky drops of drizzle on her hands and face. Any moment it would rain. She kicked Vespertine into a canter.

He stayed beside her, the same remote expression on his face.

When they reached the drive of Finn Cottage, Regan wasn't sure if Mr. McAskill would follow her, but the sound of his gelding's hooves blended with Vespertine's.

The drive wasn't long, but steep. Finn Cottage sat on a bluff that fronted the bay. Though it was built of stone, the square structure seemed bowed at the corners from the constant north wind. Her gaze shifted to the candlelight flicking against the windowpanes in her father's room. He was waiting up for her. What would she report to him?

"Tell me, how is your da's research goin'?"

"Very well, thank you."

"Is he through writin' that book about the Wicts and all?"

"That's Picts," Regan corrected him. The lie slipped too easily from her lips. She didn't like lying, but she had to hide the truth about her father's work from everyone, including Mr. McAskill. He, like the rest of her neighbors, believed Regan's father had moved into the area to research the Picts, an early Celtic tribe who had settled Scotland in 300 B.C. She could not divulge the real reason they had moved here.

"I can trace my blood all the way back to the first tribe of McAskill who descended from them." His eyes sparkled with pride as he said, "Great warriors all."

"I'm sure."

His ego sufficiently stroked, his sullen mask disappeared and his usually jovial grin dawned. "I've even found several burial urns from nearby cairns." His smile widened. "I can show you them and the burial mounds. They're just along the coast. We could explore them together on the morrow. Would you like that?"

"Most definitely." When they reached the barn, Regan said, "I would invite you in, but it's late."

"I know, but lemme put your mount away for you." He dismounted and leveled a disparaging glance at the mule. "What makes you ride such a four-legged beast?"

Regan patted Vespertine's head, then let her fingers glide along the raised scars that crisscrossed her neck. "I'd never give her up, sir. Vespertine and I are devoted. You see, I rescued her outside of Edinburgh from a cruel farmer who beat her. He sold her for hardly what she was worth. I got the better end of the bargain. She's surefooted, loyal, and smart. I'll never go back to riding a horse."

He frowned at her, at Vespertine, then reached up and grasped Regan's slender waist. "Here, let me help you dismount."

He was incredibly tall, with wide shoulders. His hands were large enough to encircle her waist. Regan realized that she had not worn a riding habit. Her petticoat peeked out beneath the hem of her dress a full three inches. However, like the perfect gentleman he was, he kept his gaze on her face and swept her off the saddle.

When her feet hit the ground, he did not step away, only gazed down at her. He remained silent for a moment, battling some inner emotion. Then he stared straight into her eyes and said, "You have tae be knowin' how I feel about you."

Regan's mouth fell open and her eyes widened in shock. After she gained some semblance of composure, she said, "You've always been very kind to us, but we hardly know each other—"

"I've been calling on your father every Sunday for a month. That's long enough tae be knowin' how I feel." His arms slid around her, then he kissed her.

She didn't pull away. His lips were warm and tasted of ale, not an altogether unpleasant sensation. Regan couldn't believe he had finally decided to marry and had settled upon her. She was not bonny, with all the freckles on her face. Her curly hair was the color of straw and behaved as such when she took the time to style it. Not to mention she was penniless. He was considered one of the most handsome and sought-after bachelors in the area. As yet, none of the local lasses had caught him.

When Mr. McAskill drew back, he said, "Forgive me. I should no' have done that, but you're so bonny."

Though his face was in shadow, Regan glimpsed the warmth in his eyes. "Perhaps we should just forget it happened," she said, still taken aback.

"I canna," he said, forlorn. "I'll be honest, you've stolen my heart."

"I—I—"

"Please listen tae me, love. I'm well off. I'll take care of you, and your family. You'll want for nothin'. I'll cherish you always."

"But this is so sudden."

"No' for me. I wanted you the moment I saw you. And

I'm knowin' your father has unpaid bills in the village; I can take care of 'em."

"My father's man of business is late with our monthly allowance," Regan lied. For the past two years they had lived off the kindness of her uncle. Uncle Inis owned a brewery. He also had five sons to support. The meager stipend he sent was not always enough to pay rent and other household expenses.

"You've no need tae explain," he said, his eyes beaming compassion.

Regan needed time to accept what had just happened, so she said, "I really should go inside."

"I'll call in the morn and we'll row out in my boat."

"Very well. Good night." Regan hurried toward the cottage, aware of Mr. McAskill's gaze on her.

She wondered at her apathy toward his advances. She hadn't felt the least spark at his kiss. Of course, she hadn't really known him long enough to feel affection for him. He was kind, and he seemed willing to overlook that she didn't have a feather to fly with or that she was as plain as Vespertine. Marriage wasn't an option she had ever considered. Although wedlock was a sacrifice she was willing to make, if it allowed her to care for her father and sister. She might not love Mr. McAskill now, but after they were engaged, when she knew him better, her apathy toward him would likely change. And she might look forward to his caresses and her wifely duties.

When she reached the front stoop, a drop of rain hit her forehead. Then another. She felt an eerie tingling as though someone's eyes were on her and paused. Her gaze shifted to the barn, where Mr. McAskill had just led Vespertine through the door. The strange sensation wasn't coming from that direction.

Instinctively she peered down the steep drive and spotted an oddly familiar dark figure on horseback, the white streak in his hair glistening in the dim light. Two dogs, so large they resembled ponies, sniffed the ground near his horse.

MacGregor looked up.

The impact of his heartless eyes hit her as though he were standing next to her. She couldn't breathe or move.

MacGregor raised his riding crop, and in a slow, calculated motion he saluted her. Something in the perverse gesture hinted that he had seen Mr. McAskill kiss her and what he thought of the whole affair.

The heat of humiliation seeped down into her arms and legs, galvanizing them into action. She fell against the door, fumbled with the door latch, and stumbled inside.

"Is that you, Regan?" Her father's voice drifted from his room.

She peeked down the hallway. Candlelight beamed through his open chamber door. "Yes, Papa."

"Need a word, my girl."

"Coming." She hurried down the hall, knowing that MacGregor would not be content with merely humiliating her. *I'll find you.* Oh, God! What next?

The wind howled down the chimneys of the cottage, sounding oddly like MacGregor's deep voice. Regan jumped and cringed against the wall. Thunder boomed. Windowpanes rattled. Rain thumped on the slate roof. She hugged her stomach and felt a wave of dread tighten every fiber in her body.

chapter 4

A *few moments later, Regan paused in front of the door* to her father's room, listening to the rain pelting Finn Cottage. She smoothed down her gown and tried to still her trembling hands before going inside.

The room was supposed to be used as a parlor, but when they had moved in a month ago, the sofa and chair had been pushed against one wall to make room for her father's artifacts and his bed. He could not walk up and down the steps. Regan felt uncomfortable at seeing his bed on the first floor; it was a reminder of his illness and that he, too, would one day leave her as her mother had.

Rows of catalogued pottery shards, bronze tools, and trays of small stones etched with ogham glyphs lined the shelves on the walls.

Emma, Regan's younger sister, sat curled in the chair near the corner, a horticulture book clutched in her hands. Her bare feet poked out beneath her pink muslin gown. The large, overstuffed chair dwarfed her diminutive frame, and she looked younger than her five and ten years.

Emma looked up at Regan, frowned as if to say, "What

has happened this time?" Then she cast an anxious glance toward their father.

Seamus Kendrick Southworth sat propped up in bed, the silent exchange between the sisters not escaping his notice. He stopped writing in a journal and laid quill, ink bottle, and book on the table beside the bed. For a moment he looked like the man he'd been before he had taken ill.

He studied Regan closely and said, "You look as pale as a condemned man watching a gallows being built. Are you all right?" He held out his hand toward her.

Regan watched the tremor in his arm and knew what effort the gesture cost him. At one time he had been a husky gentleman, a laugh always at the ready, a passion for discovery animating him. Now he was a mere shell of a man, the light stolen from his bright blue eyes.

"She doesn't look all right to me," Emma said, glowering at Regan.

"I'm perfectly fine." Regan sensed the hostility in Emma and wondered what had caused it.

Seamus scrutinized Regan, then said, "I agree with you, Emma."

Regan avoided his gaze and walked past the nightstand by the bed, watching her reflection distort in the many bottles of medication that littered the small table. When she reached her father's side, she gently clasped his hand. His clammy palm felt warm against her chilled skin. "You should be resting, not worrying over me," she said.

"How can I not be worried, my girl, when you're looking pale as whitewash?" With eyes dulled to a watery, clear blue much lighter than her own, he studied her.

"I'm fine."

"You're trembling."

"It's only the chill in the air." She heard the rain rapping on the glass and strode over to the window. Glancing outside, all she could see was her own frightened expression melting behind the dark, rain-spattered windowpanes. "You shouldn't sleep with your curtains open. You know the doctor said that cold drafts are not good for your heart."

The eerie sensation she had felt while holding MacGregor's hand hummed inside her. The same way she sensed the blood pumping through her veins, she sensed MacGregor was still nearby, still muttering under his breath, *I'll find you.* She snapped the burgundy brocade drapes closed.

"I guess I should have fastened the curtains," Emma said.

Regan glanced at her sister. "I wasn't accusing you of not closing them."

"You might as well have been." Emma stared down at the book and turned a page.

For a moment tension crackled in the air, punctuated by the tick of the mantel clock.

At that moment, Letta, a servant who had been Regan's mother's nanny, strolled into the room. After Regan's mother died, Letta had raised Emma and Regan and stayed with their father out of loyalty, since they lacked money to pay her.

Letta's stick-thin body seemed lost in the black muslin dress and the stained apron she was wearing. A cap held her gray hair on top of her head. Her gaze shifted between Regan and Emma as if she'd heard them arguing. Then she set down a cup of tea on the nightstand by the bed.

Seamus grimaced at his two daughters. He broke the silence. "Emma takes prodigious good care of me. Do you not, my love?" He didn't wait for her reply and said, "And who gives a high holy if the curtains are drawn? If I had listened to every castor-oil artist I've seen, my bowels would have played out long before my heart. Now leave off the lectures and tell me what happened tonight."

Before Regan could speak, Emma slapped the book closed, threw it aside, and leaped up. "Yes, enlighten us," she blurted, her words slurred by the rising emotion in her voice.

Regan noticed the unusual trembling in Emma's hands, the strain in her expression. She searched her sister's large brown eyes and asked, "What's wrong?"

"Nothing! What could be wrong?" Emma jammed her fists at her sides, then tears flooded her eyes.

"Something is the matter. How have I upset you?" Regan watched Emma smear the tears on her cheeks with her hand.

"If you must know, I'll tell you. I've been worried sick tonight. Do you know how many blessed nights I've sat up waiting for you and Papa to come home from an excavation, wondering if an accident killed you both? Now I have to sit up and wait for you to come home. Do you give a gnat's eyeball? No! That's all you and Papa think about, finding Avalon, traipsing about the countryside at all hours of the night. Suppose I went traipsing all over at all hours of the night? How would you feel, being left here to worry about me? Think about that."

Regan stepped toward Emma and said, "We—"

"Don't try to make it better—just don't." Emma shook her hands to warn Regan away. "You can't." Her gaze darted between Regan and Seamus as waves of tears streamed down her cheeks. "You two never stop to notice we have nothing. Look around us. Living in this drafty old cottage, hardly able to afford food."

"You've always been taken care of, my girl," Seamus said.

"Oh, yes, dragging me all over the place to these excavation sites—that's taking care of me properly." Emma stomped her foot. "I want a permanent home! I'm sick to death of moving every time I turn around! Sick to death of it all. . . ." Emma stormed out of the room, her footsteps thumping in the silence.

Regan took a step to run after her, but Letta raised her hand. "Better let me go, Miss Regan." Letta hurried out.

Regan stared at the empty doorway, then met her father's eyes; he looked as astonished as Regan felt. "Have we really been that selfish, Papa?" she asked.

"We have, my girl." Seamus's brows furrowed. "It never dawned on me that she might want a permanent home, and even . . ." His words trailed off.

"Marriage," Regan finished for him. She felt ashamed for worrying so much about her father's health and forgetting about Emma's needs. "Come to think of it, Emma was never happy when we moved so often. I had known for some time Emma didn't share our enthusiasm for your work, but I didn't know she resented it."

"She doesn't have the gypsy blood in her like you. You never were one to want to marry and set up housekeeping." Seamus fingered the edge of the sheets and said, "'Twas up to me to provide a dowry for her and a permanent home. I've failed on both counts. I've let this search for Avalon become an obsession—"

"Such a search is admirable. It is your dream. When we actually do find Avalon, Emma can have her dowry and a proper season in London if that's what she wants. When we find the proof that Arthuis is the real King Arthur, our whole world will change. You'll be famous, and all of those members of the Royal Society who scoffed at you will have to eat their words."

Her father had always believed that the King Arthur in Sir Thomas Malory's romances of the fifteenth century had been based on the exploits of a great warrior named Arthuis, who was born around A.D. 455 in what was now York. Unlike her father, most of his peers believed Riothamus, a contemporary of Arthuis's, was the actual King Arthur. This issue fueled an ongoing debate in the archeological world. If Seamus could locate Avalon, the legendary paradise to where King Arthur had been conveyed before his death and from where he had never returned, then they could find proof Arthuis was indeed the true King Arthur.

"Pride does not come cheaply." Seamus shook his head. "I've never told you this, but I had only a mere teaching salary when I married your mother. She could have married into her own class; instead she chose a penniless professor. I should have convinced her not to marry me, but I was too dashed selfish and too much in love with her to know any better. You don't look shocked, my girl."

"I'm not. I've known about this for years."

"How could you know? Your mother and I never discussed such things."

"I was six and ten when I found out. I had gone to meet you at the Royal Society. Several members leaving the building paused to put on their gloves, and I overheard them talking."

"I didn't want you to find out that way."

"It didn't matter." Regan shrugged, recalling their exact words: *Seamus Southworth is an upstart.*

Serves him right, Clarington disowning his daughter the way he did. Heard Lord and Lady Clarington didn't even attend their own daughter's funeral.

The Claringtons have probably never seen the brats.

"You must have learned more than you cared to." Sadness laced his voice.

"I did discover why you and Mama told me that Lord and Lady Clarington died the day you married."

"We didn't know what else to tell you about your noble grandparents—"

"How about the truth, that they are bigoted high sticklers, and I was better off without them?"

"That might have been the more honest response." Seamus glanced over at Regan, his expression anxious, as if he were waiting for her forgiveness.

"Never mind, Papa. I've not missed them. I had Mother, and I still have you." Regan didn't tell her father that he had become a hero in her eyes that day outside of the Royal Society.

A bittersweet smile spread across Seamus's face. "You remind me so much of your mother. She always supported me, always looked on the bright side of things. I took her for granted. . . ." He paused with a catch in his voice, then glanced toward the clock. "It has been eleven years, eight months, and three days since her death. Where did the years go? Seems as though I blinked and both you and Emma were no longer my babies, and I had spent everything on my own selfish pursuit. I should be ashamed of having to live off my brother's charity. If I were well enough, I could get a teaching position." He stared down at the sheet tangled in his fingers, the torment on his face aging him further.

Regan squeezed his hand, feeling his suffering and loss tenfold. She had never confided to anyone her guilt for her mother's death and her father's weak heart. "This is only a bad spell you're having," she said, forcing encouragement into her voice. "You shall get better, I know it. When we find Avalon, you'll be famous. You'll go on lecture tours. You'll finally have the recognition for all your hard work. You'll feel like your old self again."

"I don't see how that will ever happen. My coffers are depleted. Soon my creditors will be banging on the door. We shall have to retrench to Northhampton and live with Uncle Inis—"

"We'll find a way to stay here." Regan touched his shoulder and thought of her only option: marrying Mr. McAskill.

"You always sound so sure of yourself, lass. I wish I had your faith." He eased back against the pillows, sighed, and stared into her eyes. His regret melted into concern as he said, "Here I have been burdening you with my conscience, and you have not told me what happened tonight."

Later she would have to tell him about the narrow escape from Lord MacGregor, but she did not want to upset her father any more tonight. She forced a smile and said, "You'll be excited to hear that the tenth stone in the Druid circle lined up perfectly with Leo—just as the bard's song said."

Seamus slapped his hand over his chest. "By Jove! I never believed we'd deciphered the wording correctly." He reached over, grabbed the journal he'd been reading, and flipped to the last page. The book shook in his unsteady hands as he pointed to the song. "I wasn't sure about the tenth sister of the Lion. Wasn't sure at all," he said, his bottom lip quivering slightly.

Regan leaned forward and glanced at the poem.

Hark you searchers of mysteries
and gleaners of secrets
On Midsummer's Eve, the tenth
sister of the Lion
guards King Arthur's abode in
the spiny and untouchable circle of
Druidhean.

A year ago, Regan had been doing research in the library at Whitorn Priory and discovered buried in a trunk of burned books the song written about King Arthur. Most of the tomes had been badly singed in an abbey fire and thus forgotten. It was by sheer luck that she found the bard's song intact. It had been recorded by Benedict, a seventh-century Scottish monk.

She pointed to the word "lion" and said, "It had to be the constellation Leo and the tenth stone. What else could it have been?" She looked at her father, touched by the reverent delight in his face, a look that could only come from a lifetime of searching for a dream and finding it. "How many Druid circles in Scotland could there be where the tenth stone lines up with Leo in the summer sky precisely at midnight?"

"I had given up hope of ever finding the proper one. We have visited so many sites," he said, rubbing his thumb over the song in awe.

"I never doubted we would eventually locate it." Regan grinned at him.

"It's truly miraculous." For a moment her father's cheeks flushed red, his eyes glistened with wonder, and he looked young again.

She had not seen him so animated since before her mother had died. A wave of happiness warmed her heart. "It is, isn't it?" she said, her voice full of excitement. "Now all we need to do is dig and find the clues that will lead us to Avalon."

"We cannot excavate the site. If the rumors about Lord MacGregor's madness are to be believed, he'll certainly turn down a request to dig on his property. And that damned Sir Harry just left the island." Seamus huffed under his breath.

Sir Harry Lucas, a fellow archeologist, had been her father's rival for years. He, too, was searching for Avalon. He must have known something, or he wouldn't have poked about the island and called on her father, trying to pry information out of him. Her father hadn't disclosed anything, but Sir Harry had vowed to return within the month.

"We'll deal with Sir Harry and find a way to excavate the site, Papa." Regan tried to sound enthusiastic.

How could she ever go back there? Her gaze shifted toward the window. MacGregor was still out there—she could feel him, just as she could feel the savage bleakness on the moors of the island when she walked them. This was going to be the longest night of her life.

chapter 5

Regan left her father in high spirits, basking in the prospect of finding Avalon. But by the time she reached the top of the stairs, her happiness had faded. The image of Lord MacGregor lurked in every shadow.

Darkness filled the corner of the hallway and she paused. The only light flickered from beneath Emma's closed chamber door. She stood near a window and pressed her nose to the pane.

The rain had stopped as suddenly as it had come. Fog was rolling in from the sea, absorbing the island in its white mist.

Her pulse raced as she focused her eyes on the end of the lane. She could barely make out the road and the fence near it. No MacGregor. The sloping pasture near the drive was deserted. No movement near the barn. No shadows shifting.

Behind her, a door closed. Regan dropped the curtain and saw Letta leaving Emma's room with a worried frown.

"How is she?" Regan asked.

"Not good a'toll. Won't speak to me, still crying her eyes out."

"I'll talk to her."

"You can do more with her than me. I'll go see to your da." Letta shuffled down the stairs.

Regan listened to Letta's footsteps fade and strode to her sister's room. Four bedrooms filled the upper level, two of which faced the bay. The constant wind from the sea caused the chimneys to smoke, so Emma had chosen one of the larger chambers on the south side. Regan didn't mind the smoking chimneys. Most nights she left her window open and let the rolling of the waves lull her to sleep. Tonight, after her encounter with Lord MacGregor, she would lock every window in the house.

Regan knocked on Emma's door.

No response.

She poked her head inside and found Emma lying across her bed on her stomach. The scent of mint, basil, thyme, and rosemary overwhelmed the room.

Emma spent hours in her garden, filling her days with the lush rich colors of flowers and herbs. Wherever their father's work had taken them, Emma brought along her herbs. Sometimes they stayed long enough in one area for Emma to start a garden. When they had to leave, Emma would mope for days.

Regan suddenly realized that she'd been so involved in finding Avalon, she hadn't been aware of Emma's melancholy. Clearly gardening had become Emma's escape from worry, and until now Regan had never known how much Emma fretted over them when they were on an archeological dig.

Emma lifted her head long enough to mumble, "Go away." Then she buried her face back into the pillow.

From the moment Regan had held her baby sister when she was but a day old, she had tried to watch over her. Sometimes Regan failed miserably, like now. Emma's sobs went through her like needles.

Regan swallowed hard, approached the bed, and sat beside her sister. She stroked Emma's wavy dark hair and said, "I'm not going away until you stop crying."

After a moment, Emma turned and looked at Regan, her big brown eyes glistening with tears. "I feel horrible. I shouldn't have said anything—"

"Of course you should have, Em. How else would we have known how you felt? We've been abominable to you. I'm so sorry. You should have told us long ago."

"I couldn't. I know how important it is to you and Papa." Emma's words were muffled by the emotion in her voice. More tears trickled down her cheeks as she stared at Regan.

Regan hugged her, feeling the moisture of Emma's tears against her neck. "Nothing is more important to me than your feelings—"

"But I shouldn't have ranted like that. I spoke horribly to Papa. I hurt him. I didn't want to hurt him."

"I know. You might want to ease his mind by talking to him in the morning." Regan pushed a long dark curl back over Emma's shoulders.

"I shall." Emma sighed as though she could not believe what she had done, then said, "I know you want to make everything all right for Papa, but finding Avalon is not going to make his heart better."

Emma had an uncanny ability to read into the deeper emotions that drove people. "I know that," Regan said.

Emma turned Regan's face to hers so that they made eye contact. "You don't," Emma said, frowning. "Some things you can't change. You can't change that typhus took Mama and gave Papa a weak heart, while it left you and me unscathed. It wasn't your fault."

"If I hadn't brought it home—"

"You don't know that."

"I know. I don't wish to discuss this further." Regan leaped up from the bed.

Emma grabbed her sister's hand. "Don't let your guilt rule your life. Let it go while you still can. You can't make Papa's heart better—"

"I have to try." Regan pulled her hand free. When she turned to leave, a letter sticking out from beneath Emma's pillow caught her eye. She reached for it, but Emma grabbed it first.

"Who has written you?" Regan asked.

"No one." Emma reddened. Her face always turned red when she lied.

"Who wrote you?" Regan frowned. Emma had never kept secrets from her before. She eyed Emma with one of her motherly looks.

Emma looked torn for a moment, then tossed the letter at Regan. "You might as well read it."

Regan scanned the carefully formed strokes, the blood slowly draining from her face. "What have you done?"

Emma's expression grew defensive. "Something I should have done a long time ago."

"How did you even know our grandparents were alive?"

"I went through the trunk of Mama's things and found some old letters that she had written to her father. They had been returned to her unopened. I took a chance that they might still be alive and wrote them."

"How could you go behind Papa's back that way? Lord and Lady Clarington disowned Mama when she married. They wouldn't even acknowledge us as their grandchildren. And now you write them. How could you?"

"I was sick of moving and living like a pauper. I wanted a permanent home."

"Do you actually think these strangers give a fig about you or me, or that they would want you in their home when they would not even acknowledge Mama after she married Papa? They didn't even go to her funeral. You were too young to remember."

Emma grimaced. "I didn't know."

"I thought it was best you didn't."

"You and Papa never tell me anything."

"That's not true. I kept this from you so you wouldn't get hurt."

"How do you know they don't want me? They might."

Regan shook her head and held back her temper. "They will not. And it would kill Papa to know you wrote them—

do you hear me? This would destroy what pride Papa has left, knowing you would desert him for grandparents you don't even know and who never wanted you in the first place."

Emma twisted an edge of the pillow. "Anything's better than living this way."

"If you truly believe that, then perhaps you should go and meet them," Regan said, unable to believe Emma could be so insensitive. "All you need is a good dose of snubbing from them, and you'll see you're wasting your time."

"Papa will die soon." Emma's eyes glistened with tears. "Then what will we do?"

"Stop saying that. He's not going to die."

"Why do you keep denying it?" Emma's voice rose with frustration.

"Don't try to change the subject. We were talking about what you have done." Regan waved the letter at Emma. "This was wrong. I know you did it because you're frightened of the future. You know I will always take care of you. I've taken care of you since Mama died, and I'll never stop caring for you. Do you hear me? You and Papa are all I have in this world."

Emma didn't respond, only squeezed the pillow to her chest. "I don't care. I want to meet them."

"Fine, but I'll not be a party to it. And you'll do it without Papa knowing." Regan tossed the letter on the bed and left the room, her footfalls hammering in the silence.

Emma stared at the empty doorway as more tears filled her eyes.

The next morning Lachlan MacGregor shoved back his untouched breakfast and tossed the ham and eggs to his pets, Prince and Charlie.

The two Irish wolfhounds gobbled down the treat in single gulps. They didn't move from their spot near his chair. Their eyes stayed trained on him in that beggar way they had perfected since puppies.

"Och! Do no' look at me like that," he said. "If you're wanting more, you'll have to make yourselves useful and hunt for it."

At the tone in their master's voice, the two dogs slunk away toward the door.

Lachlan listened to the clicking of their toenails die away and watched the dust motes floating in a shaft of light over the oak table. The dining hall in the old castle had been renovated by the fourth chieftain of Druidhean. Arched Gothic windows ran the length of the walls. Gilded plaster swirled along the ceiling. A massive burgundy Aubusson carpet blanketed the stone floor. Centuries-old claymores, axes, shields, and breastplates, battered and dented, hung along the walls. The red and green tartan of the clan MacGregor fanned over the shoulders of the breastplates.

His gaze shifted to the second-floor balcony that over-looked the room. After his predecessor had taken such pains in having the room remodeled, he had hanged himself from the railing. One thing could be said of Lachlan's relatives: they all had a style that was completely their own—including Lachlan's father. Lachlan scowled at the cane leaning against the arm of his chair.

"Wipe that frown off your face. You're always frowning."

He glanced up at his grandmother, the Dowager Lady Margaret MacGregor. She glided across the room, the silk of her gown rustling in the silence. The sharp points of her cheekbones emphasized the wrinkles about her eyes and her beakish nose. An acerbic expression was etched into her furrowed brow and around her nearly lipless mouth. She was descended from the same line as Mary Queen of Scots, and at two and seventy, the old woman had perfected an imperious air that would have made Mary proud. She could intimidate the most steadfast of hearts.

Fortunately, Lachlan had never allowed the impenetrable wall over his heart to be breached. He merely stared at her with eyes darker and more calculating than her own. "Morning," he said, still frowning.

She sat, sending the curls on her white wig bouncing near her shoulders. She stared down the length of the oak table at her grandson. "What has you so preoccupied this morning?"

"Nothing," Lachlan said stoically. He watched the blue veins on her thin neck throb as she poured tea into a china cup.

"I suppose you're occupied with thoughts of the intruder last night," she said, ignoring his one-word dismissal. "We must do something. You know how dangerous the circle can be."

Lachlan didn't raise a brow at the comment. Tyg, the groundskeeper, had a sixth sense when it came to knowing everything that happened on the estate. And he always reported anything unusual to Lachlan's grandmother. He had probably told her that Lachlan had ridden out after midnight as well. "I'm seeing to it," he said, slipping a hand into his pocket and running his finger over the ivory comb he had found.

"Do you know who she is?"

"Her name is Miss Regan Southworth." He felt the carved elephant on the comb.

"Never heard of her."

"The lass is new to the area. Rents from McAskill." Lachlan's last word came out between clenched teeth.

"*McAskill.*" His grandmother's gray brows arched. "She'll find out what sort he is soon enough. Have you discovered why she was trespassing?"

"No' as yet." He would never forget seeing Miss Southworth in McAskill's arms. The image was burned into his memory. The way she had leaned against him while he had kissed her. He squeezed the comb so tightly that the sharp teeth dug into his palm.

He grimaced, dropped the bauble into his pocket, then picked up his cup.

His grandmother's keen golden eyes studied him a

moment, then she said, "Have you a plan to keep her out of the circle?"

"I'm working on one." Lachlan raised his cup and stared at his reflection in the tea. The frown on his face had turned to a devious smile.

chapter 6

Regan tipped up her face to let the sun hit her cheeks. She breathed deeply of the salty sea air. Two curlews circled overhead, their shadows arcing across the middle of the skiff in which she was sitting. It might have been a glorious day, if only she could get Lord MacGregor off of her mind.

She glanced toward shore for signs of the laird's dark presence. Thoughts of him had haunted her all night. He had even invaded her dreams. In one nightmare he had captured her, then given her to King Arthur, who had strapped her to one of the rocks in the Druid circle. Then MacGregor had tortured her with hot irons. She woke only to find her body aching and her arms twisted in the sheets.

"A ha'penny for your thoughts."

Regan glanced across the rowboat at Mr. McAskill. He kept rowing, his wide hands clutching the oars. He'd taken off his coat and rolled up the sleeves of his shirt. On his left arm, a long white scar started in the middle of his forearm and disappeared beneath the rolled cuffs of his shirt. Without missing a stroke, he kept his eyes locked with hers.

The intensity of his gaze caused a blush to burn in her cheeks. "I was just thinking it is a glorious day to be out on the water. I hate the idea—"

"That it might end?" A winsome smile eased across his handsome face.

"You have a way of reading my mind, Mr. McAskill."

"I thought after last night you'd at least call me Eth."

"All right . . . Eth." She watched the scar writhing along his skin and it reminded her of a serpent.

When she spoke his name, he smiled. Sunlight glinted off of his white teeth. "We've a lot tae discuss, my love," he said.

"I know." Regan nodded, confident he would propose to her any moment.

"How much money will you be needin' tae pay your father's debts—"

"We really should not discuss business matters before we start our new life together." Her lips stretched in a tight smile while she leveled a prim look his way.

"Right you are, forgive me. I've the dowager cottage near Bentridge Hall set up for you and your family. You can move in tomorrow."

"So soon." Regan wanted at least a six-month engagement so she could get used to the idea of marriage. "I'll have to speak to my father."

Eth rested one of the oars on his knee, bent over the seat, and captured her hand. He kissed her gloved fingers and said, "The sooner the better. I canna wait tae have you livin' on my estate. I can see you every night. I promise I'll take care of you and any bairns that come along."

Why did he not propose? Regan decided to prod him along. She leaned toward him and said, "I've no doubt you'll make a wonderful father."

He grinned proudly. "Aye, I've proven that."

"You have?" Regan's golden brows snapped together. "I didn't know you'd been married before."

"Haven't. I've eight natural children. Five girls and

three boys. I wouldna mind addin' a few more boys tae the lot." He squeezed her hand, the serpent on his arm coiling.

The truth hit Regan. She struggled to keep her composure, while every muscle in her body tensed. She felt her pulse beating against her temple; it seemed to thump out the word "idiot" over and over again.

"What is the matter? That pretty blush is gone from your cheeks. We dinna need tae be havin' bairns if you dinna want tae."

Regan stared at Eth McAskill, speechless, struck by how naive she had been.

At her silence, he searched her eyes, his expression worried. "If it upsets you, we needn't speak of bairns now. All that matters tae me—"

"Let me stop you, Mr. McAskill," Regan said, getting past the shock. "I do not want to be your mistress. I *never* wanted to be your mistress. I thought your intentions were to marry me."

"We agreed you'd call me Eth." He smiled in a patronizing way as if he hadn't heard her at all.

"Under the circumstances, *Mr. McAskill* shall do."

"No need tae go gettin' all huffed up, love."

"You're not listening." Regan struggled to hold her temper. She wished she could give him the set down he deserved, but her father still owed him rent. "Now that the misunderstanding is over," she said in a strained tone, "I'm asking you not to importune me on the subject any longer."

"You canna be meanin' that." The placid, good-natured expression fell from his face.

"I mean it, Mr. McAskill." Regan scoured him with her best indignant look and crossed her arms over her chest.

"But I still want you, love. Now more than ever."

"I admire your determination, but I'm sorry. I'll never be your mistress."

He stared at her as if her words had slapped him. Then his whole mien changed, and a slow, determined smile molded the planes of his face. "Maybe I'll just have tae make you. What would you say tae that?"

"I say your audacity knows no bounds, sir. Kindly take me back to shore. *Now.*"

He merely grinned, his eyes deepening to a strange hue that frightened her. She had never seen this side of him; a demon had taken over his body. He grabbed up the oars and pounded the water in a determined rhythm.

Regan saw that he was not rowing toward shore, but out to sea. She narrowed her eyes at him. "I warn you, I'll not be coerced into an alliance with you—"

"There'll be no forcin'—no' after the way you kissed me last night."

She glanced at the shoreline getting farther and farther away. Something dark caught her eye. Her gaze moved upward to the cliff above the beach.

Laird MacGregor straddled a huge stallion, his black attire severe against the animal's shiny pearl coat. He sat with top boots gleaming, back board-straight, wide shoulders erect. Their gazes locked, and he tipped his riding crop at her.

Her pulse quickened. Her heart hammered her ribs. Unlike when he had gestured to her last night, she did not feel repulsed by this display. Perhaps it was the current pickle in which she found herself, but she didn't mind the greeting at all. In fact, she was almost relieved to see MacGregor.

Mr. McAskill followed her gaze, glancing behind him. When he found MacGregor, the ardor drained from his expression. He made a face like he was being tortured on a rack, then he wheeled back around so quickly the rowboat rocked.

Regan caught the sides of the skiff in order to keep her balance.

He noticed what he'd done and mumbled, "Sorry." He snatched up the oars, and they pummeled the water again, leaving a large wake.

Regan had never seen such a cruel, resolute look on Mr. McAskill's face. She noticed the oars were hitting the water at a phenomenal pace. "Please turn back!" she cried.

"I'm takin' you someplace where we can get away from that bastard's pryin' eyes."

"No, you're not." Regan untied the ribbons below her chin. She sailed the bonnet over the starboard side. Her gloves went next. They bobbed on the waves for a moment, then sank, melting into the blue-green depths.

"What are you doin'?"

"I'm sorry, Mr. McAskill, our time together has ended." Before he could grab her, Regan leaped over the side.

"You'll drown!"

His bawl rang in her ears, even as the shock of the frigid sea took her breath away.

"Here, take this." He jabbed one of the oars at her.

"I'm an excellent swimmer. I'll be just fine."

"The water is cold. Let me help you!"

"You have helped more than enough." Regan began to swim toward shore.

She had expected the water to be cold, but not this icy. Her body trembled. Her teeth chattered. She felt her fingers and toes growing numb. The weight of her sodden dress and petticoats pressed down upon her. She found it impossible to lift her arms or kick her legs.

She glimpsed MacGregor bolting down the path to the beach, limping on his right leg. He must have sustained an injury from his fall last night. Her conscience tugged at her as she watched him navigate the incline with surprising agility. All the while, his gaze never left her.

Though fifty yards of water separated them, she felt those black eyes piercing her. A bizarre strength radiated from him and tugged at her, a feeling similar to the one she had experienced while holding his wrists on the cliff.

She watched him, hoping to cull some of that strength. She couldn't force her numb arms and legs to move. The pulse in her temples throbbed in her ears, getting louder and louder. Water tugged at her sodden clothes. Somehow the sea had grown hands and was steadily pulling her downward. Salty water filled her mouth. Her last glimpse was of MacGregor tossing aside his jacket, yanking off his boots,

and running toward the water. Did he think he could rescue
her? Her head went down, and she knew it was too late for
anyone to save her.

Lachlan dove beneath the surface. *Through the murky
water*, he spotted her golden hair, billowing out around
her like long tentacles. Despite the pain in his right leg, he
swam toward her. It seemed like years before he reached
her, but in reality had been only a few moments.

He clamped his arm around her chest and pulled her to
the surface. Over the crest of a wave, he saw Eth McAskill
rowing away.

Their gazes clashed for a moment.

Lachlan wanted to strangle McAskill. *We'll meet later, I
swear it.*

McAskill had somehow been able to read Lachlan's
thoughts. A smile full of malice warped his face as he
turned and rowed toward Redkirk Point.

Lachlan cursed McAskill for the blackguard he was
while he struggled to keep Miss Southworth's head above
water. He couldn't help but think about her involvement
with McAskill. What had McAskill done to cause her to
jump?

He fought his way through the waves toward shore, her
head resting on his shoulder, her breasts tight against his
arm. Strands of her wet golden hair clung to his neck and
chest. Her lips were blue and she was not breathing. In his
grasp she felt petite and lifeless.

If only he had reached her a few moments sooner. She
had saved him on the cliff. Just knowing she was there for
him and looking into her eyes had kept him from falling.
He wasn't sure he could save her life in return. An unfa-
miliar tightness squeezed his chest until he couldn't
breathe.

chapter 7

*S*omeone *was hitting her back. Regan coughed again* and spewed out salt water. A pair of strong hands grabbed her shoulders and rolled her over.

For a moment the sun blinded her, and she blinked up at the massive shadow kneeling over her. She found herself staring into a pair of pitch-black, deep-set eyes.

"*You.*" The blood drained from her face as she remembered the terror she'd felt as she had gone under and lost consciousness. "Where am I? Hell?"

"If so, we're both there." MacGregor's deep, velvety voice pierced every fiber of Regan's body.

"Could I be so unlucky?" She gingerly touched his chin. Coarse black stubble abraded her trembling fingers. "You don't feel like a dark angel." She pulled back her hand.

"I have the heart of one." He gazed straight at her. The black depths drew her; she could not look away.

He brushed back the strand of hair sticking to the side of her mouth. "How are you feeling?" he asked, while he slid his finger along her cheek.

"I'm not too sure." His touch branded her skin. An

amazing sensation of heat traveled down her neck and into her breasts. She felt light-headed, weightless, soaring. Her teeth stopped chattering. Even with her sopping clothes clinging to her body, she felt almost warm again.

"Why did you jump overboard?" he asked.

Regan glanced out toward the bay. "Where is Mr. McAskill?"

"Rowed home by now, I'm guessing." His expression hardened, and he dropped his hand.

"Then I should thank only you for saving my life." Regan almost smiled at him, but she noticed his forbidding expression and the smile never reached her lips.

"You didn't answer my question. Why did you jump?"

Regan was not about to tell him how naive she'd been when it came to Eth McAskill. She wouldn't admit that to anyone, not even Emma, who knew all of Regan's deepest secrets. Instead she said, "That is my concern."

"No' any longer." His expression turned ruthless.

"What do you mean?"

"That your conduct matters to me now."

"I fail to see how my behavior affects you."

He extended his hand toward her. "Can you stand?"

"Of course." She refused his help and managed to rise on her own. When she straightened, a wave of dizziness caught her.

One moment she was wobbling, the next she hit his hard chest. She felt his powerful arms clenching her waist, the heat of his body penetrating her wet clothes, his heart thumping against her palm. They were so close she could feel his breath warming her wet cheeks. A strange tremor of excitement traveled down to the tips of her fingers and toes.

"I—I still d-don't understand how my behavior affects you, my lord," she said past her rapid breaths.

He gazed down at her, the dark, fathomless depths of his eyes smoldering. "Only that you'll be coming to work for me. My grandmother needs a live-in companion—"

"Work for you?" True, the employment might give her access to the circle and help with her father's debts, but what was his motive in offering her a position? And she didn't like the self-assured tone in his voice. She eyed him beneath lowered brows. "What if I declined the post?" she asked, pushing against his chest to break free.

He tightened his hold. A ruthless smile inched slowly across his lips. "You'll no', Miss Southworth. Your family needs the income and my grandmother needs a companion."

She gazed up into the black, soulless eyes, disconcerted that he knew of her father's debts. "I could find a position elsewhere," she said, struggling to sound confident.

"You won't," he drawled in a silken tone, "unless you want me to speak to your father about keeping a tighter rein on you. Is he aware I found you trespassing on my land the other night?"

"You're enjoying this, aren't you?"

"One never knows where pleasure's to be found." His eyes looked deep into hers.

There was something elementally dark and fixed in them that made her feel trapped. "I'm sure you'll not find an ounce of pleasure with me," she said in an unsteady voice.

"Don't be so certain."

Regan grew conscious of his hard body next to her own. She couldn't think. Couldn't move.

At her silence, he said, "I'll be sending the carriage round for you on the morrow."

"So soon," she said, her voice a little breathless.

"I see no need for dallying, now that we've reached an accord on the subject."

"I have no choice, it seems."

"I'm glad you realize that. You're a clever lass." His black eyes glinted with a brief hint of respect. "I was knowing that the first time you got away from me."

"Not so clever. You found me."

"Running prey to ground on this island has never been a challenge."

"Regan!" Emma's scream echoed above the waves hitting the shore.

They both turned and saw Emma scrambling down the path along the cliff.

More quietly now, he said, "Dinna disappoint me, Miss Southworth, or you'll no' be liking the consequences."

His voice sent goose bumps down the back of her neck. "I keep my word," she said.

"We shall see." He dropped his hold on her and stepped back.

Regan's knees had turned to pudding and she stumbled.

He grabbed her elbow to steady her. "Be careful, I'm no' wanting anything to happen to you." His eyes blazed with the familiar searing darkness, and then he let go of her arm.

Regan was relieved when Emma ran toward her. Emma had lost some of the pins in her hair. Half of the dark brown mass straggled down around her right shoulder. She almost knocked Regan over when she threw her arms around her neck.

"You're all right?" Emma asked, her large brown eyes brimming with fear. "I saw you being dragged to shore."

"I'm perfectly sound, and I owe my life to Lord Mac-Gregor here." Regan motioned toward the sopping nobleman beside her.

Emma inspected the stranger, taking in his dripping clothes, the wet white streak of hair that dipped over his ear, the harsh black eyes. Her jaw gaped, then she blurted, "You're the MacGregor."

"One and the same." A rueful grin caught one side of his mouth.

Emma's eyes widened with apprehension.

"Lord MacGregor, allow me to introduce my sister, Emma," Regan said, watching the two black strands of hair curling near his temple. Water droplets dripped from the tips and slipped over his high cheekbones.

"A pleasure." The thin edges around his mouth softened slightly, though his arms remained crossed over his chest, and his eyes held the same intense darkness. His wet shirt stuck to his broad chest, and his soaked breeches accentuated every long muscle in his legs.

Emma managed to find her tongue. "Th-thank you for saving my sister."

"I should no' like to be doing it again anytime soon." His words held a warning. When he peered at Regan, the ruthless mask slipped back over his expression and his eyes remained opaque as two blocks of coal.

Under his close scrutiny, Regan couldn't meet his gaze. "You needn't worry," she said, her voice unsteady. "I've learned my lesson. No jumping into the sea for me."

Emma turned toward Regan. "I should hope you have. What in the world made you leap out of Mr. McAskill's skiff?"

Regan felt Lord MacGregor's eyes on her and wanted to shake Emma. "I'll tell you later." She glared at Emma.

"I'll take my leave." His tone turned abrupt with irritation. "I'll be seeing you on the morrow." He leveled a look Regan's way that could not be gainsaid, then nodded to Emma. "Good day." He limped over to where he'd thrown his boots, cane, and coat, then picked them up.

Regan watched his slow progress up the path to the cliff top, the white streak stark against his black hair. His wet shirt was almost translucent and stuck to his broad chest and flat waist. She watched the muscles ripple along his back, watched his corded thighs work beneath his clinging breeches.

He somehow sensed her observing him and turned her way, his expression resembling that of a wolverine who'd just made a kill.

Now that a hillside separated them, she held her ground and waited for him to end the staring match.

"I'm glad he's gone," Emma said.

To Regan's dismay, she realized he would never lose a battle of any kind, and she gave Emma her full attention.

"How could you ask me why I jumped in front of him?"

Emma's face scrunched up in a suffering expression. "It just came to me. I wanted to know."

"You should think before you speak."

"I don't see the harm in him knowing. I'm sure he questioned you. It isn't every day a woman jumps from a gentleman's skiff. What happened?"

"I'd rather just forget it," Regan said, unable to admit even to Emma what a fool she'd been.

Emma must have known better than to press Regan, for she said, "Mr. McAskill seemed so nice."

"I thought so, too, but no longer."

"He couldn't be as bad as Mad MacGregor. Have you ever seen such cold eyes in your life? There was no feeling in them whatsoever." Emma rubbed her arms.

"Your melodramatic description sounds like it's right out of one of Mrs. Radcliffe's novels. Have you been reading her again?"

"You read her, too. I know you sneak them out of my room." Emma rolled her eyes at Regan. "You have my copy of *The Italian* probably beneath your mattress at this very moment."

"Please don't tell Papa. You know how he disparages fiction of any kind. He would tease me for the rest of my life."

"All right, but do you not think Mad MacGregor the living image of the villain Schedoni? He has that same sinister air about him."

"He's not quite so immense and lacks a tonsure and a cowl—"

"But his eyes—" Something dawned in Emma's expression as she said, "My word, did I hear him properly? Is he sending a carriage for you tomorrow?"

"Yes."

"Why?" Concern furrowed Emma's brow.

"I took a position at Castle Druidhean."

"You're going to work for Mad MacGregor, a living and breathing Schedoni? You're ready for Bedlam."

"He's not so terrible. He saved my life," Regan said with more conviction.

"He probably did it so he could get you alone and torture

you. You cannot work for him. I've heard rumors about the MacGregors. All of them are daft. And that cursed castle where he lives is straight out of one of Mrs. Radcliffe's novels. You cannot go there."

"I have to. You know we have no means of support. If I take this position, we'll not have to move." *And Papa and I can look for Avalon.* "That will make you happy, will it not, Em? You can have a permanent home and your garden."

"But working for Mad MacGregor? You'll be in danger. You must stay away from him. I saw the way he looked at you."

Regan had, too. She could still feel his arms holding her, feel the thrall of those black eyes drowning her in their emptiness. Worse yet, she had wanted to gaze into them until she could see a warm spark of feeling there.

Her heart hammered as she took Emma's arm. With forced confidence, she said, "I'll be fine. You shall see."

"Have you stopped to ask yourself why he offered you this position?" Emma narrowed her eyes at the top of the cliff Lord MacGregor had disappeared over.

"I suppose I'll find out soon enough." She swallowed past the sudden pressure in her throat.

Lachlan galloped Phoebus across the moors, *his wet breeches sticking to his saddle.* He thought of Miss Southworth, how he had saved her, how he had banged on her back, afraid that she would die. When she had started breathing again, and those vivid blue eyes had opened, a curious tension had left him and he had felt almost buoyant.

He abhorred such moments of emotional weakness. They made him feel vulnerable. If he had learned one thing in his four and thirty years, it was to never let himself become defenseless. As if he needed proof of the creed, he glanced down at his weak leg. He squeezed the reins until his knuckles bunched beneath his skin.

Bringing her to Castle Druidhean would be dangerous,

he knew. He should stay as far away as possible from her, yet he needed to prove to himself that he could overcome this strange hold she had on him. And what better way to keep her out of the circle and find out what she was doing there than to have her underfoot? It was an added benefit that she'd keep his grandmother occupied. Lady Margaret's infernal meddling was annoying and steadily worsened with age.

McAskill was another reason to hire the lass. He could deceive women into anything. No one knew this better than Lachlan. Given the chance, the devil would find out Miss Southworth's weaknesses and work on them until he gained whatever he wanted.

Why wouldn't she speak of McAskill? Was she already his mistress? He'd find out. The thought of McAskill touching her made every muscle in his body tense. Aye, he would find out how involved she was with the blackguard, even if he had to force it out of her. He told himself it was for her own good. Yet he knew the dangerous part of him looked forward to the diversion.

chapter 8

The next morning, Regan sat on the side of her father's bed and pulled back the spoon from his mouth.

He grimaced as he swallowed. "That stuff tastes like chalk."

"It's for your heart. You must take it. Shall I put honey in it?"

"Egads, no. Then the concoction would taste like sweet chalk."

"There's no pleasing you this morning, Papa." Regan set the bottle down with the others on the table.

"How am I supposed to feel, having one of my daughters insisting that I let her go to work?"

"It's not like I'm leaving the island. I'll be only ten miles away." She hated leaving him. Since he had come down with typhus and almost died, she hadn't left his side for more than a few hours.

"Too far." He patted her hand.

"You know I must take the position. We owe practically everyone within forty miles, including Mr. McAskill." Just saying his name left a bitter taste in her mouth.

"The debts I can endure, but losing you? It'll be like losing a part of me."

At that moment Emma entered the room, hefting a huge arrangement of wildflowers. She cut her eyes at Seamus and asked, "If I have a vote in the matter, I say don't let her go."

"You don't have a vote," Regan said. "We've been through this. We need the money."

Emma said, "I can write—"

Regan knew Emma was going to blurt out "our grandparents," so she said, "No, you cannot. Uncle Inis wrote me and said he couldn't spare any money this month." She shot Emma her most intimidating stare.

Emma's face turned red with guilt and she set down the flowers on the mantel without looking at Regan.

"I'm sure he'd send it if he had it." Seamus sighed. "I suppose you must leave us, Regan." His expression turned serious. "I must set conditions on your going. One"—he ticked them off on his fingers—"you'll write me every day."

"Very well."

"Two. You shall stay well away from Lord MacGregor—and I mean that." His expression turned grave. "You'll never be in his presence alone."

"That I can manage," Regan said with eagerness. She sensed the danger in Lord MacGregor, and she had no intention of courting it.

"Three. You will keep your chamber door locked at all times."

"Right."

"Four. You shall never go out at night alone."

"But how shall I dig for clues?"

"Do it in the morning hours—when the castle is asleep."

"Very well."

"Five. You will be extremely careful, and visit your papa on your day off."

"Without a doubt."

"And I've put Old Gray in your trunk, just in case."

Regan thought of their one and only weapon, a palm-size pistol, and said, "Papa, I don't need a firearm."

"You never know, you might. And do not fail to use it if you do." His stern expression melted behind a sad smile.

The sound of carriage trappings made them share a look.

"It seems your coach has arrived, my girl," he said, his voice full of strain.

"You take care while I'm gone and do not harass Emma and Letta with your grumbling." She hugged him. He felt fragile in her arms this morning.

"I never grumble."

She grinned at him and kissed his forehead. "I love you, but you are the worst patient in the world."

"I'm going to get a consensus on that." He smiled at her and waved her out the door. "You worry overmuch. Go."

There was a brusqueness in his voice that made a lump form in her throat. She hated to leave him.

She stepped over to Emma and hugged her. Keeping her voice low, Regan said, "Take care of Papa, and remember what I said about your letter-writing habits."

"I remember," Emma whispered back, her mouth pursed in a pout.

A hard knock boomed through the cottage.

Was that MacGregor at the door? At the prospect of seeing him again, Regan felt her pulse race.

She hurried to answer the door, then froze. It wasn't MacGregor's grim countenance meeting her. If only it had been.

She tried not to stare at the patch over the man's eye. His nose had been broken many times and favored the crooked roots of a tree. His auburn hair stuck out at odd angles. A moon-shaped scar crisscrossed his left cheek and chin. He wore moleskin brown breeches and jacket, and a white muslin shirt spotted with grease stains from his morning repast. He looked like he belonged on a pirate ship, rather than land bound on the small island of Skye.

She had a hard time finding her voice. "Y-yes?"

The driver knew his appearance had shocked her, for his

mouth narrowed in a smirk. "Here tae be pickin' up Miss Southworth."

"I am Miss Southworth. You are employed by Lord MacGregor?"

The driver stretched to an indignant height and jammed his hands on his hips. His moleskin breeches pulled against a globe-size paunch. "Most of me life," he said with pride. "Worked for his da, too."

Regan hadn't realized she'd offended him until it was too late. She swallowed hard and tried again. "Since we are employed in the same household, I should know your name."

He eyed her suspiciously, as if he didn't trust telling her anything as personal as his name. He grappled with something for a moment, then said, "Tyg,'tis."

"Very well, Tyg, my trunk is here." Regan waved to the old trunk in the hall. In one pull, he hefted it onto his shoulder and carried it with the confidence of a seaman used to lifting heavy objects.

Emma strode up behind Regan and peeked past her shoulder at Tyg. Her eyes widened in disbelief.

At that moment he turned, his marred face hitting Emma full force.

She leaped back behind Regan.

Tyg threw back his head and chuckled all the way to the carriage.

Emma grabbed Regan and wheeled her around. "You can't go to that odious place. You have time to change your mind."

"I have to go."

"If ever you'll regret something, you'll regret going there."

Regan didn't realize how soon Emma's words would come back to haunt her.

• • •

Regan felt the sway of the carriage and thought of Emma. She disliked leaving with discord between them and hoped her sister would see her point of view.

She ran her hands over the indentation in the crushed velvet seat beside her. How many times had MacGregor sat in that very spot? She could almost imagine him beside her. . . .

The carriage halted abruptly. Regan grabbed the seat to keep from falling. Why had they stopped? There was another two miles to go.

Regan called out, "What is the matter, Tyg?"

"We've a visitor," he shouted down.

Before Regan could ask who it was, hooves thundered to a halt on the other side of the carriage. She leaned across the seat to open the leather blind.

The moment she pulled the curtain, MacGregor's black eyes bored straight through her. She hadn't expected to see his face a foot from her own, and she swallowed a scream.

"Morning, lass." A hint of amusement flashed in his eyes, then disappeared.

chapter 9

Do you always come out of the blue and scare the devil out of people?" Regan blurted. The predatory gleam in his eye told her he liked catching people off guard.

"When 'tis warranted." His tone was gruff, and his shoulders stiffened. The saddle protested with a creak. His horse, a huge stallion of at least seventeen hands, pawed the ground with impatience.

"I do not see the need for it now."

"I wanted to make sure you had no' changed your mind."

"I told you I keep my word. If I hadn't, would you have forced me to come?"

"If I had to."

All at once Regan felt like something small that he could crush with his boot. She gulped and couldn't help but notice his long legs beneath the tight superfine of his black breeches. He rode without a neckcloth and jacket, and looked almost wild in only a white silk shirt and trousers. There was a large V where he'd left the buttons open on his shirt. She could see where the line of black hair on his chest tapered into his broad shoulders. The constant breeze on the isle whipped back his dark locks, masking the white stripe near his temple. With his forehead bared by the wind, the chiseled planes of his face were heightened. The dimple in his square chin looked more pronounced. It struck Regan how handsome he was, and she had to force herself to breathe.

He was high enough on the back of his horse to peer directly into the window. His gaze was slipping down over her breasts.

Regan recalled the debacle with McAskill and pulled the shawl she'd donned before she left over her breasts. If he had ideas of her becoming his paramour, she would set him straight. "Exactly why are you forcing me to take this position?" She eyed him suspiciously. "I should let you know I resent being extorted in this manner. Do you always bend people to your will?"

"I'm a madmon; I can get away with it." His eyes glinted in the sun, the black depths fathomless.

"If you were mad, you would have let me drown. You are arrogant and overbearing, but not mad."

"That remains to be seen, lass," he said, his voice mellowed slightly.

Regan heard the hint of pain in his voice and felt a stab of sympathy. A halo of bleakness seemed so much a part of him. Her tone softened as she asked, "Did your grandmother have a companion before me?"

"You're the first."

"I see."

"I'll no' lie to you, she'll test your mettle."

From the gossip she'd heard, he probably was making an understatement. "She'll find I'm not as fainthearted as most young women."

"If anyone can handle her, I've no doubt you can."

Regan might have basked in the praise, but she wanted to set him straight right now, so she wouldn't end up jumping out of something besides a skiff. "I should let you know, being a companion is *all* I will be doing," she said, her formal tone leaving no doubt as to her intention.

His brow furrowed. "Dinna worry, lass. Your duties are fixed and no' likely to be changing."

"I'm glad we understand each other." It occurred to her she liked to hear him speak. His Scottish accent wasn't so thick that it was hard to understand. The lilt was polished; the words rolled off his tongue with deep sensual perfection.

"You needn't fash yourself that I'll be requiring anything from you other than obliging my grandmother."

"I'll hold you to your word."

"And I'll be holding you to your word to stay in the position once you get to the castle. Here."

He pulled a thick envelope out of his jacket pocket and handed it to her. Before she could question him about what it was, he whistled up to Tyg, then rode ahead of them.

"What did you mean, once I got to the castle?" Regan called out the window.

He had galloped past the team of bays and couldn't hear her.

Regan leaned back inside and opened the packet.

She pulled out bills from the butcher, the cobbler, and the farmer who brought Vespertine's oats and hay and their milk. Scrawled across the bottom in a bold hand were the words:

An advance on your salary.

Regan totaled up the amounts. Twenty guineas. That was more than she could earn in two years as a companion. Was this his way of making her indebted to him so she couldn't escape him? How could she ever repay him? An uneasy feeling gnawed at her. She was getting deeper and deeper into his clutches.

And why had he made that comment about her staying at the castle?

• • •

The carriage slowed. *Regan peeked out the window and saw they were on the castle's drive.* The hill they were climbing obscured her view of it, but she could see the rowans and hollies that bordered the drive. Their boughs twisted at odd angles. Contorted knots protruded from their trunks, making strange faces in the bark.

Regan leaned back and dug her fingers into the seat's horsehair stuffing. Despite her earlier display of courage for her father, queasy panic rose in her chest. She couldn't forget MacGregor's warning, or the legend that the castle was cursed. It was ridiculous to think that way. Curses didn't exist. She was sure her anxiety stemmed from having to reside in Lord MacGregor's home, where she would be totally under his power.

All too soon the carriage rocked to a halt.

Regan stepped out and saw the strange fog that coalesced around the base of Castle Druidhean. The mist oozed out of the very foundation as though the structure itself were exhaling it. There was a watchfulness in the windows as the castle raised its great crenellated head to meet the sky. Regan had visited many abbeys, castles, and ancient ruins with her father, most of them supposedly haunted. She had never felt the presence of anything remotely supernatural. But here, standing before Castle Druidhean, the shadow of it swallowing her, having it look down on her with what certainly was contempt and amusement, she felt something.

Tyg strode past her with the trunk on his shoulder. "Are ye goin' to be standin' there all day, miss?"

Regan shook herself out of her trance and followed Tyg to the entrance. The temperature near the castle was a good twenty degrees colder than when she'd left Finn Cottage. She pulled her shawl closer around her. Glancing about, she asked, "Where is Lord MacGregor?"

"Probably giving orders about seeing to you."

Regan almost wished he were with her.

Tyg rang a bell on the side and opened the huge oak

door. The wood actually moaned as it opened. The hinges crunched like someone walking over broken bones.

Regan hesitated on the threshold, feeling a gust of frigid air brush her face. An image of her father appeared in her mind. To give him a reason to keep living, she would brave this bizarre castle and Mad MacGregor's caprice and find Avalon. She could do this. Squaring her shoulders, she stepped inside.

chapter 10

A damp, fungoid odor permeated the air. Regan gri- maced and glanced around. Though it was morning, no light penetrated the castle. One candle burned in a sconce, casting hectic shadows around the foyer, a small area no larger than Finn Cottage. Nothing graced the walls but an- other bronze wall sconce and Celtic crosses that were carved into every other stone. They looked like replicas from sixth century A.D. Scotland, with their expanded wide points. The foyer ended abruptly and met a narrow winding staircase. There was no way out but up.

Tyg slammed the door, startling her. She recalled the way he had banged on her cottage door and said, "You are not one to be delicate with doors, are you?"

"If there's a need for it, I can." He winked at her, grip- ping the trunk on his shoulder.

Something in his casual manner put Regan on her guard. There was warmth in his expression, but the wrong kind. Hiding the slight tremor in her hand, she motioned toward the stairs and said, "Please lead the way."

She waited until he was several paces in front of her

before following him. A symbol in the middle of each cross caught her eye. It was an ogham mark, one with a star in the center and twelve wavy lines along its perimeter. She had never come across anything like it. She would have to sketch it. Her father would be interested in the design. She paused long enough to run her fingertips over the symbol in the middle.

A hushed sob came from the walls.

Chills crawled down her spine as she snatched her hand back.

"Shouldna go touchin' things, miss."

"Did you hear that?"

"Hear what?" Tyg snickered in a knowing way.

"Nothing." Regan felt oddly oppressed by the walls and backed up until she stood in the middle of the staircase.

"There's a reason for the crosses."

"What reason is that?"

"To keep the evil from swallowing the house," Tyg said matter-of-factly.

Regan trailed closer behind him on the narrow stairs. "Evil, indeed. There is nothing in this old place but dust," Regan said loudly, trying to convince herself.

"Ah, well, those livin' here knows better."

Regan frowned at the lace tie that held on his eye patch. For some reason he was trying to frighten her.

At the top of the stairs, a gentleman, tall and willowy, stood waiting. Rush lamps burned in indentations along the walls, their light gleaming off the top of his bald head. He had a long-jawed skeletal face that cheerful emotion had never touched. Wrinkle-free pale skin draped his hollow cheekbones and deep-set eyes. She noticed his left hand and the three fingers missing there. He appeared self-conscious and stuck his hand in a pocket.

"Are you the butler?" Regan asked. She couldn't imagine a more fitting one for the castle.

"Aye, miss." The tall man looked pleased at her insight.

"Which room she havin'?" Tyg asked.

"The green room," the butler replied in his baritone pipe-organ voice.

"That's on the family's floor. Servants ain't allowed there."

"She's tae have the green room." The butler's voice snapped with authority.

Both men faced each other the way two pugilists might, nose to nose, eyes glaring.

With a raised brow and a relenting scowl, Tyg strode down the hall, the trunk balanced on his wide shoulder, muttering.

Anyone who won a battle so easily with Tyg deserved respect. The butler had just climbed several rungs in Regan's esteem.

He turned back to her. "I'm Gillis, miss. Sorry you had to witness that."

"You handled it with great aplomb."

"There's a few things you should be knowin' aboot Druidhean." He lowered his voice. "One bein' the servants 'round here have no respect for authority." He nodded in the direction Tyg had taken.

Regan glanced down the narrow hall at Tyg. Rushlight flicked over his harsh profile. "I imagine your job is not an easy one," Regan said, sure Tyg resented direction of any kind.

"You're no' aware o' the half o' it, miss." Gillis followed her gaze and watched Tyg until he disappeared around a corner.

"Is there anything else I should know?"

"Bolt your door, miss, and never leave your chamber at night. There are dangers everywhere—'specially outside."

"What sort of dangers?"

"Strangers in the castle have a way of disappearin'. The grounds just seem tae take them away—especially the Druid circle. It's hexed, it is. Since I've been working here, and that's nigh forty years, three people have been found dead there."

"Really," she said. "What happened to them?"

"All drowned, they were."

"Were they from the island?"

"Nay. All strangers. One was a poacher new tae the area. The other two were sailors who wrecked on the rocks during a storm. Canny thing, they found their bodies in the circle. Poor devils. That's the place where the Druids made their sacrifices. 'Tis an evil place, miss. Stay away from it."

"I shall." Did Gillis truly believe in such superstitious drivel, or was he telling her this to scare her? There must be a logical explanation why the bodies were found in the circle.

"But that's no' all, miss, oh, no indeed. There's been tragedies through the whole MacGregor line since the building o' the castle. Evil walks here, miss, you can be sure o' it. Dinna ever go outside—even in the day, unless someone is with you. You can ring for me, if you're needin' assistance."

"Thank you," she said, feeling an icy blast of air brush past her neck. It chilled her to the bone.

"If you'll come this way." He turned and headed in the direction opposite to the one Tyg had taken.

Regan trailed after him down a hallway that was as barren as the foyer. Black walnut paneling ran floor to ceiling. Here, too, Celtic crosses were embedded in every other plank, forming a diagonal chessboard pattern on the walls.

She leaned past Gillis's pointed shoulder. All she could see were hallways and staircases; they gave the illusion that the castle was one big maze.

"Where are we going?" she asked.

"Tae the library, miss."

Another frigid gust of air passed her, then a raspy exhaling sound came after it. If Regan didn't know better, she'd believe the house was breathing.

Her training in science demanded another explanation. How many times had her father said, "There is always a logical reason for any occurrence that seems supernatural. One must merely search for it"? Still, some innate element in her, the same element that had sensed MacGregor's presence outside Finn Cottage two nights ago, sensed something held Castle Druidhean, and whatever It was would never yield its secrets.

Gillis came to yet another deceptive staircase. As they descended, the stairs widened. The musty dank odor had somehow been exorcised from this area, and she could smell only ancient stone and wood. They stepped down into an enormous gallery.

Here the ceiling rose thirty feet into the air. Walls were plastered and adorned with golden oak leaves, and existed despite the austere darkness that permeated the rest of the castle. Massive tapestries of hunting scenes and battles graced one wall. Embroidered on a red and green tartan was the MacGregor coat of arms. In the center of the insignia, a crowned lion wore armor. He held a shield emblazoned with an oak tree and a sword that crossed over it. Above the lion's head waved a banner with the words "srioghal mo druidhean" etched in it.

On the other wall hung paintings of ladies and gentlemen. All of the gentlemen had the distinctive white streak at the temple and the same distracted twinkle in their eyes. Most of the ladies wore a long-suffering look of sadness.

Regan paused to admire them.

"Those are the gudemon of Druidhean and their gudewives," Gillis said.

"They do not look like a happy lot."

"There's no happiness tae be had here, miss. Those paintings o' all the lairds were done before their thirty-fifth birthday."

"Why?"

"Because, miss, they all were demented shortly after. It's part o' the curse."

"All of them?"

"Well, some waited until their later years, but all fell tae daft ways sooner or later."

"Even the current laird's father?" she asked.

Gillis nodded.

What a horrible childhood MacGregor must have had

with a demented father. She couldn't help but treasure the memories of her own loving papa.

"What of their clan?" she asked, changing tacks. "There seems few of them left in the village."

"The clan ne'er came tae the lairds for help; they were afraid. After the first Laird MacGregor built here, they stopped lookin' tae the laird for guidance and help. With every generation the clan got smaller. They all took off tae parts unknown. What's left of them earn their living fishing."

"If the MacGregors have no income from crofters, their wealth must come from other sources?" Regan knew she was gossiping, but she'd been curious about how MacGregor maintained such a huge estate on such a barren island.

"The last master owned a brewery in the north o' Skye, miss. The current master sees to its running."

"Oh."

Gillis paused before a portrait of a gentleman who had dark, enigmatic eyes, black hair, and a slashing white streak over the temple. The artist had given the eyes a volatile glint that suggested madness.

"That's the master's father, Balmoral MacGregor."

"The resemblance is uncanny," Regan said, unable to draw her gaze from the disturbing black eyes in the portrait.

"Aye, spit out o' his mouth, he were."

Regan stepped over to the painting beside it. Bright red curls flowed down to the lady's shoulders. With her flawless white skin and flaming hair, her beauty was striking. Her hands were placed just so on her lap in a demure, angelic pose. A serene smile barely turned up her lips.

"Is this Lady MacGregor?"

"'Tis, miss."

"What sort of person was she?"

Gillis ignored her question and pointed in another direction. "Over here is the master's grandparents, the Dowager Lady Margaret MacGregor and the Baron Oswald MacGregor. He was the first tae receive the title from the crown. It was given t' him by the king when he married Lady Margaret, some say as a favor tae her so she could marry a Highland Scotsmon. She came from royalty, you see. A love match, 'twas."

"How nice," Regan commented. Why didn't Gillis want to speak of MacGregor's mother? "I didn't realize your master had a title other than laird of Druidhean."

"Aye, he doesn't claim it. Never uses it. The master's no' an uppity sort."

Just supposedly mad. She glanced at Oswald MacGregor. He had auburn hair, with the same white streak, and a long drooping mustache. He had a twinkle in his eye that suggested life amused him. On the canvas he did not look mad at all. Clearly, when the portrait had been painted, he'd been in charge of all of his faculties.

Lady Margaret looked young in her portrait, no older than twenty. She had platinum blond hair and striking brown eyes, and the artist had captured her looking down her nose at him. Regan knew by the portrait that she would have her work cut out for her being this lady's companion.

"We should move on, miss."

Regan trailed him in silence.

Gillis passed a door and motioned to it. "The dining hall, miss."

"Oh." She'd never find it again unless she had a map.

"We break the fast at nine, luncheon at two, and dinner at eight. Dinna be late, miss. The master canna abide tardiness."

"I see," she said, more to herself.

"You'll find, miss, things'll go better for you here if you keep on the master's good side."

"Another useful bit of information. Thank you, Gillis." Maybe the master of the house needed to be inconvenienced once in a while. A perverse part of Regan wondered what he'd do if he were.

Finally Gillis drew up short before a set of double doors. Regan gingerly touched the carvings on one of the door's edges. Small Celtic crosses with the same ogham symbol were chiseled amid vines and leaves.

He opened one of the heavy doors, its hinges rasping a protest. He waited for Regan to walk inside. "This is the library, miss."

Regan took in the massive room. It was so large, Finn Cottage could fit into it. A fire hissed and spit in a hearth vast enough to roast a whole cow at once. Firelight flicked over a huge red Indian carpet. "This is a lovely room," Regan said, awed.

"'Tis one o' the master's favorites."

When she glanced at the walls, her jaw dropped open. Lines of books curtained the room from floor to ceiling. Not just any books, but thick tomes with gilded covers and crusty spines, a confection for Regan, who had spent most of her life in libraries.

"This is truly unbelievable," she said, unable to draw her gaze from the shelves. She'd never seen so many ancient texts in one room.

"All the MacGregors favored books, miss."

"They're lovely," Regan said.

"Wait here, miss. I'll be telling the master you've arrived."

At the prospect of seeing MacGregor in his own home, her heart sped up, her pulse throbbed in her ears. The castle didn't seem half as intimidating as its owner. When she turned around, Gillis was gone.

She strode over to the bookshelves. The history section was some twenty feet wide. Her gaze traveled lovingly over the titles: *The Histories of Scotland and of Ireland, The History of Scotland: From the Regency of the Earl of Morton in 1572 to the Declaration of American Independence in 1782, A True Narrative of the Proceedings of His Majesty's Privy Council in Scotland.* The titles went on and on, feasts for the eye.

She found one, *The History of Skye*, written in Scottish Gaelic. She eased the heavy book out and gave in to the impulse that her father said was one of her shortcomings, to inhale the scent of the book. She closed her eyes and let the aged ink and foolscap fill her senses, then she gently turned the pages. The brittle paper crinkled in a welcoming way she had grown to love. It had been handwritten by Prior McEwan and printed in 1653.

Regan became so absorbed in the book that several long moments passed before she felt an overpowering presence behind her. She assumed it was MacGregor, but when she turned, she dropped the tome.

Book met stone. The bang echoed through the cavernous room.

Regan gulped and sucked in her breath. Two wolfhounds eyed her. They were tall, waist high, and had the largest paws she'd ever seen.

In tandem they bared their fangs and growled, crouching toward her.

Regan was ten again, facing a pack of wild dogs. The huge black pack leader had stepped toward her, his fangs exposed, strands of saliva coming from his mouth. He had growled, then attacked.

The old scar on her thigh began itching. *That's where they'll tear into me,* she thought. She couldn't breathe. Fear stole up into her throat and she felt strangled by it.

The dogs inched closer. . . .

chapter 11

Lachlan strolled into the library and found the lass cornered by Charlie and Prince. He took in her pale face, the clamped jaw, the protruding veins in her beautifully slender throat. Her eyes were locked on the dogs, and she didn't seem aware of his presence.

"Off." The harsh sound of his voice made the dogs back away.

She didn't move, only stared at the spot the hounds had just left.

Lachlan crossed the room. Now that he stood in front of her, he noticed her arms, stiff at her sides, yet trembling. Her breasts heaved beneath the bodice of her gray dress. He could feel the pressure of the terror in her. It disturbed him to see her so frightened. "Lass, are you all right?" he asked.

She continued to stare at the floor.

He stepped up to her and shook her slightly. "Miss Southworth."

She gulped in air, as though she remembered to breathe; then she looked at him with terror-stricken blue eyes. He knew terror, knew it intimately—and what it could do to a person. To see her so beset by it was his undoing. An unruly overprotective feeling swept through him as he dropped his cane and picked her up. She felt stiff as marble in his arms.

He limped to one of the chairs before the fire and sat, urging her head to his chest. "Relax, you're going to be all right, lass."

He felt her snuggle against him and began to stroke her neck, working the taut muscles. He cradled her for what seemed like an eternity, hating the fact she was terrified and he could do nothing about it.

"I'm such a dolt," she said in a vulnerable voice. "I'm so very sorry."

"Are you frightened of just large dogs, or all dogs?" He felt strands of her blond hair curling around his fingers as he continued to rub her neck. For the first time he noticed the tiny dimple in her angular chin that hinted at a strong willfulness.

She hesitated a moment, then spoke. "All dogs. I was attacked once when I was little."

"What happened?"

"We were living on the Isle of Wight. It was such a barren place. The cottage we rented was secluded. Our nearest neighbor was a mile away. There had been a pack of wild dogs running loose. My father had warned Emma and me not to go outside without him."

"But you went." Lachlan was certain the lass was as strong willed as a child as she was now.

"Yes. We needed eggs for breakfast. I went out to get them. I didn't see the dogs until it was too late."

"How did you survive?"

"My father. He was following me out, saw them, and shot them. He saved me, but one dog tore a place in my leg." At the recollection, her face contorted.

Lachlan wished he could take the bad memory away, but he couldn't. "Well, we're owing your father a debt." He stared at the dimple and wondered what it would feel like to place his lips there.

"I do owe my father everything. He's a very special

man. I'd do anything for him." She glanced up at Lachlan. Her eyes had turned back to their bright periwinkle blue.

How many gentlemen's hearts had been lost to those beautiful eyes? He remembered her kissing McAskill. How could she let someone like McAskill touch her? What irritated him even more was the fact he could feel himself becoming aroused. He slipped his hands beneath her back and knees, and stood.

"Where are you taking me?"

"Over here, lass." He set her down in the chair beside his. "You'll be all right now."

She glanced up at him, looking slightly baffled. "Thank you for your kindness."

"Och, you should no' be thinking of me as kind." His annoyance came through in his voice. He sat in the chair opposite hers, feeling cold air hitting his chest where her warmth had been.

"You paid off my father's debts. That was generous of you," she said, her expression turning into a mixture of curiosity and uncertainty.

"Dinna think I did it with a benevolent heart. I take debts seriously. You'll be getting half your salary. The rest will go back toward what you owe me."

"I see. And here I had been fretting over how I shall repay you. You've already figured that out." She sounded vexed as her gaze shifted to the fire.

Lachlan didn't want her believing he was anything other than indifferent. He had to keep her at arm's length. "Has Gillis apprised you of the dangers in Castle Druidhean—especially the circle?" He stressed the word "circle."

"He has, but I find these so-called dangers very hard to believe."

"Make no mistake. There's danger in the circle, the worst kind."

"I'm not easily intimidated by superstition. My father is a man of science. We do not believe in sorcery or magic."

"You'll be a believer before you leave here." Lachlan

added just enough menace in his voice to see her shudder. "What brought you to the circle the other night?"

She hesitated. "I, uh, was taking a walk and got lost."

"I see." *Little liar.* Getting the truth out of her wouldn't be easy. He found himself looking forward to the challenge. "The interview is over. Good day, Miss Southworth."

She rose.

He tried to keep his gaze from her, but he couldn't. He watched the firelight flick along her golden hair pulled back in its tight chignon, watched her dress caress her slender curves as she rose. He felt the ache in his groin and grimaced. Would he ever be able to control his lust when she was near him?

She wouldn't look his way as she stepped past the chair.

Footsteps sounded behind them. Lachlan rose to see his grandmother walking toward them, poised in her queenly stride.

He found his cane, aware of the abeyant fuse burning in his grandmother's eyes. "Dowager Lady Margaret MacGregor, meet Miss Southworth," he said with breezy indifference.

Miss Southworth curtsied. "Pleased to finally make your acquaintance, my lady."

Lady Margaret turned her intimidating gaze on the lass. "So you're here, are you, gel?"

Miss Southworth met his grandmother's gaze head on. "I just arrived. I can read to you later if you like."

"Read to me?" Lady Margaret bristled with indignation.

In Lachlan's preoccupation with the lass, he'd forgotten to inform his grandmother of her position. "She's to be your companion." He threw the words out like cannon fire.

Lady Margaret's bottom lip trembled as she struggled to check her ire.

Miss Southworth's brow furrowed. "Is there some mistake?"

"Nay, lass," Lachlan said.

Lady Margaret waved angrily toward the door. "You can go, gel. I'll call for you if I want you."

"Yes, madam." Miss Southworth covered the length of the library, her fearful gaze on Prince and Charlie, who sat in the middle of the room, watching her.

Lady Margaret waited until her new companion had left, then stomped her foot. "For the love of Mary!" She shook her finger at Lachlan. "What am I to do with a companion? I do not want a companion, especially some meddling, snotty-nosed gel who hasn't lived in the world long enough to know how to avoid evil."

"I couldn't think of anyone better suited to keeping an eye on her than you." Lachlan couldn't reveal his primary aim in the lass staying under his grandmother's watchful eye instead of his own. He didn't want to admit it even to himself.

"I'll not bear the brunt of your perverse sense of humor."

"To be sure, I'm finding no humor in this."

Lady Margaret looked deep into his eyes in that direct way of hers, as if she were reading his inner thoughts. "I see how things are."

Lachlan met the formidable golden eyes, knowing if he glanced away, it would be a sure sign of vulnerability. "If you've something to say, out with it."

"You're attracted to her. You have that same silly besotted look your father had when he looked at your mother," she said, her tone bitter.

Lachlan kept his expression as stony as ever. "You're imagining things. She's here so we can keep her out of the circle, that's all." And away from McAskill's clutches.

"I know you came home yesterday with your clothes sopping."

Lachlan wasn't surprised that Tyg had been quick with his report. "She almost drowned jumping from McAskill's skiff," he said nonchalantly.

"Do you know why she jumped?"

"She'll no' say. I was hoping you'd question her about it."

Lady Margaret frowned, looking unsure whether she'd read Lachlan's feelings properly. "Well, well, I shall find out what the gel was doing."

His grandmother had taken the carrot he'd dangled in front of her. Her curiosity far outweighed her sense of being inconvenienced. "Does that mean you'll be having her as your companion?" he asked.

"I'll have the gel and see she doesn't give us any trouble."

"I'll no' have you abusing the lass while she's here."

"I would never misuse her."

Lachlan knew better. His grandmother loved exerting her power over others. She had a sadistic side that could easily get out of control. "See that you take care no' to hurt her," he said, starting for the door.

"Let me leave you with some advice, my grandson. Do not lose sight of the fact you've chosen never to marry."

"I'm no' likely to be forgetting it." Lachlan limped out of the room, his cane tapping hollowly on the floor.

Prince and Charlie had been sitting quietly. They rose and trailed him like two dark shadows.

R*egan followed Gillis and thought of her encounter* with MacGregor. When the dogs had attacked her, he had surprised her with his kindness.

She recalled sitting in his lap. When she looked into his mysterious black eyes, they had held her in a kind of trance. She hadn't wanted to move. How easily she had stayed put and let him massage her neck with his large magical hands. Her skin still tingled from the contact. She would have continued to sit there had he not grown so distant and set her down in another chair.

When he had warned her about the circle, his eyes had turned brutal. Even now she could feel the harshness in them. She shivered. His expression had stayed that way when he had questioned her about her motives for trespassing.

She couldn't tell him about Avalon. If word leaked out that she was interested in the circle, Sir Harry Lucas would not waste any time getting there first. He'd risk anything to find Avalon before her father. Archeologists could be a cut-throat lot. Sir Henry had once broken into a monastery's library to pilfer a sixth-century tome he thought would lead him to Avalon. He even bragged later about slipping past the monks. Since he was a nobleman, he made a sizable donation to the monastery and avoided being prosecuted. No, Sir Harry must never find out.

Gillis turned a corner. Regan noticed that all the doors in this particular hallway, like the library, had carvings of vines and leaves with Celtic crosses incorporated into them.

"What sort of person is Lady Margaret?" Regan asked, breaking the silence.

"Rigid, miss. Breathes fire sometimes. I've seen her send many a servant running from here."

"How many servants?"

"Dozens, but they weren't worth keeping. She weeds out the chaff, she does."

Perhaps servants left the castle not because people thought it was cursed, but because the curse was Lady Margaret.

"Here's your chamber, miss." Gillis paused next to a door. He motioned to a room two doors away. "There's Lady Margaret's room, so you're no' alone on this floor."

"Where are Lord MacGregor's apartments?"

"The north wing, miss, at the opposite end o' the castle. Ne'er go there. He likes his privacy."

"I do not intend to."

"If something happens in the night, you can always ring the bell."

"The only help I'll need is with Lady Margaret."

"Can't help you there, miss. Remember tae bolt your door and dinna venture out come nightfall. You'll be a'right."

"Thank you." Regan stepped inside.

A creak sounded behind her and Regan knew she wasn't alone. As she wheeled around, a figure stepped out from behind a wardrobe door and immediately began screaming.

Startled, Regan screamed, too.

chapter 12

❦

Regan realized it was a scrawny girl and not an unwanted intruder.

The girl leaped back behind the wardrobe door, and her shrieking stopped. In a frightened voice she whispered, "Our Father, who art in heaven, hallowed be thy name . . ."

"Hello," Regan said, raising her voice.

The Lord's Prayer grew louder. "Thy kingdom come, thy will be done . . ."

"Gillis didn't tell me you'd be here. I'm Miss Southworth. You must be a maid." Regan didn't walk over for fear she'd frighten the girl even more and she'd crawl into the wardrobe and never come out.

The girl stopped praying and stuck her head past the door, the sides of her white cap fluttering near her cratered face. Pimples filled the girl's complexion. Her whole visage was one florid oval. Regan couldn't help but feel sorry for her. Emma dabbled with herb salves for skin. Regan would send a note to her directly for something to help the girl.

"Yer Miss Southworth?" Her golden, earthy eyes looked skeptical and filled with fear.

"Yes." Regan walked farther inside the room.

"Wallace's grave! You shouldna go scarin' a body like that."

"I'm sorry."

"I truly thought you were one o' the clooties runnin' aboot the place. You ne'er knowin' what you'll be findin' around here." The maid approached her, seemed to realize she'd forgotten something, and curtsied.

"Let's dispense with formalities, shall we?" Regan smiled at her.

The girl drank in the kindness, obviously starved for it, and said, "I'm Darcy Kincaid, miss. I'm the Lady Margaret's maid. I hav'na been a maid long."

"I'm not surprised. You look all of five and ten."

"True you are, miss. Me ma made me come into service here. We're poor, you see, and I have five brothers and sisters. Ma says I'd ne'er get a position anywhere else with a face like I got." Darcy stepped over to Regan's trunk and pulled out another dress. "That's the way 'tis 'round here, if you hav'na noticed. All the servants are misfits here. They canna find another position anywhere else. I guess 'tis good that we have somewhere tae work. I just wish it were no' in a haunted place like this. Me ma gave me this when I came here." She laid one of Regan's brown serviceable day dresses on the bed and pulled out a St. Christopher's medal from inside her collar. It dangled from the chain and glistened in the light from the fireplace.

"I didn't bring one of those. I suppose I should have, but I'm not Catholic."

"Oh, we're no' either."

Regan grinned. "Ah, well, I'm sure it works whether you're Catholic or Protestant."

"Kept me safe, it has." Darcy dropped the medal back into her nonexistent bosom, picked up Regan's dress again, and walked toward the wardrobe.

Regan took in the room. It was cozy, small as castle chambers go, done all in shades of green. Lime green velvet curtains hung at the window and matched the counterpane on a four-poster bed. A jade-colored chaise stood by the fireplace, where a fire blazed, sending orange reflections leaping around the room.

"What am I tae do with this?"

Regan saw Darcy holding Old Gray by the barrel. "I'll take it." She eased the pistol from Darcy's grasp and placed it on top of one of the pillows.

"Good thinkin', bringing that." Darcy nodded her approval. "Ne'er know when you'll need it in this place." She fished out the small shovel and lantern Regan had stuffed in the bottom of her trunk. "What's this for?"

"One never knows when one might need digging implements. I like to be prepared for any situation." Regan smiled and laid them back in the trunk. Ignoring Darcy's perplexed look, she asked, "Do you know anything about Lord MacGregor's father and mother?" Regan hated resorting to gossip but she wondered why Gillis had been so reluctant to speak of Lady MacGregor.

"Hech! I'm knowin' what I heard. But you'll no' tell the Lady Margaret I told you. She's says she'll fire me if I repeat gossip tae anyone but her."

"I won't tell." Regan chuckled, her first laugh since coming here.

"'Tis true. She did say that." Darcy looked wounded.

"Oh, I believe you." At the moment Regan could believe almost anything about someone with the last name of Mac-Gregor. "So what do you know?"

"Well, I know that the old Laird MacGregor died on All Hallow's Eve, twenty-two years ago. Me ma says she remembers it 'cause the day afore she was walking past the castle grounds and saw a huge black dog, with eyes like fire"—Darcy fluttered her fingers in front of her own eyes—"walk outta the grounds. Then, poof"—she motioned through the air—"it disappeared right afore her eyes. Me ma thought she was the one dying and took tae her bed. When the Mad MacGregor passed that night, me ma was ne'er so happy. She leaped outta bed and made haggis for us all."

Regan had heard of the Celtic legend that people about to die were visited by a monstrous black dog. She had never believed it, but since coming to Castle Druidhean, she was sure the woman must have seen something unexplainable. "What did he die from?"

"Madness. They said 'fore he was locked up, he would go huntin' in thunderstorms and curse at the lightnin'. Some say that toward the end o' his life, he had tae be kept under lock and key right here in one o' the towers at the castle. He was cursed with the madness by the ancient ones, like all the Laird MacGregors—so me ma says."

"What of the Lady MacGregor?"

"Hech, now, there's a story tae be told." She paused and thought a moment and twisted the ruffle of her cap in her fingers. "I need tae be gettin' the tellin' right. Gives me gooseflesh e'ery time me ma tells it. Maybe if I do it right, you'll be gettin' them, too. Let's see, it goes like this: Two years after the old laird died, Lady MacGregor disappeared. When the magistrate investigated, the family said she'd ridden out alone on the moors. The master hisself likes doing that—must get it from his ma. Anyway, her body was ne'er found. Some believe the evil in the house got her. The magistrate thought it was foul play, but ne'er could find the body, or a weapon, or a reason."

"The present laird must have been only a boy."

"Four and ten he was. Me ma knows 'cause her firstborn, me brother Teddy, shares the same birth date."

"I'm sure the lady must have gotten lost on the moors and died in a bog, or been caught by the icy winds. They can blow up very quickly, so I've been told."

"I dinna like tae think about it, no' while I'm forced tae work here." Darcy shrugged.

Regan found herself asking, "What is your impression of the current laird?"

"Dinna know, miss. Keeps tae hisself, he does. I try tae stay far away from his side of the castle. Ne'er shows his face in the village either. People are still scared o' him. It's the hexed white streak. His thirty-fifth birthday is coming up—he could go daft at any time. I never look at him when I'm forced to pass him in the halls. All's I need is a hexed white streak with this mug." She pointed to her pimpled face.

"I can assure you, looking at the white streak will not put a hex on you. If so, I'd have one." Regan recalled looking into those dark eyes and wanting to remain on his lap. He definitely had hexed her in other ways.

Hours later, Regan dressed for dinner. Her wardrobe consisted of four neutral-colored dresses and two dinner frocks that Regan hadn't worn because she never had an occasion to go out in society. Dark grays and browns never showed dirt, and for an archeologist that was essential. Emma called Regan's clothes frumpish. Regan thought they were sensible. Since she was trying to make an impression on Lady Margaret, and gray always showed a certain stolidity of character, she opted for a bluish gray crepe dinner gown with a white collar and gray gloves. She made sure her hair was caught in a tight chignon and then left her room.

Following Darcy's instructions on finding the dining hall, Regan kept her eyes peeled for those monster dogs. She definitely did not want to make a cake of herself in front of their master again.

After several hallways and turns, Regan realized she was somewhere in the bowels of the castle. But where?

Halfway down the hall burned three rushlights sitting on ledges built into the stone walls. Beyond the glow of their dim fire, complete darkness loomed with foglike thickness. What she could see of the hall branched off into endless stairwells and passages.

She cupped her hands and yelled, "Hello!"

Her voice echoed back to her from every direction.

A sound came from behind her. As she turned, something flew at her.

She covered her head and ducked. Two sparrows fluttered past.

The birds, more scared than she, dived into the darkness, instantly engulfed by it. She heard the beat of their wings keeping time with the pounding of her heart. She listened until she couldn't hear them any longer.

"Hello!" Her voice took on a frantic tone.

Distinct, heavy footsteps thudded behind her. She wheeled around.

No one.

She felt someone watching her. "Who's there?"

Only the whisper of the cold draft in the house answered her.

The footsteps again, this time coming from the inky blackness.

Her skin began to crawl as she raced back the way she had come.

The footsteps followed.

Her heart hammering, she forced herself to turn at the top of a staircase and look over her shoulder.

The hallway was empty.

Hiking up the hem of her dress, she flew down the stairs two at a time. She was sure it wasn't a ghost following her, but more than likely Tyg, and she had no desire to meet him in an empty part of the house.

When Regan reached another hallway, she turned a corner and careened into a broad chest.

chapter 13

Lord MacGregor caught her before she fell. "Och, what's the matter, lass?" He frowned down at her and didn't take his hands from her arms.

"I was lost," she said past her rapid breaths.

"That all?" He eyed her expectantly.

"I think someone was following me."

"This old place makes strange settling noises. It can be unnerving if you're no' used to them."

Regan was certain she'd heard footsteps, but there was no point in pressing the matter. She hadn't actually seen anyone, so she said, "This castle is quite unique."

He was so close she could feel the heat of his body. Her gaze slipped down over him. He wore a midnight blue tailcoat, his broad shoulders filling it without padding. His white linen shirt was stark against a black waistcoat.

She glanced upward to the black curls just touching the top of his white linen cravat, which he'd tied in the Irish style. He'd brushed back his hair, the snowy streak making a perfect rectangular blaze above his ear. One wayward strand of hair spiraled near his temple. He had shaved, but the shadow of his beard had already come back. She didn't think any man could be so handsome. Regan felt an awareness of him at the very center of her being.

He slid his hands slowly down her arms as he said, "To be sure, the castle has its own temperament."

Tingles shot up her arms and pooled in her breasts. "I—I shouldn't tell you this . . ." She paused, feeling the gentle pressure of his fingers through the long sleeves of her gown.

"What?"

"You may think I'm daft."

"No' you." His gaze dropped to her lips, to her breasts.

Heat seeped over her like warm honey as she said, "Do you ever sense that the castle is alive?"

"Aye, I'm knowing it is." His fingers paused on her wrists, then he found the bare skin of her wrists just above the end of her gloves.

Her knees went weak. All she could think about was the rough rasp of his fingertips against the tender skin on her wrist. "It is a fascinating edifice," she said, forcing the tremor from her voice.

"But not as fascinating to you as the circle."

Regan jerked her hands from his grasp. "Of course it is. I'm interested in any archeological sites on this island. If you know who my father is, then you must know he's writing a book about the Picts." She hoped the lie would appease him.

He studied her critically. "So you were helping your da with his book the other night?"

"Yes." That was only part of a lie.

"And McAskill, is he helping your da, too?"

"I fail to see how that is any of your concern."

He grabbed her shoulders. "What is he to you?"

"Nothing but a landlord. Why do *you* dislike him so much?" she fired back, hearing the animosity in his voice. She remembered the expression on Mr. McAskill's face in the boat when he'd seen MacGregor. She felt his fingers digging in her shoulder and said, "You're hurting me."

He gained control of his emotions, then dropped his hands. Without glancing at her, he turned and said, "We're late for dinner."

Regan followed him, but at a safe distance. He had frightened her. What would he have done if he'd lost his temper? Earlier he'd been so kind in the library when she'd been terrified of the dogs. He was an enigma, this dark Scottish lord. From now on she'd stay on her guard around him. She still wondered what Mr. McAskill had done to MacGregor to cause such resentment. After having seen firsthand the sort of man Mr. McAskill was, she couldn't begin to imagine what had passed between them.

I n the great hall, Lachlan sat at the head of the table. Miss Southworth was in the middle. Too close, he decided as he watched her nibble at the roasted brisket on her plate. From behind her long golden lashes, she flashed a leery glance at him, then at the dogs, who lay on either side of his chair. He wanted to assure her the dogs would not come near her. On the other hand, he wanted to capture her in his arms and ravish her Cupid's bow mouth. His yearning for her was getting stronger, while his willpower was getting weaker.

He hadn't meant to lose his temper with her earlier. But he'd been provoked with himself for wanting to kiss her, and then he had seen the image of her in McAskill's arms. His iron self-control had slipped. If she had been with any other man on the isle, he wouldn't have minded. What if she were in love with McAskill? The thought had eaten at him since he had seen them both in the skiff.

He knew he'd have to send her away as soon as he was sure she would not dig in the circle any longer. But first he had to find out what had brought her there. He didn't believe that story about helping her father. She would not have been out in the middle of the night if she wasn't after something specific, something she wanted kept secret. Her expression had closed down when he'd questioned her about it.

He watched the candlelight flick over her golden hair, setting on fire the yellow and red highlights. She wore it pulled back in a tight bun, adding a severity to her oval face. He remembered seeing it fall down her back, and he fought an urge to go over and shake it loose.

Her skin wasn't pearly white, as was fashionable on the mainland, but tanned a light bronze. He'd read that some ladies in London took tincture of lead to make their skin pale. Lachlan had never liked women with that ghostly, translucent white skin. It reminded him of death, and he'd seen enough of death. At least Miss Southworth looked healthy.

He was glad she didn't follow fashionable modes. She didn't need to follow fashion; she made her own. He couldn't help but admire her courageous, independent spirit. Most women would not have risked their lives to help him up the cliff. Most women would have run from the castle the moment they sensed its cursed spirit. Not this lass.

She glanced down the table at him, breaking the silence. "I had hoped Lady Margaret would join us. I would like to have spoken with her."

"Her arthritis is acting up." Lachlan knew better. Lady Margaret had realized she'd been coerced into taking the lass, and she was stewing over it.

"Oh." She made a face at her plate, then sipped her claret.

A hush settled between them. The hiss of the burning logs in the hearth, coupled with the moans within the castle, filled the silence.

She ate another piece of beef, then said, "What was your childhood like, living on the island?"

Lachlan frowned at the thought of his childhood. No one had ever asked about it before. His first instinct was to say nothing, but he had heard the genuine note of interest in her voice. He found himself saying, "No' a very happy one."

"Were you close to your father?"

He felt his leg ache as he thought of his father. "I never felt like I knew him. He went mad when I was a young lad."

"I'm sorry." Her brow wrinkled with emotion.

"Dinna pity me, lass. All we MacGregors know our lot in life."

She laid down her spoon. "Perhaps you should not forget you are allowed a little happiness."

"There's no happiness to be found here."

"I'm certain you are wrong. You have to look for it."

"If you're searching for something out of your reach, you're sure to never find it."

"You must have good memories of your mother."

"I never discuss her." When Lachlan saw her frown, it was obvious he had added too much emphasis to his voice. Since he wanted to change the subject, he asked, "What aboot your childhood? Was it happy?"

She chewed on a fingernail in thought, then said, "We were very happy, up until Mama died."

"How did she die?"

The memory made her eyes gloss over with emotion. "I lost my mother to typhus." She paused, looking at him but not really seeing him. "I'll remember that night to my dying day. We were living in London in a town house on High Street, near Wearmouth Bridge. It was all Father could afford on his teaching salary. Usually a steady stream of carts, carriages, and all manner of humanity moved past High Street. Before the fever came to our house, I used to love to listen to the boisterous laughter that could be heard all hours of the day and night. But that evening, the silence was stifling." She rubbed her arms as if she'd felt a chill, waited a moment, then continued.

"A fog had moved over London and paralyzed it. The unusual silence had a deafening, millstone quality that strangled the air right out of our little house. Every sound caused me to jump. Emma, Papa, and my mother were all sick. I was alone, save for the doctor tending them." She hesitated, her face distorted by the memory.

He prodded her. "What happened, lass?"

She inhaled deeply, then said, "Despite the doctor's warning, I went into my mother's room and crouched at the side of her sickbed. I was too fearful to move. I listened for each of Mama's ragged breaths. After each breath, I prayed for another, and another. I wanted the silence to go away, but it wouldn't. I kept praying. Sometime during the night I fell asleep. In the morning, the doctor woke me. I saw the regret on his face, then I looked at my mother. She was pale and still. I felt guilty that I hadn't been able to stay up long enough to pray for the silence not to take her. You see, I was convinced it was the silence that had taken her from me."

"I'm sorry." The pain on her face awakened a place inside Lachlan that he hadn't known existed. "But your father and sister lived."

"Yes, but it weakened Papa's heart."

"Did you get typhus?"

"Yes, I was the first to come down with it. My fever lasted only a day with hardly any symptoms. I was fortunate, so the doctor said. I didn't think so." Anguish etched her face, and her eyes turned darker blue. "I remember the agony of every hour of those weeks when I thought Emma and Papa would die like Mama. I spent every moment praying to God not to take them. There was a red rash on their bodies. They were delirious for days, thrashing about in the bed. Every time I went into the sickroom, the smell of the fever overwhelmed me. I couldn't help them. Some nights I lay awake all night, afraid that if I closed my eyes, I'd wake up and they'd be gone like Mama."

"How bad is your father's heart?"

"He has spells. It has weakened over the years. I don't know what I'd do if . . ." Her words trailed off. Consternation slipped into her expression as if she realized she'd shared more than she cared to.

Sympathy for her pulled at him. He could sense her dread of the future. He wanted to say something that would comfort her, but insignificant words could not do that, so he remained silent and waited for her to speak again.

It took a moment for her to gather herself, then she said, "I'm no longer hungry. Please excuse me."

He watched her leave the room, the silk of her gown rustling in the silence. He wanted to go after her and hold her, but he fought the urge. If he gave in to the desire, he'd want to do more than just hold her.

L*ater that night, Regan heard yet another creak outside* her door. She lifted her head from the pillow and felt for Old Gray. When she touched the warm metal, she laid her head back down, assured of her safety. How could she ever fall asleep in this place? The castle seemed to come alive at night with groans and creakings.

She thought of what she'd told MacGregor. She'd never spoken of her suffering during that time to anyone. How could she have opened up to him like that? Perhaps it was the moment of vulnerability she'd seen in his face when he'd told her of his own father. His childhood must have been horrible—growing up with a mad father, then having his mother disappear. She couldn't forget how strange he'd acted when she'd questioned him about his mother.

Her mind turned to more pressing matters: Avalon. In the morning she would go out to the circle and begin digging. She would disregard Gillis's and MacGregor's warning about the evil there. The only true evil on the grounds was in the form of Tyg. Regan rolled on her side, beat the feathers in the pillow, and snuggled her head down. She forced her eyes closed.

The sound of angry voices outside her window brought her eyes open again.

chapter 14

R egan threw back the covers. When her feet hit the cold
stone floor, she grimaced and tiptoed to the line of tall,
Gothic-shaped windows. She pulled back the curtain and
pressed her nose to the glass.

Her chamber, on the west side of the castle, faced the
courtyard. Moonlight threw a dim haze over the yard and
the yews growing in a line along one side of the bailey.
Their misshapen limbs stretched out in all directions, ready
to attack any unsuspecting intruder.

MacGregor's dark form stood near one of the trees. At
the sight of him she felt her stomach knot. He was speaking
to someone hidden beneath the canopy of leaves. She
couldn't hear clearly, so she flicked up the latch. It took a
few heaves but the window creaked open.

She grimaced. Had MacGregor heard the noise?

He didn't seem to notice and shook his cane at someone.
"Damn you, come back here!" he said.

Regan heard heavy footsteps hitting the courtyard flag-
stones, then the slam of the gate.

MacGregor pounded his cane against the tree trunk in frustration, making Regan flinch.

He paused and something caused him to glance up at her window.

Regan leaped behind the curtain, her pulse racing. Why was he so angry? And who had been with him? He certainly had a temper. She'd already seen that.

Och, you should no' be thinking of me as kind. His words rang in her mind. A nagging apprehension swirled in the pit of her belly.

R*egan woke at dawn. She wanted to go out to the circle* before the servants rose. Later she'd sketch the strange symbol on the walls for her father. He'd enjoy researching it.

As she dressed, she listened to the noises within the walls. Even in early morning, the house had its peculiar aberrations: the moanings, the strange sighs, the icy drafts that never seemed to tire. One wafted through her room, sending goose bumps down her skin.

She hurried over to the wardrobe to locate her shawl. She was certain Darcy had laid it in the drawer, but she couldn't find it.

When she gave up looking, she closed the wardrobe. As she turned, the bright yellow and red paisley wool caught her eye. The shawl lay draped over a ledge beneath the window, as though someone had been wearing it and carelessly tossed it there.

She would have sworn she'd seen Darcy fold it and put it in the wardrobe's drawer. She picked up the wrap; the wool felt ice cold. A strange sensation forced her to glance around the room. Why did she have a feeling the walls were grinning at her? The hairs along her neck rose.

"Regan Southworth, you're being utterly ridiculous," she said in her sternest tone. "The castle did not take this shawl."

She threw the wrap over her shoulders, snatched up a lit

candle, and gingerly opened her door. The hinges creaked slightly. She made a face as she peeked her head out into the hall. The rushlights had gone out during the night, leaving the hallway in total darkness. She raised the candle, saw no one was there, then stepped out.

She tiptoed down the hall. When she neared the stairwell, she heard voices. She darted behind a corner, blew out the candle, and pressed her spine against the cold stones.

As the people climbed the stairs, she recognized Tyg's and Gillis's voices.

"'Tis your turn tae watch the circle tonight," Gillis said.

"Master didn't say we had tae be takin' turns."

"He said we're tae keep the miss away from it. You'll be takin' your turn at it."

Regan grimaced. They were watching the circle. How would she ever get near it?

"I'll take me turn when I'm good and ready," Tyg grumbled. "If you're knowin' what's good for you, you'll stay out o' my way."

"Cross me, and you'll regret it." Gillis's voice had a pernicious quality that seemed foreign to him.

"By, I'll cross you. You've no authority over me."

"I will if you continue tae be a slacker. I've had tae finish the chores I gave you yesterday. If you think you can hide behind Lady Margaret's skirts and no' pull your weight, think again."

"I do me work," Tyg hissed.

Regan imagined Tyg's face swollen with rage, and she had to admire Gillis's pluck.

"Half the time."

"You callin' me lazy?"

"Aye, you're too lazy tae stroan."

"If you know what's good for you, you'll shut your trap," Tyg said.

"Don't threaten me. I know where you were the night the Flame disappeared."

Regan heard a thump like a shoulder hitting the wall. She could visualize Tyg with a knife, slicing poor Gillis's throat with one sweep of his burly paw. She stepped out from behind the corner.

"Good morning, all." Her loud voice tolled through the stairwell.

Tyg and Gillis glanced up the stairs at her.

Gillis had Tyg up against the wall, not the other way around. His elbow was thrust up under Tyg's neck. Choking noises came from his throat. Regan's eyes widened in surprise. Gillis must know how to defend himself.

Gillis saw her and broke away from Tyg.

Tyg rubbed his throat.

With a breezy air of indifference, Regan said, "Lovely morning for a walk."

"Aye, miss?" Gillis said, his eyes trained on Tyg.

"By, you shouldna be leavin' your room." Tyg readjusted his eyepatch that had been knocked over to the side of his nose.

Regan glimpsed the deep hollowed-out socket and had to look away. "I thought I might do a little exploring. The interior of the castle is fascinating."

The hatred between the men temporarily thawed, and they shared a her-mind-has-gone-begging look.

Tyg spoke first. "No' a good idea tae explore the castle alone."

"I'm afraid he's right. Anyway, Lady Margaret'll be lookin' for you soon, miss."

Regan glanced at Gillis. "Is it her custom to rise at dawn?"

"Aye." Tyg nodded.

Would she ever get to the circle? Tyg and Gillis were watching it at night. Lady Margaret rose at dawn.

"Shall I bring a tray up for you?" Gillis asked.

"That will be lovely. Thank you." Regan headed toward her room. She recalled Gillis mentioning the Flame. What was the Flame? she thought with a frown.

• • •

Half an hour later Regan had finished a quick sketch of the symbol on the walls for her father and had written Emma, asking if she might work her horticultural wizardry and brew up an herbal salve for Darcy's face. She stuffed both items in an envelope and was about to ring the bell for Gillis when a knock sounded on the door.

"Come in," she said.

Gillis opened the door. "The Lady MacGregor wishes you tae take your meal in her parlor."

"Thank you."

Gillis looked embarrassed and said, "About a moment ago. I'm sorry you had tae come upon such a fray."

"I heard the last part of it." Regan watched for his reaction.

He stared down at the teapot, his mouth hardening, the three stumps on his left hand moving as his thumb and first finger tightened on the side of the tray.

"What is the Flame?"

"Nothin', miss. Better you forget what you heard." Blood infused his hollow cheekbones. He shifted on his feet as if he wanted to run away. The hand missing three fingers clenched and unclenched.

Regan waited for him to say more. When he didn't, she was certain he wouldn't take her into his confidence. She handed the letter to him. "Please, would you post this?"

"Done, miss." Gillis grabbed the letter with his good hand, and relief masked his expression as he slammed the door.

Now more than ever, she was determined to find out about the Flame.

Temporarily pushing the thought away, Regan smoothed down the Egyptian-brown muslin day dress she was wearing and repinned the few blond wisps that had come loose from her bun. When she stood before the dressing table, she saw her plain face, made even plainer by her brown dress. Before meeting MacGregor she had not cared about her appearance. She frowned at the freckles on her nose. No help for them. Why should she care if she wasn't beautiful? She was here for only one thing, Avalon.

Regan reached to put away the comb she'd been using only moments ago and noticed it wasn't there. She glanced around and spotted it on the ledge beneath the window, exactly where she'd found her shawl earlier that morning.

"What is this?" she said to the room at large. "I know I didn't put that comb there." Or had she? Her brow furrowed. Was she losing her mind?

In two steps she stood before the window and picked up the comb. The ledge gave slightly beneath her fingertips. Regan tossed the comb on her bed, then bent and saw the board that formed the ledge was warped from humidity. She tried to press it down and the oak moved several inches.

She examined the wood more closely and discovered a nail driven in one end, like a makeshift hinge, so that the board could swing completely free from the wall.

She pulled on the unfixed end, and it opened with a *plunk*. The smell of dampness wafted up from a five-inch-wide space between the wall and the sill. Cobwebs formed bridges across the opening. Regan glanced past them at a book hidden down in the bottom.

She batted away the cobwebs, retrieved the book, and flipped through the pages. It was a diary of some sort. She didn't have time to read it, so she put it back in its hiding place.

After securing the board, she headed for Lady Margaret's chamber. She paused before two doors. Gillis had said one was Lady Margaret's chamber and one the parlor. But which was which? Regan decided to knock on both doors. As she raised her hand, the door next to her opened, and she looked into Tyg's disagreeable visage.

Regan wanted to step back but refused to give him the satisfaction of knowing he'd frightened her.

"Go in, she's waitin' for you." He nodded toward the door.

Regan hurried past him, taking care to give him a wide berth, feeling his one eye boring into her.

Lady Margaret's parlor was three times the size of her own room. It was done all in lilac hues, the brightest and by far the prettiest room she'd yet to enter—save, of course, the library. The only thing that spoiled it was the dowager herself.

She sat on a sofa, eyes narrowed, face twisted in a sneer. The yellow silk dress, black wig, and powdered face made her look like a wasp queen. Had the lady a stinger, Regan would be dead.

"Come in, gel, and close the door. Do you always keep people waiting?"

"I came as soon as I could." Perhaps she had taken longer discovering the diary than she'd thought.

"Sit down." Lady Margaret waved to a small table that had been set for only one.

"Are you not eating?"

"I've already eaten with my grandson."

"Oh." So Lord MacGregor rose at dawn, too.

"Let us get on with this interview to see if you'll suit. Tell me a little about yourself." Lady Margaret narrowed her eyes at Regan while she picked up her sewing.

"I came to Skye with my father and sister."

"From what part of England are you?" She poked the needle into the canvas.

"All over, really."

"That is no answer."

Regan wondered if this interrogation was more to appease the lady's curiosity than to see if Regan was suitable. She tried again. "My father's a teacher and archeologist. We never stayed in one place long. But I was born in London."

"Is there nobility in your family?"

"My mother's father is a baron."

A gray brow shot up. "Really! What is his name?"

"I'd rather not speak of him. I fail to see how my relatives have anything to do with how well I perform my job."

Irritation flared in the dowager's golden eyes, then her lips disappeared as her mouth hardened. "Well, well, you're a bumptious young person."

"I wasn't trying to be." Regan was certain that if the lady didn't get her way, she could be as moody and unpredictable as her grandson.

"You do speak your mind, which, to a point, I can admire in one so young, but know that I'll not stand for insolence." Her next words sounded pried from her lipless mouth. "I suppose you'll do, gel, but let's speak plainly. There'll be no setting your cap at my grandson. Do I make myself perfectly clear?"

"You needn't worry," Regan said. "I can promise you, if I were in the husband market, which I'm not, he'd be the last man on earth I'd ever want to marry." Was he already engaged? Why should she care?

"I'll take you at your word, gel." The loose skin beneath Lady Margaret's chin stretched as she pursed her wrinkled mouth. The expression caused her pointed cheekbones and nose to become sharper and more pronounced.

Regan wasn't sure who had won that round. At least she hadn't let the lady pry into her father's work. Given Lady Margaret's lioness disposition, Regan knew she'd have to set a few boundaries or the lady would run roughshod over her.

After a moment of tense silence between them, Lady Margaret's eyes turned crafty. "How well do you know your landlord?"

"Not very."

One of her gray brows arched and she looked incredulous. "That isn't what I've heard, gel."

"Then you've heard incorrectly. We are not well acquainted. Mr. McAskill is nothing more than my father's landlord, and it shall stay that way." Regan was certain Lady Margaret must have known about her jumping out of the skiff. Her grandson must have told her. She couldn't help the blush that stole into her cheeks.

Lady Margaret eyed her skeptically.

Before the lady could pry further, Regan decided to slip in a few inquiries of her own. She adopted a casual tone and asked, "Has my room always been a guest room?"

"Why? Is it not suitable?"

"Yes, very." Regan thought of the diary, and said, "It is such a pleasant room, overlooking the courtyard as it does, I wondered why it was not favored as a chamber."

"No one would use that room. It was the late Lady Mac-Gregor's sitting parlor before I had it remodeled."

"Oh." Had the diary belonged to Lady MacGregor?

A lengthy silence settled between them while Regan ate. When she was done, Regan asked, "My lady, who or what is the Flame?"

"Where did you hear that?" Lady Margaret narrowed her eyes at Regan.

"From a servant."

"Which servant?"

"I cannot say. I didn't recognize the voice."

"It's to be that way, is it?" Lady Margaret drummed her fingers on the edge of the sewing hoop.

"Yes."

When Regan wouldn't glance away, the lady said, "I'm sure you'll go snooping around until you find out. The Flame was the nickname of my son's wife." She stressed the word "wife" with contempt.

"Oh." Regan tried to appear indifferent. Lady MacGregor? Gillis had been speaking about Lachlan's mother and the night she disappeared.

One of Regan's puzzles had been solved, but she had another. She waited a moment, feeling the full force of Lady Margaret's gaze, then said, "Did you hear voices last night?"

"I slept like the dead. Why, did you?"

"Yes. Outside my window in the courtyard. I'm sure it was Lord MacGregor arguing with someone."

"You shouldn't be eavesdropping. You'd do better to mind your business." The words were a barbed command. Lady Margaret turned her nose up at Regan and said, "The interview is over, gel. You'll find a list of things to do today, there." She pointed to a rosewood writing desk near a wall.

A piece of foolscap lay next to a quill and inkstand. Regan scanned the list:

> *Direct Darcy with laundry*
> *Clean out garment closet*
> *Sort hairpins*
> *Comb wigs*
> *Write correspondence*

The list went on and on, enough work to keep her busy for a year. Lady Margaret didn't want a companion, but a slave. Regan felt Lady Margaret scrutinizing her for a reaction—no doubt it was a test of Regan's endurance.

Regan forced a smile and said, "I'll get on this right away."

She left the lady squinting at her needlework and closed the door. In the hall, she met Darcy maneuvering an armload of Lady Margaret's dresses.

"Let me help." Regan caught several gowns that were slipping off the top.

"Obliged, miss. Got tae get these down and launder 'em. The old carlin"—she nodded toward the parlor—"said she wanted every speck o' dirt off 'em. 'Tain't a bit o' dirt on 'em. Just laundered 'em last month."

"I'll help you." Regan was used to helping Letta with laundry.

"Hech! Forgot the drawers. Just be a minute." Darcy plopped the tower of dresses in Regan's arms and scurried toward the room.

To avoid the possibility of another encounter with Lady Margaret, Regan decided to wait for Darcy near the stairs. Unable to see over the stack of garments in her arms, Regan carefully made her way down the hall. When she reached the stairwell, she felt the dresses slipping and tried to get a tighter hold on them.

Suddenly someone shoved her from behind, then she was falling. . . .

chapter 15

Dresses flew out of Regan's hands as she tumbled downward. She envisioned falling and breaking her neck. Luckily the stairwell was U shaped with a landing in the middle, so she went down only six stairs, though they felt like a hundred. She lay on the landing, trembling, aching, feeling the frigid breeze within the house brushing past her.

Regan forced herself to move enough to glance up and see Tyg running down the stairs toward her. How had he arrived here so quickly?

"You hurt, miss?" He bent to help her, his expression one of genuine worry.

"I don't know," Regan said, feeling sore all over. "Someone pushed me."

"Probably a ghoulie. We have some what likes a good jest."

"It wasn't a ghost who pushed me." Those had been human hands she'd felt on her back. "Did you see anyone?"

"No' a soul." He shook his head and shrugged.

He avoided her gaze and she couldn't help but wonder if

he had pushed her. But how could she prove it? It was his word against hers. He'd been here longer. Who would believe her?

Footsteps pounded the stairs. She turned and looked up into MacGregor's stony black eyes. In his kilt and white shirt, he was William Wallace, Robert Bruce, and Bonnie Prince Charlie forged into one, the quintessential Scottish lord. His presence filled the whole stairwell.

He held his cane in one hand and a musket in the other. A gunpowder purse was draped over his left shoulder as if he'd just come from hunting. He set the cane and gun down, then stepped past Tyg and scooped her up. "Are you all right, lass?" he said, his voice rough with concern.

With his eyes searching hers, his hot breath on her lips, and his powerful arms cradling her, Regan wasn't sure if she was all right at all. "Y-yes," she forced out.

He glanced over at Tyg. "What are you knowing of this?"

"Nothin'. I was coming down the hall and saw her fall off the top step, then I come runnin'."

"It was an accident. I lost my balance." Regan looked askance at Tyg.

He shifted awkwardly under the close scrutiny and began picking up the dresses.

Darcy appeared at the top of the stairs, drawers hanging from her hands. Observing Regan's disheveled appearance, she immediately dropped her gaze and stammered, "Wh-what's h-happened?"

MacGregor spoke. "Miss Southworth had an accident. I'm taking her to her room. Carry on."

Darcy snatched the dresses out of Tyg's hand, then hurried down the stairs. Tyg frowned, then followed her.

As MacGregor climbed the stairs, Regan felt his chest and abdomen pressing against her hip. She glanced over at his ebony hair curling around his collar. Several strands coiled in front of his ears, and she longed to reach up and push them back. Regan rested her head on his shoulder and breathed in the scent of his white linen shirt, starch, and his own woodsy male scent.

"You shouldn't be without your cane. Put me down. I'm sure nothing is broken." She stared at the thatch of black hair on his chest, prominent against his light shirt.

"You could be hurt."

"I'm not." Regan noticed the dark shadow on his unshaven chin. Virile masculinity oozed from him. "How long has Tyg worked for you?" she asked, her voice growing unsteady

"He's been here as long as I can remember. He's a trusted retainer." His brows furrowed with worry. "Did he have something to do with your accident?"

Regan hedged a moment, knowing it was her word against Tyg's. Finally she said, "No."

He looked relieved. "What were you doing on the bloody stairs with those dresses anyway?"

"Helping Darcy."

"Lady Margaret had you helping her?" he asked in disbelief.

"No." Regan didn't want to cause strife between him and his grandmother.

His lips thinned as if he didn't believe her, but he said nothing.

Regan heard the click of toenails and glanced over his shoulder at the dogs following behind them. She immediately tensed.

"You needn't fear them," he said.

"Are you sure?"

"Aye, they'd never attack unless ordered to."

The look on his face disquieted her.

He reached her chamber and slammed the door before the dogs made it through. He gently laid her on the bed. His hand slowly slid from beneath her back and knees, making her pulse race. She expected him to move away, but he straightened and stared down at her, a cryptic expression on his face.

"You can go now," she said, her insides churning at his close proximity to her bed.

"No' until I inspect your wounds."

"That's unnecessary. I'm fine."

"I'll be seeing for myself." He crossed his arms over his chest and splayed his legs, resembling a Celtic warrior about to go into battle.

"The devil you will." She sat up on her elbow and ignored the twinge in her back. "Surely you know the impropriety of your even being in my room. Now leave this instant."

He didn't speak or move, just towered over her, a determined gleam in his eye.

"I mean it, MacGregor." Regan picked up a pillow and shook it at him. It wobbled in her hands like a giant piece of bread dough. "Get out!"

He didn't move.

"If you think I'm going to amuse you by letting you humiliate me—"

"I can think of better amusements." He snatched the pillow out of her hands and tossed it on the bed. A hint of a wicked grin twitched one side of his mouth as his gaze flicked over her body, lingering on her breasts.

Regan didn't know whether to be offended or not. "And I can think of other things I should be doing." She threw her legs over the bed's side to stand.

In one effortless motion, he plopped her legs back on the mattress. "I'm needing to check the extent of your injuries and you'll be letting me."

Regan's heart pounded as his dark gaze impaled her to the bed. Her voice wavered as she said, "I assure you, I'm fine. It would take more than a tumble down a few steps to harm me. I once fell into a pit in a cave and I came out with only a sprained ankle. I'm hale and hearty."

"I'll no' take chances." His raven eyes glinted a warning.

"I don't see—"

"I'll no' quarrel with you. Now take off your dress and

petticoat, or I'll do it for you," he said, his nostrils flaring with mounting anger.

"My dress *and* petticoat?"

"Aye, how else am I to see your wounds?"

"You're enjoying this, aren't you?" She glowered at him.

"Dinna fash yourself. I'll get no enjoyment out of this. You have nothing I haven't already seen."

So he'd been with other women. It wasn't a surprise. What surprised her was the stab of jealousy she was feeling. "I hope you'll have the common decency to give me a bit of privacy."

Satisfaction gleamed in his eyes as he turned around. He kept his arms crossed over his chest and waited.

"No peeking."

"Be quick about it."

"Very well, but keep your back turned." Regan kept one eye on him as she untied her dress. Her father never had money for pins, or for a maid, so Regan and Emma were forced to make their dresses more serviceable and less fashionable with bodices that laced down the front.

She pulled the brown muslin over her head and tossed it on the bed. Next, off came her sturdy walking shoes, then her petticoat. Clad only in her chemise and drawers, she slid beneath the covers.

"You're no' done," he said. "Let down your hair."

She frowned at the back of his head. Did he have eyes back there? "Why my hair?"

"Need to check for head injuries."

"For the love of King Arthur. My head is not sore, but talking to you about it is likely to make it so." She jerked the pins out of her hair.

She shook out her hair. Blond curls tumbled down to her waist. She made sure he wasn't peeking, then jerked the covers up to her chin. The sheets felt cold against her exposed skin and she shivered.

"All right, let's be done with this," he said.

She held the sheets up around her throat and watched him turn.

His kilt fluttered slightly. When she glanced up, she saw he was no longer angry. Was that pleasure in his eyes?

"Where to start?" he said, his voice laced with the kind of excitement a boy might have before he attacks an apple pie. He stopped near the side of the bed, eyeing her dress.

Something in the intimate way it held his attention caused Regan's breath to freeze in her lungs. Her gaze dropped to his bare knees. She gulped and lied, "Only my back hurts."

"I'm glad you're finally being honest aboot injuring something. Roll over."

Regan hesitated, saw his implacable expression, then turned on her side. She was relieved not to have to face him.

The edge of the cover lifted. Though she couldn't see him, she felt his penetrating gaze roaming along her back, his overwhelming presence bending over her. Her whole body began to tremble, but not from the cold.

Regan closed her eyes, while a blush burned from her head to her toes.

He pulled the covers down to her waist. Cold air touched her skin. He brushed aside the hair that had fallen down her back, and she heard his breathing grow shallow and rapid.

"Does it look bad?"

"Bad enough." His hand touched a spot near the top of her chemise.

"Ouch!"

"You've got bruising here," he said, concern in his voice. "Lie on your belly."

She rolled over, feeling the scratches on her sore knees and elbows. He kept the sheet over her buttocks and legs, and for that she was grateful. As it was, she wanted to shrivel up and melt into the sheets. She buried her face in the pillow.

The moment his hand touched her, she jumped.

"Hold on, lass." His fingers slid along her spine.

She felt his rough palms brush her soft skin, leaving tingles in their wake. The heat of his hands had magic in it that flowed along her back, down her arms and legs, and spread to her breasts.

He hit a sore spot and she jerked. "Tender?"

"Yes."

Those searching hands moved up her neck, then he buried his fingers in her hair. Warmth oozed down her neck.

"Hmmmmm!"

"What?"

"No bruises."

"I told you so."

He dropped the sheet over her. "Your back took the brunt of the fall. I'll send the maid up with liniment. You'll stay abed the rest of the day," he said, his voice strained.

"I'm really all right."

"You'll obey me or else."

"Or else what?"

"You're no' wanting to know, believe me," he growled.

Before she could turn around, she heard his stiff footsteps beat a quick retreat to the door. When she turned, she glimpsed a stony expression carved into his handsome profile. He slammed the door.

Regan turned to pick up her dress. The small mirror hanging above the writing desk caught her attention. He had been facing in that direction, ogling her. No wonder he'd looked so diverted.

"Scottish rogue." The thought of him watching her while she disrobed caused a strange reckless anticipation within her. She stared at her reflection in the mirror, her white shoulders peeking over the top of her chemise, her blond curls falling down to her waist, her large blue eyes inflamed with anger. She didn't look too terribly unbecoming. In fact, she looked like a different person, rather like a wanton. She hoped he'd gotten an eyeful.

"You're dissolute, Regan Southworth," she said to the mirror.

Admit it, you didn't want him to leave.

She would have sworn the words had issued from the walls. But that couldn't be. She fought a desire to escape the room as she quickly reached for her clothes.

O*n the other side of the castle, Lachlan strode toward* the north wing and heard:
You want to go back to her.
Lachlan was used to the castle voice. He'd never admit to anyone he heard it. His father had heard the same voice, told someone about it in his later years, and been put under lock and key for it. Such a fate would befall Lachlan sooner than he cared to admit, so he ignored the castle's utterings.

He had retrieved his gun and cane from the stairwell, and now felt them slipping in his sweaty palms. He realized his hands were trembling as he shifted the musket to the crook of his arm and thought of Regan Southworth. To be sure, she couldn't be ignored. He'd just seen all her bonny parts. The sight of her undressing would be burned into his memory until he died. The perfect outline of her high proud breasts, the hardened nipples pulling against the thin chemise, the sensual way she unpinned her hair and shook it out, letting it fall down to her waist.

As he had watched her, he kept wondering if McAskill had seen her undress, and he'd felt a jealous rage the like of which he'd never experienced.

When he was close to her, he felt the control she had over him. He'd spent his entire life mortaring a wall of indifference around him; it had helped him survive his childhood and bear the unbreakable chains of the past that kept him tied to Castle Druidhean and all its secrets. But every time he was near her, he felt another stone in the wall crumble. Despite the castle's insidious advice, he had to keep her at arm's length. He had made up his mind long ago that he would never care for a woman, nor would he ever marry and pass on the madness in his blood. Never.

Lachlan listened to the soft pad of the dogs' paws behind him and reached the north wing, his favorite part of the castle—up until today. Today the air was suffocating. The smell of burned rushes hung bitter in the air. The walls here were whitewashed, and near the ceiling, embedded in the plaster, stag horns clawed out from the walls, forming a twisted, writhing arch.

The north wing had fallen into disrepair until Lachlan had come into the title and refurbished it. Here was where Lachlan the boy had escaped his father's drunken tirades and his mother's indifference. He had dubbed it the Hidey Biel. He had always cherished the solitude of the Hidey Biel, forbidding entrance to any of the servants save Gillis. Only recently, with Miss Southworth in the house, had he realized how secluded and truly isolated this part of the castle was.

As Lachlan paused before his chamber, Gillis opened the door. "Good day, lad."

Lachlan handed him the musket. "See this is put away." There was a six-hundred-year-old rule in Castle Druidhean that all weapons were kept under lock and key. It had come about after the fifth Laird MacGregor had shot his wife. He'd shot the servant he'd found in her bed, too. Then he'd shot the magistrate and several of his men when they had come for him. His life had ended at the end of a hangman's noose.

"Aye." Gillis took the gun and read Lachlan's expression. His long face wrinkled in a frown. "What's wrong?"

"Nothing."

"Beggin' your pardon, but I've seen you grow up. I know when somethin's botherin' you. Is your leg painin' you? The poultice no' workin'?"

Gillis was the one fixed person in Lachlan's life who never wavered. He had always been there for Lachlan, much more so than his own parents. Gillis was more than a servant; he was a friend. "It's not my leg," Lachlan said.

"Then it must be Miss Southworth worryin' you."

"Has she asked you aboot my mother?"

"No' yet." Gillis had turned away, and Lachlan couldn't

see his face. "Are you knowing what she's wanting in the circle?"

"Nay." Lachlan thumped his cane in his hand, and caused the dogs to raise their heads near his side. "But I intend to find out. If she asks prying questions about my mother or her disappearance, say naught and tell me at once."

"Aye." Gillis's brows dropped over his deep-set eyes.

"Has she said anything about McAskill?"

Gillis shook his head. "No' a word. How deeply you thinkin' she's involved with him?"

"I'm no' sure." Lachlan ground his teeth together until they ached.

"You canna be lettin' her go on with him. He's a skellum if ever there was one."

"I know."

"Have you told her what sort he is?"

"No' yet."

"Maybe 'tis time you did."

Lachlan didn't answer him and scratched the ears of the dogs.

"You've feelin's for this lass?"

Lachlan's silence was answer enough.

"That's no' such a bad thing in my way o' thinkin'."

"It's bloody well dangerous." Lachlan frowned down at the top of Charlie's head.

"You should have married long ago, lad, and had an heir."

"We've been through this. I'll no' propagate this madness. 'Tis ending with me."

Gillis stared down at the gun in his hand. "There's always a chance the madness willna affect your bairns."

"I'll no' take the chance."

"I can see there's no' talking tae you. How long will Miss Southworth be with us, then?"

"Until I force her to leave." Lachlan whacked the cane in his palm once more.

chapter 16

❧

Regan sank into the soothing heat of the liniment Darcy had rubbed on her back. Physically she felt much better, but MacGregor had sent word that she was supposed to stay in bed again today. Regan had never lain in bed for two straight days in her life, until now. After her mother died, she'd had to care for Emma, who had been only three at the time. Then when her father had become ill, she'd had to take of him. She felt almost guilty having lain in bed for such a lengthy period. The longer she stared at the walls, the more she felt like they were closing in on her.

Most of the hours she had spent in bed had been occupied with thoughts of MacGregor. Yesterday played over and over in her mind, how he had set her down on the bed and demanded she undress. She recalled the feeling of his hands stroking her back and neck, his fingers delving into her hair.

At the mere thought of his touch, the skin along her nape burned. An intense warmth seeped through her. She admonished her wanton side for it. She wasn't here to fall under his dark spell, but it was happening.

Her gaze shifted to the window ledge. In all the excitement she'd forgotten about the diary. She wanted to discover who had written it.

Though her body was slightly sore, she got out of bed. She hurriedly dressed, choosing a tan dress made of China crepe; then she swung open the board and pulled out the diary.

The spine crinkled as she bent it. The handwriting was hardly legible, with hurried strokes. She read the first page:

March 3, 1774
Today Lord Balmoral MacGregor sent me four dozen roses after my performance. He's been in the audience all this week. Though the gentleman is very striking, with that strange white stripe in his hair, I'm afraid he'll have to do more than send roses to impress me. Diamonds might do. I've heard he's very wealthy and owns an island in the Hebrides. He's asked me to dine with him. I refused, of course. It doesn't do to appear too interested. I wouldn't have any admirers if I did.

Regan recalled Gillis telling her MacGregor's father's name had been Balmoral. She was certain now Lady MacGregor had written the diary.

March 5, 1774
Today a lovely diamond bracelet arrived from Lord M. He must have read my mind. Perhaps I will let him take me to dinner. Lar's just told me the theater is losing money and he can no longer keep it open. Oh, the life of a thespian! I dread finding another theater, not that I will have trouble in that quarter. They love me anywhere I go, but I hate the thought of leaving Bath behind. It's so alive with gaiety and pleasures and amorous, rich admirers.

March 12, 1774
Lord M informed me he's in love with me. I've done
nothing to warrant his attentions—maybe my dis-
couraging him has inflamed his desire. He asked me
to marry him. I almost laughed in his face. Noblemen
do not marry actresses—Sir John proved that axiom.
He knew I loved him to distraction, but would he pro-
pose? Uncaring, unfeeling rogue. I shall never love
another man, but I will never let him know that, nor
poor Lord M. When he had proposed, he had looked
at me with such adoration and sincerity, and all I kept
thinking was, he's a fool to be ruled by his heart.
Tonight is my last performance. The theater will close
on the morrow. I could take on the role of Lady Mac-
Gregor, be pampered for the rest of my life, and not
have to ever work again. What shall I do?

Someone rapped on the door.

Regan slammed the cover closed. "One moment." She
slipped the book back in its secret place, then said, "Come
in."

Emma stepped inside.

A wide smile broke over Regan's face.

For a moment the two sisters only stared at each other
across the room. Then Emma ran toward Regan.

Regan ran, too.

They hugged at the foot of the bed.

"I miss you," Emma cried. "It's not the same at home
without you. I have no sister to scold me."

Regan hugged Emma tighter. "I miss you, too, Em. And
if you need scolding, I'm sure I can think of something."

Emma giggled. "You're horrid."

"I know." Regan's smile disappeared. "Have you taken
my advice and ended all communication with our grandparents?"

"Yes," Emma said in a pout. "I know you were right."

"I'm glad you think so now. How is Papa?"

"Anxious for news of you." She paused as if remembering

something and said, "He said to tell you the symbol you drew is some sort of ancient sign that was used by the Celts to keep evil spirits away."

"Oh," Regan said, not surprised.

"He looked very pleased when you sent it."

"I'm sure it took his mind off being sick."

"He's still worried about you."

"Assure him I'm fine and not to worry. Did you get my letter?"

Emma nodded and pulled a small jar out of her purse. "For Darcy. I made it this morning, so it's fresh. Tell her to apply it twice a day."

"You didn't have to bring it so soon."

"I wanted to see you. Mr. McAskill offered to bring me as far as the gate—"

"He what?" Her little sister had been alone with that roué? Regan grabbed Emma's shoulders. "You didn't come alone with him?"

"Letta rode with us. She's with him now. He said he'd wait for me in the village. He's not so bad. He says he loves you and wants to propose."

"Rubbish! He can't love anyone. He's a vulgar, rag-mannered bounder. Did he send you here to peddle this Banbury tale?" Regan asked, getting angrier by the minute at Mr. McAskill. She should have told Emma exactly what had happened out in the skiff.

"Well, he did ask me to." Emma's brows met in consternation. "I said I would. I'll tell him you're not interested, but why do you think so ill of him?"

She told Emma about McAskill's indecent proposal and his threat to compromise her and that she'd jumped to escape him.

Emma looked worried. "Goodness, I had no idea he was such a blackguard."

"If you are alone, stay well away from him."

"I'll have to ride home with him."

"I believe he'll behave with Letta there."

Emma stared into Regan's eyes. "Something besides McAskill's worrying you. What?"

"Oh, Em, the Dowager MacGregor is a horrid old spiteful she-lion." Regan didn't want to worry her about the tumble down the stairs, so she said, "And the castle . . . well, I vow I can hear it breathing—but do not tell Papa I said that. He'd ridicule and tease me forever."

Emma glanced around the room. "I believe you. There's something singular here, I can feel it." She shivered and rubbed her arms.

Regan thought of Tyg and said, "It's the living who haunt this castle, I'm quite sure of it."

A fierce knock made them both jump and glance at the door.

The pounding didn't sound like it came from a mere hand but from something more rigid. MacGregor's cane? Regan's heart thumped in anticipation of having him in her room again. Her face flushed as she thought of how he'd last seen her.

She steeled her courage and squared her shoulders, abruptly aware of the bruises on her back. "Enter," she said.

MacGregor strode inside, looking not quite so savage as he had earlier. He wore a black frock coat, tight trousers, boots, a white linen shirt, and a cravat. He'd washed and shaved and his hair, black and glistening, was still wet, the white streak cutting a sharp line past his right ear. The heavy cloud of his presence invaded the small room.

At the sight of him Regan felt her mouth go dry. He appeared more handsome every time she looked at him. "To what do we owe this pleasure?" Regan asked.

"I came to see how you're feeling, lass." He glanced at the mirror, and for a brief moment amusement softened his granite-like features.

"How nice of you." Regan glowered at him.

His lips strained against a grin. "I'm hoping you're better?" His gaze dropped down the length of her body and back up again with bold frankness.

"Much." The hungry gleam in the predatory black depths made Regan's pulse race.

"Are you all right?" Emma's face contorted with worry.

"I had a little fall, but I'm fine now."

His gaze shifted to Emma. He bowed slightly and said, "A pleasant surprise, Miss Emma."

His scrutiny caused Emma to step over and slip her hand into Regan's. She managed a fumbling curtsey, gulped, and said, "I—I just came to see Regan. I'm leaving now."

"I'll escort you home."

"Thank you, but Mr. McAskill is waiting in the village—"

His brow darkened, causing Emma to step even closer to Regan.

Regan frowned at Emma, wishing she hadn't mentioned their lecherous landlord.

MacGregor's hand tightened around his cane in a death grip. "I'll be leaving you to your visit," he said, his tone curt. He turned and exited the room, slamming the door behind him.

Regan and Emma jumped.

Emma let out a sigh. "Why does he dislike Mr. McAskill so much?"

"I do not know, but I heard him arguing with someone two nights ago in the courtyard. I couldn't see the person's face, but I was certain it was a man. I heard more than one muffled deep voice. I wonder if it was McAskill?"

"Why do you think it's him?"

"Lord MacGregor was very angry when the person left."

"I'd hate to have Lord MacGregor angry at me."

"I would, too." Regan frowned.

O*utside Regan's room, Lachlan whistled for the dogs* he'd made wait at the end of the hallway. They bounded toward him, sensed his irritation, and crouched near his side.

He hooked the handle of his cane on his wrist, bent, and

petted them. "Well, tykes, we know where she stands with McAskill."

Petting the dogs didn't stop his blood from burning. She must be in love with him, and the sweet-faced sister was passing love notes between them. He'd find McAskill and face him man to man. For Regan Southworth's own good, he'd make sure McAskill never came near her again.

chapter 17

As Lachlan rode, he could see the Cuillin Hills behind the small spattering of crofter cottages that made up the village. Several women stood gossiping, their arms loaded with baskets of fish. When they saw him, their jaws dropped open and they lowered their gazes.

Behind the women, children stopped playing in the sand long enough to gawk at Lachlan.

One little boy pointed at him. "Assa! 'Tis Mad MacGregor. Look! Look! He's got the cursed stripe in his hair."

The two women grabbed their children. One of them said, "Dinna look at him. You'll be hexed."

One boy refused to obey and received a cuff on the head. The boy staggered back behind his mother's skirt.

Lachlan glanced away, feeling a dull empty ache gnawing at him. His whole life he'd felt like an outcast among his own people. They shunned him for being cursed. After all, he was the Mad MacGregor. Och, maybe he *could* hex someone by looking at them—if he tried.

He spotted McAskill's carriage sitting in front of the O

Whistle tavern, a small establishment at the end of the village. Cane in hand, he walked inside.

The smell of cooking cabbage, haggis, and pipe smoke lingered in the air. Lachlan spotted a woman in a corner wringing her hands, staring at him the way she would at Old Nick himself.

The hum of conversation stopped. Five men turned at the bar to look at him. When his identity registered, one man choked so hard on his ale that it spewed all the way across the bar.

"'Tis Mad MacGregor"—a twitter went around the room.

The men glanced everywhere but at him.

"Should be goin'," one said, and leaped up.

"Wife's waitin'." Another one scrambled off a stool.

"I'm with you."

"Me tae."

"Bad time a day tae be into the bitters."

All five men scurried toward the door, elbowing each other to see who could get out first.

A sixth man at the end of the bar hadn't moved. McAskill. He wore his blond hair pulled back in a queue, and there was no mistaking his arrogant, rawboned profile. Lachlan felt his hatred foam up and churn in his gut.

McAskill turned, a sardonic grin splitting his lips. His white teeth glistened like a shark's. "Haith! If it isn't the spavie Mad MacGregor himself, gimping into town. Frightened everyone away, I see, but you were always good at that, weren't you, lad?"

Lachlan gritted his teeth before he spoke but held on to his temper. "I'm warning you to stay away from Miss Southworth and her family."

McAskill laughed, the superior sound filling the tavern. After he'd made his point, his expression straightened. He gripped the handle of his mug and glared at Lachlan. "I'm no' seein' how she belongs tae you."

"She's under my protection."

"That mean you're givin' her the roger?" He laughed

again. "How do you like slippin' between her legs? She's no' bad. Nice soft curves." He winked at Lachlan.

Lachlan's fingers clenched into fists. The lion head on his cane dug into his palm. Jealousy tightened every muscle in his body. "Stay the bloody hell away from her. You ken?"

"If she has a choice between me and a mad spaven like you, which are you thinkin' she's goin' tae choose?"

Lachlan wasn't sure. The uncertainty burned in the pit of his belly like acid. "It'll no' take her long to figure that you're no mon at all."

McAskill's eyes blazed as he crashed his mug down on the bar and broke it. Jagged pieces of the pottery jutted from the handle he held. "We'll see who's a mon."

The crash brought the brawny Robert MacTavish, the innkeeper, through a door. He saw Lachlan and fear passed over his expression. But his worry over a brawl destroying his tavern was greater, for he dove in front of McAskill and shoved him back.

"Sit there, Eth. There'll be no fightin' in here."

"Be off." McAskill swung hard and connected with MacTavish's jaw.

The man staggered and fell flat.

Lachlan heard the woman sitting in the corner scream as she ran out of the bar.

"'Tis just you and me now, lad," McAskill said, brandishing the broken mug handle as he stalked toward Lachlan. "I've been waiting for this for a long time. I still owe you for the scar on my arm."

"Let's have a go, then."

McAskill dove at him.

Lachlan sidestepped and swung his cane. It met McAskill's hand with a loud thump.

McAskill stumbled past him and dropped the jagged mug handle.

"I'm preferring a fair fight." Lachlan threw aside his cane.

McAskill swung around and raised his fists. "All right,

if that's the way o' it, lad. I'll whip your arse to hell and back."

"Come on, then." Lachlan took up a boxing stance.

McAskill swung at him.

Lachlan dodged back, but not quickly enough. McAskill's fist caught his left eye. Lachlan staggered into a table. Chairs and table toppled over. He caught his balance and shook off the pain. "That all you got, old mon?" Lachlan taunted.

McAskill smiled, white teeth gleaming. "You've seen nothing yet, spavie." McAskill dove for him.

Lachlan was ready. McAskill was a sloppy fighter, led with his right, but always too slow and low. Lachlan feinted left. His fist landed right between McAskill's eyes. He felt the bones in McAskill's nose give beneath his fist. Before McAskill reacted, Lachlan caught him again in the ribs. Again in his jaw.

McAskill's eyes rolled in his head. He teetered and collapsed onto an overturned chair. Broken wood flew in all directions.

Lachlan waited for his nemesis to get up, but McAskill stayed put, sprawled in a nest of broken wood, his eyes closed. Lachlan was about to leave, when someone struck him from behind. Everything went black and he felt his body crumple.

R*egan walked beside Emma toward the village. A lone pair of seabirds circled over the tiny crofts. The streets looked deserted. Even the dock was empty.*

When McAskill and Letta hadn't met Emma at the gates, they had gone in search of them. Regan wanted to speak to him anyway and tell him to leave her family alone. Landlord or not, she didn't want him anywhere near Emma. If he didn't like what she had to say, they would move.

Emma glanced ahead of them and frowned. "Isn't that Letta running toward us?"

"I believe so." Regan saw Letta's thin arms waving wildly like an angry chicken's wings.

"What in the world could be the matter?" Emma asked.

"I don't know." Regan ran to meet Letta.

Letta had run so fast, she couldn't speak for a moment. She grabbed her knees and waited to catch her breath.

"What happened?" Emma blurted.

Letta stood and said, "Oh! He's killing him! He's killing him!"

"Who's killing who?" Regan asked.

"Mad MacGregor's killing Mr. McAskill in the tavern."

"Take Emma to the castle and wait for me there."

"But I want to see him kill Mr. McAskill," Emma cried. "You never let me see anything."

"Go with Letta!" Regan leveled one of her because-I-said-so glances, then hiked up her dress and started running.

Regan had never run so fast. Eth McAskill was the least of her worries. With his bad leg, Lachlan was no match for Mr. McAskill, nor did McAskill seem like the type to fight fairly.

She reached the tavern, heart pounding. Inside McAskill lay on the floor. Splintered wood surrounded him, and several large chair legs rose and fell on his chest as he breathed. His head rested against an overturned table.

Several feet from him, Lachlan lay on the floor. A man stood over him with a club in hand.

"What have you done?" Regan rushed over to Lachlan, elbowing the man aside.

"I could no' have 'em breakin' up me place." The man dropped the club at his side and swallowed hard, his expression panicked.

Blood oozed from Lachlan's left eyebrow and down his temple, veining the white streak in his hair with a stream of red. His eye had almost swollen shut. Staring at Lachlan's still body tore at her insides. "Oh, my God! If you've killed him, I'll see you hanged!" She bent and listened to his chest. When she heard the steady thump, she let herself breathe again.

"Didn't hurt him, did I?" the man said, the club trembling in his hand.

"His heart is beating."

"I knew I'd just knocked him out. That's all I did. Do it all the time."

"Not to a nobleman. Do you know who he is?" Reproach filled Regan's words.

The man nodded his balding head. "Mad MacGregor." He frowned, the realization of what he'd done crashing down on him. His face turned the color of burned ashes. "Jesus, Joseph, and Mary!" the man howled.

"Where can I tend him?"

"Upstairs."

"Help me take him up there." Regan used a brigadier general's tone that sent the man into action. "Who are you?" She slipped one of Lachlan's arms across her shoulder.

"Rob MacTavish." He laid the club on the bar and rushed to help her.

"Well, Mr. MacTavish, we're going to be gentle with him."

"Aye, me lady." He pulled Lachlan's other arm over his broad shoulders, then hefted him off the floor.

Regan didn't bother telling him she wasn't a lady as they both managed to carry him up the stairs. Not an easy feat, she realized. Lachlan was a large man, and she had to let Mr. MacTavish carry the brunt of the weight.

He led the way to a tiny room with a bed. The sheets were dingy brown and had holes. "Is there a better room?"

"Only ones with pallets in 'em. This is my room." He sounded offended.

"Oh, well, it shall have to do. Careful." Regan relinquished her hold, and MacTavish laid Lachlan on the bed. "I'll need warm water and clean bandages. Send word to the castle that Lord MacGregor's been hurt and I'm here with him."

"Must I do that, me lady?" He looked worried.

"Well, perhaps we can wait." Regan knew the man could be imprisoned for striking a nobleman. "Send for Dr. McGuirk."

"He's no' there, me lady. I'm knowin' 'cause he's with Tim Kent's wife up tae Blaven in the hills. She's havin' twins and a rough time o' it. He's liable tae be there for days."

"We'll just have to take care of Lord MacGregor until he returns. Hurry with that water."

"Right away."

"And make sure you get Mr. McAskill out of here."

"Aye, me lady."

Regan waited until the door was closed to run her hand over Lachlan's head, feeling for knots. She found a lump half the size of her fist. "MacGregor, you have to be all right. Please be all right."

She pressed her hand against his cheek. His skin felt clammy. If something should happen to him . . . Fear tugged all the air from her lungs, and her throat constricted until tears burned her eyes.

chapter 18

Lachlan woke to a pounding in his head . . . and something else: a warm cloth moving over his right brow and temple. A pair of gentle fingers glided along his cheek.

"Please be all right."

The words came to him from far off, the drumming in his head dulling them. He couldn't tell who'd said them.

He felt warm lips feather across his own. Sweet, gentle lips. He breathed deeply and recognized the distinctive feminine scent of Regan Southworth. She used no perfumes, yet her hair and skin were redolent with the aroma of clean air, an herb garden, and her own tantalizing scent.

He tried to open his eyes. One stayed shut and ached. He remembered the lucky punch McAskill landed to his face. With one eye, he saw the lass's face close to his. Her eyes were shut, and he felt her lips brushing his.

When she made a move to draw back, his arms closed around her. He splayed his hand behind her head and pressed her face closer. Och! He had waited so long to kiss her. If this were an illusion, he didn't want it to end.

Lachlan ran his tongue along the crease of her lips,

feeling them tighten. "Open your mouth, lass," he whispered against her lips.

She did as he asked, and he thrust his tongue deep into her sweetness. His tongue mated with hers, and he couldn't get enough of her. He wanted more. He caressed the flesh along the back of her neck, while his other hand learned the curve of her spine.

He was so enmeshed in the feeling of her, in the taste of her, that he hadn't realized she was pushing on his chest, trying to break free of him. He recalled McAskill's comment about her curves. Bitter jealousy swept through him, even as it hit him this was no dream. He dropped his hold on her.

Her eyes registered surprise, then she said, "You're injured." Her breathing was ragged and her breasts tugged rapidly at the tight-fitting bodice of her dress. "You must have lost your head for a moment."

"I'm pretty sure I didna kiss you first. Are you always putting your lips where they dinna belong?"

"I—I don't know what came over me," she stammered, and chewed on her fingernail. "I was worried about you."

"I'm no' needing your worry." His self-control had gone astray again. "Where am I?" he asked.

"The tavern. How are you feeling?" she asked, her face red.

"Like dross that's been thrown in the middens. Someone hit me from behind. Where the hell's McAskill?"

"He's gone home. I believe he was out cold like you. What possessed you to fight him?"

He couldn't acknowledge the real reason he'd come here, so he glanced over at a water pitcher in the room and said, "I need a drink."

"Not until you tell me why you hate McAskill so much."

"I'll get it myself." He threw his long legs over the side of the bed. She was sitting on the mattress beside him, and he was forced to push his way past her. When he tried to stand, the room wouldn't hold still.

She grabbed him around the waist and locked her hands

behind his back. He was so tall her head only came to the top of his chest, and he felt it pressing over his heart. Lachlan gazed down at her blond head so close, felt her body tight against him, and it was all he could do not to wrap her in his arms and kiss her again. He swallowed hard.

"See, you shouldn't have gotten out of bed." She gazed up at him with reproach in those vivid blue eyes.

"And you should never have come here, lass. Why *are* you here?" Lachlan stepped out of her reach and plopped down on the bed. He waited for his head to clear and his desire to dissolve.

"I came to tell Mr. McAskill to stay away from my family—especially Emma."

"Then you're done with him?"

She jammed her hands on her hips, incensed. "Done with him? I never started with him."

"I saw you in his arms."

"A stolen kiss is what you saw."

"Didna look that way to me." He tried to keep the jealousy out of his voice but failed.

"Well, it was."

"What aboot when you jumped out of his boat?"

She hesitated, then said, "If you must know, he asked me to be his mistress. When I said no, he attempted to compromise me. I had to do something."

"You're no' his mistress then?" He felt an unbidden excitement that he shouldn't have been feeling. He searched her face and held his breath, waiting for her answer.

"You think—you think . . ." She didn't seem able to repeat what he'd said. Her eyes blazed at him. "I should slap your face for that comment, but since Mr. McAskill has done that for me, I'll leave it—just remember how it felt." She headed for the door.

He leaped up, grabbed her wrist, and pulled her around to face him. "You're bonny when you're angry."

"A compliment will not smooth this over." She tried to break free of his grip, but he held on tight. "And stop looking at me like that. I've never been any man's Cyprian.

Why on earth should I want to become a man's warming pan—especially McAskill's? I certainly have more intelligence than that—"

He cut off her tirade by placing his hand over her mouth. "I was hoping you did, lass." He stroked the side of her cheek and felt a shudder go through her.

For a moment he just stood there, his hand pressed against her mouth, staring down at her. He felt her soft lips against the roughness of his palm, her breath on his skin, the silken smoothness of her cheek as he caressed it.

Emotion warred within him. She was an innocent. How could he have not seen that? And he wanted nothing more than to ravish her lips again. But he knew how dangerous those kinds of feelings were. He'd be no better than McAskill for giving in to them. His expression hardened, then he dropped his hands from her mouth and wrist.

"We should be going, lass."

"You cannot walk."

"Och! We MacGregors may be mad, but it'll be a cold day in hell when we canna get up after a bloody brawl." He forced his legs to stay steady as he limped over and found his cane propped against the edge of the bed.

Lachlan felt her watching him leave the room. Despite his attempts to tamp it down, he couldn't forget waking up to her lips on his, or her saying, "I was worried about you." He'd never had anyone fuss over him but Gillis. He didn't like seeing this caring side of her; it made him want her even more. He tried to frown but his eye ached and he grimaced instead.

O*n the way to the castle, Lachlan led his horse,* Phoebus, while Regan rode in the saddle. Lachlan's strides were surprisingly straight and steady.

Silence stretched between them as he seemed to drift away behind a mist of aloofness.

Every time she remembered giving in to that imprudent impulse and kissing him, a new wave of heat burned her cheeks. When she had bent down to kiss him, she had thought he was unconscious. More than once, she had conjured ideas of what his lips would feel like.

The experience with Lachlan had been nothing like McAskill's smashing of her mouth—or any kind of contact she could have imagined. She had felt the urging pressure of his tongue down to the tips of her toes and fingers. Every sense in her body had vibrated. But she had thought the bump on his head had made him delirious and he didn't know what he was doing, and she had broken away, more frightened by her own desire than his. Worse than being embarrassed, she'd had to suffer his apathy afterward. The kiss hadn't meant anything to him at all. It had only caused him to grow more distant.

"Please stop this instant," she said. "I need to walk. I have a cramp in my leg." A little lie couldn't hurt. She really wanted to be down near him so he couldn't forget she was with him.

He held the bridle and waited until the horse fully stopped; then he stepped around to help her dismount.

He grabbed her waist and swept her down. When her feet hit the ground, they shared a long look.

"Does it hurt much?" Regan reached up to touch the side of his swollen eye, but he backed away as if she held a torch in her hand.

"I'll live." He turned and began walking.

She fell in step beside him. "You never told me why you hate McAskill so much. You must have as good a reason for disliking him as I do," she said. "What has he done to you?"

He remained silent for a moment, staring straight ahead at the castle coming into view. He seemed reluctant for a moment, then finally said, "At one time I used to call him a friend."

"What happened?"

He withdrew again behind the remoteness he wore like a badge. "It's a long story."

"We have another mile to walk."

He turned to look at her. Maybe it was a trick of the

bright sunlight on his face, but his usual formidable and distant expression had mellowed slightly. "I've never spoken of it to anyone," he said, his gaze boring into her face, somehow delving directly into her soul.

Regan met his look squarely. "I would never repeat it, or harm you in any way. You can trust me. Please believe that."

"Can I, lass?"

"I give you my word of honor."

"I dinna trust easily," he said.

Regan felt a tiny thread of hope. He might open up to her for once. She didn't hesitate in saying, "I swear on my honor to keep anything you tell me in confidence."

A satisfied gleam shone in his eyes. "Very well. And since you've just sworn on your honor, you can call me Lachlan from now on."

"Lachlan." Regan tried the name, intrigued by how natural it sounded on her lips.

He walked beside her and said, "When I was eight, my mother decided I should go away to England to be educated. I returned when I was twelve and my father went totally mad and had to be restrained. He didn't live long after that." He paused, lost in thought.

Regan saw a frightened little boy facing a demented stranger who was his father. "How awful that must have been for you," she said with a catch in her voice.

"I expected it all along and knew it would come one day."

His acceptance was the saddest thing of all. Her heart ached for him.

"I had no friends here," he said, continuing. "I met McAskill while out riding on the moors one day. We became friends. He was six years my senior, but the age difference didn't matter much—at the beginning." He paused, his eyes narrowing.

"He can be very charming when he wants to be."

"Aye, so charming that when I was fourteen I found him kissing my mother in the great hall."

Regan clenched her jaw to keep it from dropping open. All she could manage to say was a shriveled, insipid, "Oh, I'm sorry."

"I lost my temper when I found them and leaped on McAskill. He was older and stronger than I. He pinned me against the wall and kept hitting me with his fist." He wore a pained expression as he relived the incident. "I knew he'd kill me, so I grabbed a broadsword off the wall. I brought it down across his arm. He stumbled from the house, vowing to seek revenge on me. We've hated each other ever since."

"I suppose your mother must have seen what sort of person he was and been glad to see the backside of him."

"She said I'd acted foolishly. We argued. I knew they'd both been using me for their affair."

"How horrible," she whispered.

"Those were the last words ever spoken between us. She disappeared that night." He tossed out the words with a strange confrontational tone.

Regan swallowed hard. She was overwhelmed by his opening up enough to speak of his mother. Perhaps he wasn't so hard underneath that icy facade. She slipped her arm through his and said, "I wish I could change the past for you."

He didn't pull away as she expected he would. "It's part of the curse, lass. We MacGregors are destined for unhappiness."

"You cannot believe that."

"I do. We're all marked by it. There's no changing it," he said, a hint of melancholy in his voice.

"Superstition is the bane of common sense." She used one of her father's old adages. "I do not believe in curses. We make our own destiny."

"You're wrong, lass. There's no controlling madness."

"If you accept it, you cannot."

"What is that supposed to mean?" He glowered at her.

"That perhaps by believing you'll go mad makes you do just that."

"Are you saying all my ancestors went mad because they expected to?" he asked, incredulous.

"I'm just saying that sometimes if you wish an illness on yourself, then you will become ill."

"A person canna force madness in his head. If you'd seen my father chained to his bed and my grandfather as well, you'd no' be saying it was in their bloody heads." He let her arm drop and moved several steps ahead of her, his strides stiff as he pulled on Phoebus's reins.

Regan watched his broad shoulders sway as he walked, and an overwhelming dismal feeling pulled at her.

She wanted to make Lachlan see that he could have a life different from the hopeless one he imagined for himself. But he seemed so resigned to his fate. As she watched his boots crunch down the heather, a knot formed in her throat.

At some time, she wasn't sure when, he'd become as important to her as finding Avalon. She couldn't allow him to throw his life away because he believed he'd go mad one day. Somehow she'd have to convince him that he could be happy, maybe even fall in love and marry. She owed him that much for saving her life.

A fter Gillis had made sure Emma and Letta had arrived home safely, Regan sat in her room with the diary in hand. Lachlan had avoided her at dinner, and she'd been forced to eat with Lady Margaret and evade her questions about the fight in the tavern. Not surprisingly, she had heard a lot of the details from Tyg already. When Regan couldn't stand any more prying questions, she had excused herself, saying she had a headache.

Regan opened the diary to where she had left off.

April 30, 1774
Today I was married. In the eyes of church and state I'm now officially Lady MacGregor. I've played many ladies, but never dreamed I'd actually become

*one. Balmoral insisted we marry in Bath and get it
over with before we returned to Scotland. I'm sure
he's doing it because his family would never approve
of me. I should not care if they did. I needn't suffer
them. I'll just have them removed to the other side of
the island. Ha!*

Loud voices sounded outside in the bailey.

Regan laid the diary aside and crept to the window. Mac-
Gregor and a man stood near the same tree as before. This
time the man was in view. He had a cap pulled over his
head and his back was to her. He was stocky and shorter by
several inches than MacGregor, and definitely smaller in
stature than McAskill.

Regan had left a tiny crack in the window and now
pressed her ear to it.

"You canna tell me what tae do," the man in the hat said.

"I can and will. You'll do as I say."

"I'll no' listen tae you. I can go where I want."

"No' without someone with you."

"I dinna need anyone. And what aboot her?" The man
motioned toward Regan's window. "You said you'd let me
meet her."

"I will in due time."

"Nay, you're keeping her all to yourself. That's no' fair.
I'd share her with you."

Regan stepped back and dropped the curtain. She didn't
appreciate being spoken of as if she were a warming pan in
a cold inn. Shared indeed. Why hadn't Lachlan introduced
her to this man? Once and for all she'd find out who this
person was. She headed for the door.

chapter 19

Regan checked the hallway. The way was clear, and she slipped out of her room. When she reached the staircase, a door slammed behind her.

"Miss Southworth, what are you doing out of your room? I thought you had a headache."

Regan turned to look at Lady Margaret stepping away from her chamber door. "I—I was just on my way to the library."

"You must not be as indisposed as you said." She gazed at Regan suspiciously.

"I assure you, my lady, I did have a headache," Regan said, feeling the need to defend herself.

"Well, it hasn't seemed to harm you, so I'll expect you in my room tonight. You'll bring a book."

"Very well." Regan kept the disappointment out of her voice.

"And make it something light. Scott's poetry will do."

"All right." While in Lady Margaret's sight, Regan stepped down the stairs at a leisurely pace. The moment she was clear of her prying eyes, she snatched a tallow candle burning in a sconce, cupped her hand around the flame, and descended the winding stone stairs two at a time.

The foyer was in complete darkness. At the last step, Regan drew up short and held up the candle. The dim light flicked over the suffocating tomblike area.

All she could hear were her own short breaths, amplified in the quiet. She forced herself to step down onto the floor, again feeling the strange sensation that the stones had eyes and were watching her. When she reached the massive front door, she shoved on it. Every bruise on her back objected as she threw her weight against the oak.

It creaked like the hull on an ancient galleon.

She slipped out and left it ajar, knowing she'd have to come back that way. She headed around the right side of the grounds, skirting the strange mist near the castle's foundation and the deep ditch where the moat had been.

She trailed beside the crumbling defense wall, hopping over cracked stones that had fallen to the ground. Finally she reached an arched tunnel that she felt certain led to where she'd seen Lachlan and the man speaking.

Here the stones were carved with the Celtic crosses, too. Moss grew along the interior and water dripped from the ceiling. Mice scampered within the globe of candlelight, then disappeared into the darkness.

A burst of wind blew through the tunnel. The candle flickered, then went out. Left in total darkness, Regan groped her way through the passageway.

She came to an opening and stepped out into the bailey. Moonlight beamed over the bailey and glinted off the ancient stone paving.

Empty.

She headed back through the tunnel and past the mist. As she searched the moors behind the castle, she saw a burning lantern, the man carrying it, and his companions— MacGregor and the two dogs. They paused before a crofter's cottage, the man patted the dogs, then they stepped inside.

So the man was a renter of MacGregor's. Why had he

wanted to be introduced to her? And why was MacGregor so concerned about the man's welfare? Later she'd find out who he was.

B y the time Regan ran back through the front door and found the books of poetry Lady Margaret had asked for, her heart was pounding. How long had it taken her? It seemed like hours.

Regan met Darcy coming out of Lady Margaret's room. She looked harried and flustered. "Hech, miss, if you're havin' tae go in there, I pity you," she whispered to Regan. "She's ripe tonight. Cranky as an old fishwife, she is."

"Do you know where Gillis and Tyg might be?" Regan wondered which one was guarding the circle.

"Why, miss?" Darcy's red brows narrowed.

"I just wondered." Regan shrugged.

"If there's something you're needin', I can get it for you."

"No, I'm perfectly fine." Regan had promised her father to go out only at dawn, but that was before MacGregor had ordered the circle watched and before she'd learned Mac-Gregor and Lady Margaret rose at dawn. If she wanted to go, it'd have to be at night.

Regan looked at Darcy's face and changed the subject. "My sister brought a salve to me. It's on my writing desk. It's for your complexion. I'm sure it will help. She's wonderful with herbal remedies."

Darcy beamed a smile at her. "Thank you, miss. I'll get it."

As Darcy hurried down the hall, Regan gripped the books in her arms and strode inside Lady Margaret's room.

The lady lay in a four-poster bed, her nightcap sitting slightly askew. When she met Regan's eyes, her expression soured.

"Well, it took you long enough."

"The library is so vast, I had trouble finding Scott."

"Why, are you blind?"

Regan held her temper, unwilling to give Lady Margaret one moment of enjoyment, for Regan knew she thrived on making others feel like fools. "If you want the truth, I'm not used to such a treasure trove of books."

"So you dawdled in the library, when you knew I was waiting for you."

"It won't happen again." Regan stared directly into her cold eyes.

"Well, well." Lady Margaret's mouth puckered. The tiny lines that were her lips disappeared into wrinkles. "See that it doesn't." A felinelike expression moved over her face, suggesting she knew Regan was lying.

For a moment their eyes clashed.

Regan refused to glance away and lose the small ground she'd gained with the lady.

"Perhaps you might consider reading to me this century, gel."

Regan started to sit on the stuffed chair near the side of the bed, but the lady said, "Don't sit there, gel. I'm hard of hearing. Get that writing desk chair there."

It was a small salon chair with wooden spools for the back and no stuffing in the seat. Another test of mettle, Regan thought. She strode to the side of the bed and plopped down next to Lady Margaret.

"Wh-what are you doing?" Lady Margaret sputtered, then slid to the opposite side of the mattress like a cobra had slithered up beside her.

"If you are hard of hearing, what better place to sit than on your bed?"

The grand lady glared at her for two long minutes, her contentious nature distorting her expression. Then she seemed to comprehend what Regan was about. Her contempt abruptly lost to a trace of a smile. "You are as impudent a young person as I have ever encountered." She jerked the covers up around her stomach in a haughty fashion.

"I believe we've already established that, my lady." Regan grinned at her, turned to the first page of *The Lay of the Last Minstrel*, and began reading. "The way was long, the wind was cold, the minstrel was infirm and old . . ."

She had spent many hours reading to her father, and though it had only been two days since she'd left him, she missed their nightly discussions about finding Avalon. She longed to see the hope in his face when she returned home with clues to Avalon's whereabouts.

She glanced over at Lady Margaret. She didn't look at all sleepy—her eyes were wide open and centered on Regan.

Regan hoped she'd fall asleep soon. Her curiosity about the crofter was itching to be satisfied, and she wanted to see if she could get to the circle without being discovered.

A fter another half hour of Scott, the stubborn Lady Margaret had finally succumbed to sleep. Regan slipped out of the castle.

Moonlight was her only light source, and she had to weave her way along the well-worn path she had discovered that led directly to the crofter's cottage.

Candlelight glowed from a side window. As Regan drew closer, she noticed well-tended beds of poppies, marigolds, mugwort, and goldenrod surrounding the cottage. Emma would have loved to get her hands dirty in the flower beds.

Regan parted several bushy marigolds and crept up to the window. Through a slit in the curtains she saw MacGregor sitting directly in front of the window. The back of his wide shoulders and the black hair falling over his collar filled her line of vision. His head was bent and his voice droned on as if he were . . . reading? Why was he reading to that strange man?

Regan couldn't see the other fellow, or where he was inside the room. She tilted her head and tried to look past MacGregor's broad shoulders, but she couldn't make out anything.

At least she knew where MacGregor was. Now she had

to find out who was guarding the circle. As she turned, a twig cracked beneath her feet.

The dogs inside barked once. MacGregor stopped reading.

She flinched and waited breathlessly to see if the dogs would be let out.

Muffled low voices came from inside, then MacGregor continued the story.

She released the breath she'd been holding, stepped out of the flower bed, and hurried back up the path toward the circle.

It was a good thirty minutes before Regan walked around the castle and reached the circle. The shoreline was farther than it had looked from the castle, all of a mile, and without a lantern she had had to step carefully over the rocky terrain.

When she heard the waves crashing, she knew she was close. She hid behind the cover of a thicket, surveyed the area, and waited. She didn't see anyone about. If luck was on her side, Tyg and Gillis were back in the castle, arguing over who would watch the circle.

Her heart pounded with anticipation as she headed toward the stones. Before she stepped inside, she recalled Gillis's warning about three men having died within the ring.

Though she knew there was a logical explanation for the deaths, she still felt an overpowering desire to leave this place. She inhaled deeply, then stepped between the huge stones and entered the circle.

Once inside, all sound became muted, as though she had entered a huge drum. It seemed impossible for the stones to cause such a strange phenomenon. No doubt her father could explain it away by a principle of physics. Couldn't he?

She surveyed the ground. The first details any seasoned archeologist looked for was the evidence visible on the surface, so she bent low until she was eye level with the ground. Oddly enough, no vegetation grew inside the circle, most likely because the stones blocked out most of the sunlight. A tiny ray of moonlight shone through the stones, and she could see a three-foot by six-foot indentation in the center of the circle. Clearly something had been buried here.

She used the shovel she'd brought with her and dug into the soil, carefully scooping the dirt away in small increments. When she'd moved several inches of soil, the tip hit something hard.

She felt the ground. Her fingers connected with something metal. Gently she dug it out of the ground and picked it up. Using her thumbnail, she flicked clods of dirt from it until she met with a gold band. It was a ring of some kind. She slipped it into her pocket. Her first artifact to inspect. Her father would be ecstatic.

She heard a noise behind her. She dropped the shovel, leaped up, and saw Tyg stepping out from behind the thicket of gorse and hawthorns. His expression was harsher than she'd ever seen it. A memory flashed of him standing at the top of the stairs after she'd been pushed. Each vertebra in her spine turned to ice.

chapter 20

Tyg stalked toward her, his expression murderous. *"You shouldna be out here. Strange things happen on the grounds here at night."*

"I was just walking."

"I'm no' believin' your lies."

She forced herself to assume an air of disdain, though her insides churned. "I do not owe you an explanation." It took all of Regan's courage to lift her chin in a haughty manner.

"Maybe I'll just go tae the master and tell him what you're doin' out here."

"You do that, and I'll tell him about you pushing me down the stairs."

Tyg frowned and clenched his fists. "I ne'er pushed you."

"Who was it, then?"

"I dinna know, but it wasna me. I saw you fall and came tae help."

He sounded sincere, but she still didn't trust him.

At her silence, he said, "You'll leave this place now and

go back tae the castle." His words drifted out into the din of the waves.

Regan wanted to tell him he couldn't order her about, but under the circumstances it might be better to back down now and try again before dawn. She didn't want to explain to MacGregor what she had been doing here.

As she left, she felt Tyg's eyes on her and picked up her pace. Halfway to the castle, she noticed someone on the path. In the moonlight she could make out a broad silhouette and a limp. MacGregor.

Regan tried to look unruffled and approached him. Though darkness hid his face, she could see the furious shadows in his expression.

"What were you doing out here?" he asked.

Regan quickly thought of an excuse. "I was looking for a comb I lost the night you found me. It belonged to my mother."

The line of his lips tightened in a way that suggested he was holding back something. "You were warned no' to leave the castle at night," he said.

"I know. I just wanted to find my comb."

"That's no' the only reason you were out here, lass." He stepped closer.

As he towered over her, she felt raw power flowing from him. There was a dark side to him that frightened her; she sensed it radiating from him like the back draft from a fire.

His fingers bit into her shoulders. "Tell me, lass. I want the bloody truth."

"I already told you. I am researching something in the circle for my father's book." She couldn't tell if he believed her or not behind his fierce expression. Even though she cared for him and she wanted to tell him about Avalon, she couldn't take that chance, not with Sir Harry Lucas coming back to the island. He was a wily little man and would stop at nothing to find Avalon before her father.

"You'll never come out to this circle again. Do you ken, lass? Never."

"Please, I need to excavate the site to see if my father's theory about the Picts having erected the stones is true."

"Why didna you come and ask permission to dig instead of sneaking out here?"

"I knew you thought there was evil there and you wouldn't let me," she said, wincing at the fury in his voice.

"You're bloody well right. You canna go near there again. People die in the circle. I'll no' have you harmed." He grabbed her shoulders and shook her. "Are you hearing me?"

She felt her teeth rattle as her fear rose. She had never seen him so angry. "Yes," she managed to say. "Let go! You're hurting me."

He stopped shaking her and seemed to realize what he'd done. Regan thought he would step away from her. He didn't. One moment his hands were on her shoulders, the next they crushed her to his chest. Then he captured her lips.

chapter 21

🍃

If *Regan cared to admit it, she had thought of kissing him
again* since the tavern incident. The scenario had played
over and over in her mind. What she had failed to imagine
was the way she burned out of control the moment their lips
touched. Every sense in her body ached from his hard body
pressing against her, his hands gently moving toward her
buttocks, the way he embraced her as if he didn't want to
let her go.

He stroked all of her desires alive. She pressed closer,
needing to reach that impervious place inside of him.
Boldly she sucked on his bottom lip.

He groaned and deepened the kiss. His tongue eased
past her lips. His breathing grew ragged.

Regan wrapped her arms around his neck and ran her
fingers through the hair at his nape. She felt him shiver and
wondered at the magic her touch had on him.

He slid his hands down the curve of her spine and covered her bottom, kneading her flesh.

Regan felt him shudder and knew he was reining in his
desire, hiding behind the armor that protected his heart. She

wanted to feel it crumble, to feel him surrender totally to her. "Let me in, Lachlan," she whispered against his mouth.

"You'll no' like what you find."

"I'll take my chances."

"But you see, I canna take the chance." He placed kisses over her nose, her cheeks, her chin, then trailed his tongue down her neck. His hands moved to cup her breasts.

Regan moaned and arched her back.

He made a savage sound deep in his throat. Then he broke away from her, chest heaving, the willpower it took him to withdraw tensing his whole body. "Och, if I dinna get you back to the castle, we'll both regret it."

Speak for yourself, Regan wanted to say, still trembling from their fevered embrace, still wanting him to touch her.

"Lachlan! Lachlan!" The voice came from behind them.

She glanced past Lachlan's shoulder at the crofter. He ran toward them, the dogs bounding at his side. He wore the same cap and dark clothes she had seen him in earlier.

The man skidded to a halt near her. His teeth gleamed in a wide smile. It was the first sign of true openness she'd seen since coming to the castle, and it warmed her.

"You're bonny." Boyish wonder filled his voice.

Something in his manner was too innocent for a man of his age, and Regan realized he might be slow. "Thank you," she said.

"What are you doing out of the house?" Lachlan asked, his tone impatient.

"I wanted tae see what you found, Lachlan." He turned to Regan. "We heard the dogs growl. Lachlan decided tae see who it was. I guess he found *you*."

"Yes." Regan smiled at the man. He was shorter and thinner than Lachlan and looked younger by several years.

"I told you not to go out at night." Lachlan leveled a look at the man that made him take a step back.

"Dinna fash yourself, Lachlan, I just wanted tae see what you found." The man thrust out his jaw. "You canna stop me. I gotta a right tae see."

"Go back home. I'll be there in a minute."

The man didn't move, only stared at her. "Are you in love with Lachlan?"

Regan felt her face redden. Lachlan blinked, then he glowered at the man.

"Who are you?" the man addressed her, ignoring Lachlan.

"Regan Southworth. Who are you?" Regan queried back.

"Quin, Lachlan's brother."

"Ah, I should have seen the resemblance." Regan noticed below the brim of the Quin's cap the distinctive white streak at his temple. He had a strong square jaw, a patrician nose, and dark eyes and hair. The only difference between him and Lachlan was size. How could she have missed the similarity?

"Nice tae finally meet you, Regan Southworth." Quin's smile broadened. "I saw you kissing Lachlan."

"I—I—"

"Go back to the house," Lachlan interrupted her.

"I'm going, but I'm thinking you should continue kissing her, Lachlan. Come on, tykes." Quin slapped his sides, and the dogs followed him.

When Quin was out of hearing range, Regan said, "Your brother is very sweet."

"He likes everyone."

"Why doesn't he live in the castle?"

"He's afraid to stay there. I've tried to get him to live there so I can better keep an eye on him, but he refuses."

"I'm sorry. Perhaps I can persuade him."

"No one can." Lachlan laced his hand with Regan's and guided her toward the castle.

Regan fell in step beside him, waiting for him to remove his hand, but he didn't. She reveled in his long fingers intertwined with her own, the heat of his skin hot against her palm. There was something comforting in the connection, something she couldn't explain. It warmed her all over. His brooding presence at her side felt terribly right for some reason, like he belonged there.

They walked toward the castle, their footsteps harmonizing with the sound of the waves and the shrill of the crickets in the heather. Neither one of them spoke, savoring the moment of contentment.

Regan broke it by asking, "What are we going to do?"

"About what, lass?"

"The kiss."

"It was only a kiss." His voice took on that closed, detached quality Regan knew well. "It'll never happen again." He dropped her hand and walked ahead of her, his steps wooden, the cane hitting the ground harder than usual.

"Are you sure of that? I know why you won't admit you kissed me. You're frightened of your feelings. They'll not go away. Neither will I."

"I have no feelings, lass. They were done away with long ago. As for you, you'll be leaving when your position here ends."

Regan watched his stiff strides. Melancholy and sadness seemed to weigh him down. She fought an urge to run after him and shake him. Despite the dark side of him that scared her sometimes, despite his hiding behind the barrier of aloofness, she was attracted to him. But maybe his heart was so hardened that he could never return anyone's affection.

Regan told herself it didn't matter if he cared, that she was here only to find Avalon. Why then did she feel such a stabbing ache way down deep in the pit of her belly? The feeling traveled up in her throat and threatened to choke her.

Regan halted beside Lachlan at her chamber door. She heard a commotion behind her, then the dogs bounded past her to get to their master. Quin must have sent them back to the castle. They lumbered up beside Lachlan, clumsy in their massiveness.

Regan cringed and stepped away from them.

Lachlan eyed her reaction, his expression impatient. He opened her chamber door and said, "In you go and stay there."

Regan pursed her lips at him. "You can't order me to stay in my room."

"Seeing as this is my castle, I can."

"You can't keep me prisoner."

"Either you stay in your chamber, or I'll be tying you to the bed. Now which is it?"

After he'd insisted that she take off her clothes when she'd fallen down the steps, Regan didn't doubt he'd follow through with this threat. "This is insufferable."

"No' in my way of seeing it." A devilish light gleamed in his eyes.

"I resent being treated like a child." Regan stomped past him. "Infuriating Scotsman," she said under her breath.

"Better than being an infuriating Sassenach." He slammed the door behind her.

"Ohhhh!" Regan glanced around for something to throw and couldn't find anything, so she whipped off her sturdy walking boot and sailed it at the door

It hit its mark with a hollow thump.

She was unsure which angered her more, that he had kissed her and turned so aloof afterward, or that he had confined her in her room.

No matter how infuriating he was, she wouldn't have been able to keep him at arm's length had he kissed her again. A pair of dark brooding eyes rose up in her mind. Regan tried to shut out Lachlan's face, but she could still feel his hands on her bottom, his tongue exploring her mouth, his hard body pressed against hers. She yearned for him to touch her again.

Such feelings disconcerted her, for she knew he had no real affection for her, only lust. She didn't think he was capable of warm sentiment. He'd probably never had anyone nurture him or show him affection. His father had been mad. And his mother? After having read Lady MacGregor's diary and learned how self-involved she had been, Regan couldn't imagine her capable of loving anyone. Perhaps if Regan showed him tenderness, his heart might soften.

She frowned and jammed her hands into her pockets. Her fingers met with the ring she'd found in the circle.

She bolted the door and pulled the ring out of her pocket.

Crusty bits of sandstone and mud adhered to it, but she could see several diamonds winking out through the debris. Her hand trembled as she picked up the pitcher from her desk and poured water into the bowl.

She dropped the ring in the water. Carefully she flaked off the debris with her fingernail. When she was done, she stared down at an emerald the size of a large pearl. Eight half-carat diamonds surrounded it. Her excitement over the find waned. It was a very expensive lady's ring and, by the modern design, made within the last century. It wasn't a sixth-century artifact nor could it help her find Avalon.

Regan wiped it off and decided to question Lady Margaret to see if she had lost it. If it wasn't hers, perhaps she might know whom the ring belonged to.

She stored the ring in her trunk, then fished the diary from its cubbyhole. Something about the diary was spellbinding. If she continued to read, perhaps she could understand Lady MacGregor, which might help Regan understand her son.

May 15, 1774
I have to admit Balmoral is the most attentive of husbands. He buys me anything I wish for. I suppose he isn't a bad sort, and his lovemaking doesn't bore me. It was a shame our honeymoon in Bath could not go on forever. Of course, I shall never love him. He keeps asking me if I do. I lie to him to silence him. He avoids my questions about his home. I wonder why?

June 1, 1774
I loathe this castle, and I'm sure it hates me. I feel it watching me. It will be the death of me, I'm sure of it. My crone of a mother-in-law despises me and thinks I'm not worthy of her son. She also knows I do not care for her or her son. What have I done? I'm

*miserable here. This island is barren, the castle
drafty and morose. There is no society or pleasure to
be had. I should never have left the stage. To top it
off, Balmoral seems like a different man now that he's
home in this abysmal prison.*

I n the north side of the castle, Lachlan sprawled on the
sofa in his room, watching Gillis hang up his frock coat.
He couldn't get the lass out of his mind, or that habit she
had of looking at him behind those long ginger-colored
lashes. The way her blue eyes had flared at him when he'd
forced her into her room. He'd come a hairbreadth from
shoving her inside and having his way with her.

He recalled watching her undress in the mirror, the way
she had shaken her hair loose, how it fell over her thrusting
breasts with their perfect nipples hidden behind the thin
chemise. It was the most erotic sight he'd ever seen. And
kissing her a wee bit ago. Och! He had been unable to control his desire to taste her lips. She had felt so sweet and
giving in his arms. She had whispered shivers down his
body, rallied every ounce of his lust. He could still feel her
breasts filling his palms. No woman had ever aroused him
like she did. What was she doing to him? He groaned.

"Were you sayin' something?" Gillis looked at him as he
hung up Lachlan's waistcoat.

Lachlan had forgotten he wasn't alone. He cleared his
throat and said, "I want a constant guard on the circle."

"The lass pokin' aboot, is she?"

"Aye. I found her near there."

"You dinna say. I warned her tae stay away from it."
Gillis shook his head, firelight gleaming off his bald pate.

"She's a hard head, that one."

"You knowing what brought her out there?"

"She said it had to do with her father's work, but I know
it's more to it than she's saying."

Lachlan stared at Prince and Charlie lying before the
fire, watching the firelight play along their fur.

"She's a shrewd one, that miss. If you ken my meaning."

"I ken it." Lachlan drummed his fingers on the top of his cane.

"Did you find Tyg on guard at the circle?"

"I did, but the lass got past him."

"He's a worthless carl." Gillis snorted his disapproval.

"No' when it comes to Quin and my grandmother."

"Aye," Gillis said, envy lacing his reply. "He's all sweet-meats and cakes tae them, but I'm knowin' what he's really made of."

Would the rivalry between the two servants ever end? Lachlan wondered. Gillis couldn't get past the fact that Quin, as a child, had become devoted to Tyg. It had always been one of the sticking points between them.

The other was Lady Margaret. She had hired Tyg after he had barely escaped a press-gang and she'd found him half-starved and beaten near the docks. Lachlan knew she hadn't done it out of the kindness of her heart, but because she was desperate for servants to work at a cursed castle. After that, Tyg's loyalty to her never wavered, even when it meant spying for her. And Lady Margaret rewarded him by showing partiality toward him. Tyg ate up the attention like a starved stray.

"Do you think that old carl will be able tae keep the miss out o' the circle?" Gillis asked, as he turned down the covers on Lachlan's bed.

"I dinna know."

Gillis shot a contemplative glance Lachlan's way. "Maybe I should go and keep an eye on her room, just in case she decides tae go back out there."

Lachlan scowled. She had sent him running to the opposite end of the castle like a hound with his tail between his legs. He would gain his self-control back and prove to himself he could. Before Gillis's hand touched the door, Lachlan leaped up and said, "I'll go."

"Are you sure?" Gillis's deep-set eyes gleamed with uncertainty.

"Aye." Lachlan slammed the door on his way out. No lass was going to get the better of him.

A knock on Regan's chamber door brought her gaze up from a page in the diary. She shoved it in the writing desk, unbolted the door, and let Darcy inside.

Her red hair was tucked up under her cap at odd angles. "Oh, miss, you're back. I've been fretting over you. I saw you go out."

"I'm fine. I . . . uh . . . was searching for a comb I lost by the circle."

"Hech, miss, you shouldna go near the stones. They're wicked."

"I've heard that."

"If you're interested in stones, you should see the one in the middle keep. Embedded in the floor, 'tis. Mighty strange tae look at. Got that curious writin' on it like what's all over the walls."

"Can you take me there?" Regan asked, her archeological curiosity piqued.

"I—I couldn't. I couldn't. I never scamper aboot the castle at night. Please dinna ask me tae take you. Tomorrow I will."

"Can you tell me where it is?"

"Aye, but you shouldna be going there alone. Hard telling what's down there. 'Tis in the older part o' the castle. Gives me crawlies thinkin' aboot it." Darcy added a touch of drama to her voice. She shivered and clutched the doorknob in a white-knuckled grip.

"I'll be fine. How do I find it?"

With more admonishments to wait until morning, Darcy directed Regan on the shortest route.

Regan listened, her eagerness to see the stone growing by the moment.

• • •

Twenty minutes later, with paper and charcoal in hand, Regan paused before an interesting dome-shaped corridor. Inside her pocket, Old Gray thumped against her thigh. Darcy's warnings had convinced her she might need a little extra protection—especially if she ran into Tyg again.

Four staircases, each leading north, south, east, or west, branched out from it. The constant draft within the castle blew stronger here and the temperature felt colder.

She immediately spotted the rock embedded directly in the center of the area. Specks of black granite sparkled like ravens' eyes on the stone's silver gray surface. Two feet by four feet, with slightly rounded corners, the stone had been chiseled by ancient cutting tools—probably in the second century A.D. Her father would love to see this little gem.

Regan bent and looked at the Celtic text. The letters were in a strange style she'd never seen before. She began sketching them.

As always, Regan felt the eerie sensation of being watched. The muted footsteps that so often echoed through the castle became clearer. For a moment the sound bounced off the walls, and she couldn't tell from which direction the footsteps were coming.

Beyond the globe of the two candles she'd brought with her, she could see nothing but cavelike blackness. An icy breeze fluttered past her, rustling the hem of her dress, chilling her hands. The wicks flickered in the tallow.

Don't go out, she prayed.

The draft blew harder, as if a door opened, then . . . blackness engulfed her.

Shadows pressed in around her.

The footsteps again, getting closer.

This time she had come prepared for trouble. She pulled out Old Gray and cocked the pistol. She had one shot. And it was only one person, by the sound of the footsteps. Her breathing halted as she aimed the pistol toward the footsteps.

chapter 22

❧

Lachlan reached Regan's chamber and knocked. The door fell open, and he peeked inside to an empty chamber.

He picked up her shawl and let the dogs sniff it. "Find her," he ordered.

The dogs trotted out of the room, their noses to the ground.

He followed them down the hallway, more afraid than angry. If she had gone back out to the circle after he told her not to . . . An image came to mind of her lying dead in the circle, as he'd seen the three men who had died there.

"Hurry, tykes," he commanded the dogs.

They trotted faster, guiding him down the stairwell.

Regan fought to keep from trembling, but she couldn't help it. The footsteps drew closer.

"Who's there?" Regan gulped and tightened her grip on the pistol.

She could feel a presence in the darkness.

"Stop right there," she said. "I have a gun."

A deep laugh cut through the air and made Regan's blood freeze. She aimed the gun in the direction of the laugh. "Tyg, is that you?"

"Leave this castle, if you're knowin' what's good for you," a deep voice said through the pitch blackness, inching closer.

Regan couldn't tell if it was Tyg or not.

Strange how being blinded by darkness heightened the senses. She heard the person's deep breaths as if they were next to her ear, and then an arm reaching for her.

Regan pulled the trigger, but the gun didn't fire.

A pair of strong icy fingers grabbed her wrist.

She wrenched away, drew back, and crashed the gun against the person's head.

The attacker cried out and staggered back.

She ran, not knowing which way she was heading. One thing was certain. It wasn't a ghost who had tried to grab her.

As the dogs led Lachlan through the gallery, he heard heavy footfalls.

The dogs barked.

He saw Regan as she turned a corner.

Their eyes met.

She ran toward him, her face pale, her body trembling, fear glistening in the liquid blue depths of her eyes. The moment she reached him, she flung her arms around his neck.

"'Tis all right, lass. What's the matter?" Lachlan held her, feeling her heaving breaths burning his chest. "Where have you been?"

When she gathered herself, she said, "I don't know how I found my way here. I just kept running and running, then I saw the lights burning in the gallery. Someone wants me to leave."

"I dinna ken your meaning, lass."

"I heard footsteps. Someone threatened me . . . I hit the person and ran."

"Whoa, lass, start again. Where were you?" Lachlan cupped her chin and made her look at him. Her eyes were wide and misty with fear.

"I went to see the stone."

"You mean the circle of stones?" Lachlan said, baffled.

"No, the stone. Darcy told me about a stone embedded in the floor of the ancient part of the castle, where the four corners meet," she said, impatience creeping into her voice.

"The Tender stone, you're meaning."

"If that is what you call it. Anyway, I wanted to quickly sketch the symbols on it. I thought they might interest my father. It's some sort of old text I have never encountered before."

His brow wrinkled in a frown. "I told you no' to leave your room."

"Such archeological finds cannot wait," she said, her tone inflexible. "All I wanted to do was look at the stone. But a breeze blew out the candles, then someone tried to frighten me by warning me to leave. I didn't want to tell you, but it wasn't an accident when I fell down the stairs— someone pushed me."

"You should have told me." Lachlan's jaw tensed at the thought of someone harming her.

"It was Tyg." Her eyes searched his face for a reaction.

"Tyg? Are you sure?"

"Well, no. But he was at the top of the stairs after I fell."

"What about the voice you heard. Was it Tyg's?"

"It was raspy and deep. I cannot be sure. Can we go back there? I want to finish examining the stone."

"All right." He found it hard to believe Tyg was trying to harm her, but he couldn't discredit what she had said. He would have to watch her closely and question Tyg. He felt her hand slip into his, and he clasped it tightly.

• • •

Regan felt so much safer with Lachlan walking beside her. And having the huge dogs nearby didn't hurt either. She was almost getting used to them. Almost. The steady click of his cane was like a balm to her nerves, though his nearness caused her insides to quiver. She could still feel the huge wall of reserve that he kept up between them.

Lachlan held a candelabra up before them, and the light pierced the dark bowels of the castle.

"Lachlan, why do you think someone's trying to drive me away?"

"I've no idea."

"I wonder if it has anything to do with the circle of stones. Three people have been found dead there. And surely everyone knows that I was out there when we first met."

He frowned and said, "Why would that have anything to do with it?"

"What if there is a murderer here?"

"There's no bloody murderer loose here, unless you count the evil that has plagued my family for generations."

"It wasn't a Druid curse that harmed those men. What do you remember about their deaths?"

He hesitated a moment as if gathering his thoughts. Light from the candles flicked in his black eyes as he said, "Nothing much. They were all drowned. Somehow their bodies ended up in the circle."

"It doesn't make sense. The sea never rises as high as the cliff."

"Sometimes when there's a storm it does. Two were sailors and their ships had wrecked on the rocks. The Druid spirits that dwell there took their lives for sacrifices to their gods. Pure and simple."

"Surely you don't believe that?"

"'Tis a known fact that lights dance around the circle. Sailors have seen them for eons as far as three miles out into the bay. Aye, I believe it."

Regan wanted to argue with him, but she knew pressing him would not get past his superstitions. Their footsteps melded together as they traversed another hallway and came upon the stone. Regan's sketch pad and charcoal still lay on the floor.

The dogs sniffed at them.

Regan bent and picked them up. "Do you mind if I finish sketching the stone?" she asked.

"Nay." He leaned against the wall, crossed his ankles, and rested the cane near his leg.

"Do you know where this stone came from?" she asked.

"There's a tall legend attached to the Tender stone. 'Tis said a great Druid priestess carved the stone to mark the funeral pyre of her lover, an English warrior king, and placed it over his grave to ward off evil."

"Do you know anything about the king?" Regan asked, hiding her sudden excitement.

"Nay, only that he was wounded in battle, came to her, and died in her arms." His eyes took on a strange black hue as he stared down at Regan. "Theirs was a forbidden love, because she believed in Celtic gods and the old way, and he was a Christian. 'Tis said that he built her a great fortress here on the isle where they could meet, but the ruins were washed away. All that remains of their life together is this one stone. Legend had it that it protected those who owned it from harm, and the first MacGregor was gifted with it by his clan."

"Really. What an extraordinary tale." She strained to keep her features calm, while her insides were doing cartwheels. Could Sir Thomas Malory have heard of this same myth in his travels and fictionalized the account, for the sake of telling a good tale, naming the Druid priestess Morgan and making her Arthur's half sister? When in reality she'd been something much more ordinary, his mistress.

In the Arthurian legends, Morgan ruled the island of Avalon and was versed in leechcraft, and Arthur was sent there after he was wounded. The real priestess had probably tried to revive her lover and been unsuccessful. In her heart, Regan believed Arthuis had been her lover and this was his burial stone. He had been laid to rest on this island. But where?

"Please, go on," she said, keeping her voice from growing impassioned.

"There's no' much to tell. The first Laird MacGregor instructed his architects to incorporate the Tender stone into the castle, but it did him no good. He went daft all the same."

"Oh." Regan bent down and ran her hand lovingly over the rough texture.

"It is said the priestess killed herself after her lover died."

"She must have loved him very much." She gazed into Lachlan's eyes.

He didn't glance away, and the swirling inkiness there held her spellbound. "I'm thinking she did," he said. "She loved him so much she took her life when he died."

Had he actually mentioned the word *love*? "I admire her greatly for her courage," she said, her voice barely above a whisper. "I wouldn't want to live without the man I loved."

He stepped toward her. "And would you be keeping secrets from the mon you loved?"

"It all depends." Regan began sketching furiously.

He inched closer. He was so close, her arm brushed his trousers.

"On what, lass?" His voice held a deep velvety note of distrust.

"Do you not agree that some secrets are better not spoken aloud?"

He leaned over, grabbed her hands, and pulled her up to face him. His gaze tunneled directly through her as if searching for all her guarded secrets and desires. "I'm not talking about insignificant confidences, lass, I'm talking about the kind that can harm you." He cupped her chin and ran his thumb over her lips.

Regan felt the heat of his fingers move over her lips and

send tingles down her neck. "Why are you looking at me like that?"

"I'm wondering what secrets you're hiding." He slipped his hands around her waist and pressed his body against hers.

"None, really." Regan felt herself being forced back by his powerful chest.

When he reached the wall, he leaned against it and pulled her close. "You're lying." He feathered a kiss across her lips as his knee slid between her thighs, sending hot prickles along her skin.

Desire thickened in the pit of her belly, and a thin film of perspiration broke out over her body. The sketch pad dropped from her fingers. Next the charcoal.

He kissed her again; this time his lips stayed on hers for only a moment. "I canna protect you if I dinna know what you're after. What made you go to the circle, and why is this stone so important to you?"

"It has to do with my father's work. That's all I can tell you." Regan felt him ease her hips against his leg, pressing against a sensitive spot that made her throb all over.

"You can trust me," he said, his breath ragged.

"Can I?" She could no longer fight the strange influence he had over her. She grew bold and found herself running her hands over his powerful chest.

He groaned. "Aye, lass, you can."

"I'm not sure," Regan said, kissing his chin, feeling him straining to hold back his emotions. "You frighten me sometimes."

"Are you afraid now?" he whispered against her lips, his eyes glowing with desire.

Regan felt his hot breath on her mouth, smelled the clean linen of his shirt and his own delicious male scent. She breathed deep of him and said, "No."

He kissed her, thrusting his tongue once in her mouth only enough to make her want more. Then he moved his leg enough to allow him to slip his hand between her thighs. He touched her where no man had ever touched her.

Regan's mouth opened in surprise and amazement, then he was stroking her through her clothes and she could only cling to him.

He drew back enough to whisper against her lips, "What are you after, lass?"

"Arthur . . ." Regan kissed him, plunging her tongue into his mouth.

Lachlan drew back and pressed tiny kisses along the corners of her mouth, teasing her again with his lips and, God, . . . those wonderful fingers.

Her mind reeled from her own longing and the madness his restraint caused her.

He groaned and finally gave in to his desire. He deepened the kiss, while his free hand found her breast.

Regan arched against him, liquid fire singeing her whole body.

"Miss Southworth, are you down here?" Gillis's voice echoed from afar.

"We're here," Lachlan said, abruptly setting her away from him.

Her knees too weak to hold her, Regan braced her hand against the wall to keep from falling, and said, "You cannot deny that just happened."

For a moment his face softened, then a mask of chagrin drew it back into its tight closed lines. "I should never have let it," he said.

Gillis appeared, took in her flushed face and Lachlan's annoyed one, and said, "I went tae the miss's room tae see if you needed something 'fore I turned in, and found it empty. I got worried and searched for you."

"Did you pass anyone on your way down here?" Lachlan asked.

"Nay." Gillis's brows met over his sunken eyes. "Something happen?"

"Aye, someone threatened the lass." Lachlan motioned toward Regan. "Take her to my wing and dinna leave her until I get there. I want a look around."

"But whoever it was is long gone by now," Regan said.

"Aye, but the dogs may be able to lead me to him."
Lachlan picked up a candle, then he and the dogs walked
down a hallway.

"Be careful," Regan called to him.

He turned to look at her and appeared pleased that she
was worried about him. "I will," he said, the rough edge in
his voice gone.

She watched his large shoulders sway as he disappeared
from sight. Regan pulled out Old Gray and looked at it.

"You've a gun, miss?"

"Yes, my father insisted I bring it"—she glanced down
the barrel—"but it's not loaded. My father always kept it
loaded. I don't understand."

"Maybe someone unloaded it."

Regan stared down at the pistol. At the thought of Tyg
sneaking into her room and deliberately taking away her
one assured form of protection, Regan felt the bite of real
fear.

chapter 23

🌿

As Lachlan strode deeper into the core of his home, he felt a frisson of uneasiness. The dogs had picked up a scent near the Tender stone, and they were leading him into the darkest, oldest part of the castle. He never came here. This was the nucleus of the structure, the heart of its curse. He could feel the visceral pull of its force, as if his body were magnetized and this area were north.

Already his chest was tightening, his breath quickening. His nose had grown numb from the cold, and he could see his breath condensing in front of him. The murmurings and sighs were louder here.

To get his mind off the area, he thought of his encounter with Regan. Why had someone threatened her? Perhaps she'd been correct. Maybe it had something to do with the circle. The evil in it reached far, all the way inside the castle walls.

He frowned and recalled losing control and kissing her. He'd hoped to get the truth out of her. But somewhere along the line, he'd forgotten about his goal, and all he had wanted was to drown himself in her.

He could still taste her lips, feel her breasts and the soft, giving spot between her legs. If Gillis hadn't come upon them . . . He grimaced and tried not to think of what would have happened.

He remembered holding her, and using her own desire to force the word "Arthur" from her. The name didn't make sense to him. It provoked him that she wouldn't trust him enough to tell him the truth.

The dogs stopped suddenly.

Lachlan frowned as he held the candle up and watched the hounds pounce on two thick raw steaks on the floor.

Someone had known he'd use the dogs, and the culprit had left the meat to throw him off the trail. He'd find the bastard and hold him accountable for what he had done. He didn't want to believe it was Tyg. Tyg had always been a loyal servant, and Quin was attached to him.

Lachlan called the dogs and headed back in the opposite direction, relieved to withdraw from that part of the castle. He'd have to question Tyg.

Regan followed Gillis into Lachlan's chamber. The room was twice the size of Lady Margaret's. A large, canopied medieval bed filled the middle of the room. The carved posts were as wide as her waist.

A little sitting area stretched near a massive hearth, where a fire spit and hissed at them. Eight arched windows lined one wall; velvet royal blue curtains that matched the bed's counterpane framed them. Despite the warmth from the fire, a weighty dismal feeling pervaded the room—an oddly familiar feeling, identical to the cloud of remoteness that surrounded Lachlan.

Her gaze shifted back to the hearth, next to which a cage held a sleeping baby rabbit. She strode toward the rabbit. "Is this another one of Lord MacGregor's pets?"

"Oigh! I forgot tae put the wee thing back in the stable. The master was tending it today."

"He was?"

"Aye, miss, sometimes he rescues young 'uns like that one you see there from harm. This one he found after its mother was eaten by a fox."

Regan knelt and touched the soft wool blanket Lachlan had curled inside the cage for the baby rabbit to cuddle against. She could see Lachlan finding the rabbit and cradling the frightened animal next to his powerful chest. She couldn't help but smile. Was this the same blustery Scotsman who warned her he had no feelings left?

"Gillis, you seem to know Lord MacGregor better than anyone. Tell me, does he love his brother?"

"Aye, miss. Master Quin means more tae him than anyone in the world. He's always worrying over Master Quin, always has protected him since he was born."

"Why does he push everyone else away?"

"He's afraid."

"Why?"

"I've known the lad since he was born. He closed off his feelings tae survive. You canna know the misery the poor lad has seen. He had tae watch his grandfather go mad, then his own father. It takes its toll, miss. It can make a mon's heart hard as stone."

"I imagine it could," Regan said, wondering if anything could penetrate such a tempered heart.

"I remember the times when he was a wee lad and Lady Margaret would make him go and visit his father locked up in the keep. 'Twas a terrible thing tae see, the lad shaking all over, afraid of his own father. He'd never let on tae anyone, and he'd visit his father, but I could see his fear. And 'tis ingrained in him. That's why he's bent on never marrying. He's no' wanting anyone tae see him like that." Gillis made a face at the memory.

"But you said some of the lairds didn't go mad until their later years. What about his life now? He could be happy if he let himself."

"If you find a way of making him see he can enjoy his life, miss, I'll forever be grateful. I'm sure he's set in his beliefs now."

"What of his mother? Was she a good influence on him?"

"Nay, miss. Never took a moment's time with either of the lads. I hate tae say it, but it was a relief when she disappeared."

"Why do—"

Lachlan strode in through the doors, frowning.

Regan clamped her mouth shut.

Lachlan scowled at her. "Go ahead, you can finish what you were going to say aboot me."

"I was just telling Gillis that I didn't know you had a soft spot for baby rabbits. Is that not right, Gillis?"

Gillis nodded and shared a guilty look with her.

Lachlan's brows dropped over his eyes. "'Twas a wee tiny thing," he said, his voice gruff and uncomfortable.

"Did you find anything or anyone?"

"Nay."

Regan could tell by the slight inflection in his voice he was hiding something from her.

Lachlan turned to Gillis. "I'll take the lass back to her room."

"Aye." Gillis gave Regan an encouraging glance.

She knew he was remembering their conversation on changing Lachlan's view on life. She shot him a look that said, "I'll try," then watched him leave the room.

Lachlan's black inky gaze swept over her in a slow, lingering way.

A burning sensation spread low in her belly. "What did you find?"

He seemed hesitant to tell her, then said, "Someone tried to throw the dogs off the scent of the trail."

"At least we know we're dealing with someone who is clever."

"Aye."

"Did you question Tyg?"

"Aye, found him near the circle. He said he never left it."

"Maybe it wasn't him."

"I dinna know, but I'll find who did it and he'll wish he were never born."

The savage tone in his voice made her shiver. Regan motioned to the cage and said, "May I pet the rabbit?"

"Aye."

Regan carefully eased it out of the small opening. Its pink, frightened eyes stayed on the dogs and it trembled in her arms. "I promise, I won't hurt you. So I'm not the only one afraid of dogs," she said to the rabbit, feeling Lachlan watching her.

Regan felt the tension in her chest lessen as she stroked the rabbit's tiny head. "You should name it."

"I'll no' be keeping it. I'm taking it back to the wild in a few days. It's gotten bigger and better able to fare for itself."

She heard the distant steel in his voice. Forming any kind of attachment must be nigh to impossible for him. How could she help him?

His gaze caressed every part of her body.

Regan felt the warmth of his dark eyes swirling inside her. She remembered him kissing her near the stone, the way he'd touched her everywhere and how she'd let him. He crossed the room toward her, those black eyes devouring her.

When he was a foot from her, he said, "'Tis no' a good idea for you to be in here, lass. Put the rabbit back and I'll walk you to your room."

Regan set the rabbit in the cage, closed the door, then stood. "Can we talk a little?"

"Trouble is, I'm wanting to do more than talk." He frowned at his bed, then grabbed her wrist and guided her toward the door.

"What did you have in mind?"

"You're no' wanting to know."

She saw his dark, thunderous expression and grinned. Maybe she was getting somewhere with him.

"Why are you smiling?" he asked, not looking at her, keeping his eyes purposefully straight ahead of them.

"Do you have eyes in the side of your head?"

"No, but I can feel you smirking."

"Really."

"Aye, and you'll bloody well stop it."

"You may be able to drag me through your castle and pretend I don't exist, but you cannot keep me from smiling at you," she said under her breath.

"I heard that."

"I hope so." Regan saw his brows plunge so low over his eyes, his lashes disappeared. She was beginning to enjoy annoying him. Perhaps that was the only way she could break down the cocoon of indifference that embraced him. He might even get so aggravated he'd kiss her again.

When they reached her chamber, Lachlan flung open the door and scanned the room. "All clear."

Regan stared at the shiny black hair curling over the edge of his collar and fought a desire to touch it. She stepped closer. Her lips were inches from his neck. "Are you sure?" she asked in her most sultry voice.

His shoulders stiffened. His fists clenched. Every muscle in his body tightened. "Aye," he said. "In you go." He stepped back so she could pass him and refused to look at her.

Her goal to seduce him into another kiss dissolved when the dogs lumbered up near her leg.

"Ah!" She hopped back, eyeing the large gray beasts. They always seemed to come upon her when she least expected it. And they always had their tongues hanging out, and the little tips of their fangs showing.

His expression turned impatient. "'Tis high time you get over your fear. I'm going to show you there's nothing to be afraid of." He grabbed her hand.

"No, please." Regan tried to pull away.

He forced her hand down on the head of the dog closest to her, then he covered her hand with his own and kept it there. "See, they'll no' hurt you."

Regan flinched and tried to draw back, but the unrelenting pressure of his hand kept her fingers on the dog.

"Nay, lass, dinna show them you're afraid."

"But I *am* afraid." Her hand trembled as he moved it down the dog's spine. She felt the coarse fur brushing her palm. "You're doing this to punish me for smiling."

A ghost of a grin twitched a corner of his mouth. "I can think of better ways to punish, lass. You'll get over the fear."

"You don't know that. You have no idea what it feels like." She felt the warmth of his hand seeping through her skin and traveling up her arm.

"I do."

"How?"

"I've been afraid before." He hesitated a moment, then lifted her hand to stroke the dog again. He seemed lost in thought as he watched their hands moving over the dog's fur.

"Tell me what you're thinking," she urged, hoping to keep his attention with her.

After a moment, he said, "I was remembering the west tower. I used to have nightmares about it. I always dreamed I was tied to a bed there and I couldna get loose. . . ." His words trailed off.

Regan swallowed and felt a catch in her chest. "Was that where they kept your father?"

He nodded.

She wanted to hug him and make him forget, but she knew it was a vulnerable moment for him and he'd turn away from her if she gave him sympathy. "You were small and afraid," she said. "It was a natural fear."

"Aye, natural." He glanced over at her and frowned. It was one of those expressions he wore when he'd said more than he had realized.

"This is Prince," he said, his tone growing brusque. He forced her hand over to the other dog. This dog's gray whiskers were longer than the other's, and he had more white on his chest. "This is Charlie."

He glided her hand down Charlie's spine. He stood behind her and his arm was over her back. Regan turned, and their faces were inches from each other. He stared at her lips. His head moved toward her lips. . . .

At the last moment he jerked back.

"Now you pet him by yourself." He pointed at Charlie.

Regan hated that cold restraint in his voice—it battled with the passion in his eyes. While he'd spoken of his own fear, Regan had forgotten to be afraid. Now that he'd withdrawn his hand, she wanted to recoil, but he was watching her to see what she'd do. She forced her hand to stay on Charlie, though she cringed on the inside.

"See, they'll no' hurt you. You ken that now."

"Yes."

"We'll do it again, until you answer me like you're meaning it," he said, somehow reading her thoughts with disconcerting accuracy. Yearning filled his expression as he lazily perused her body.

She could almost feel his hands caressing her breasts, his lips ravishing her. Her eyes sought his. The yearning between them pulsed in the air. She reached out to touch his arm, but he stepped back.

"Go to bed, lass."

"Will you be nearby?" she asked, suddenly back again in total darkness, feeling the person who had warned her to leave grabbing her arm. She didn't want to be alone.

"I'll be sleeping here tonight." He threw the words out and glanced into her room.

"Here?" Regan's eyes widened. If he'd dropped the Tender stone on her, she could not have been more surprised.

chapter 24

"Dinna think I meant inside there." He nodded to her room. "I'll be outside your door."

"Oh." Regan couldn't help but feel a stab of disappointment.

A door opened and Lady Margaret appeared, holding a candle. The shadows in the hallway heightened the wrinkles on her face and the dark circles beneath her eyes.

Lachlan grimaced when he saw her and asked, "What are you doing up?"

"My fire has gone out. I cannot sleep unless my chamber is warm. What the devil is going on? No one is where they're supposed to be. I've rung the bell but not a soul answered. Are there no servants to be found in the castle?"

"Can I warm it for you?" Regan asked.

"You canna," Lachlan said adamantly. "Your life was just threatened."

"Threatened? I find that hard to believe." Lady Margaret narrowed her eyes at Regan.

"'Tis true."

"If that is so, she must be guarded."

"I'll be doing it tonight." Lachlan glanced over at Regan, his dark gaze drinking her in.

"Surely Gillis or Tyg can do it."

"Nay. I'll be protecting her." His concerned expression warmed Regan.

Lady Margaret eyed them, then pursed her lips in annoyance.

Regan saw the soiled edge of Lady Margaret's dressing gown. She remembered seeing it in the clothes that she'd helped Darcy carry before someone had pushed her down the stairs. The train looked as though it hadn't been laundered at all.

"You've soiled the bottom of your dressing gown," Regan said, and watched for the lady's reaction.

"That scatterbrained Darcy rarely takes her duties seriously. I told her to use more soap in the wash."

Lachlan pointed inside Regan's chamber. "In you go, lass." He turned to the dogs. "Watch her."

The dogs shifted and stood on either side of her like two gray, shaggy sphinxes.

"I really don't want them in my room." She warily eyed the huge fangy beasts so close to her legs.

"I'll feel better, lass, if they stay with you."

Regan saw his concern and her fear of the dogs no longer seemed tantamount. She heard herself say, "Very well, if you insist."

The dogs were following her when Charlie caught a whiff of something on Lady Margaret's hands and paused long enough to lick her fingers.

"Wretched creatures," Lady Margaret said with a huff. "Why do you insist upon letting them inside?"

At the tone in her voice Charlie cringed and followed Regan inside.

Lachlan's answer was cut off as he closed the door. Regan listened to his deep muffled voice and felt the emptiness of the room. She glowered at the dogs. Her hand trembled as she pointed to a corner. "Go. Lie down."

They didn't move, only kept their dark eyes trained on her.

"All right, be insolent." Regan eased around them. "Do what you like. I ask only that you stay away from me." With one eye on the dogs, she found her trunk and opened it.

Down in the bottom of the trunk, she saw a tiny mound of gunpowder and a lead ball, evidence that someone had unloaded Old Gray. She had stashed the leather satchel containing additional gunpowder and shot in the wardrobe, inside a hatbox. When she opened the top, the pouch was still inside the box.

She took it out and carefully reloaded. Her father had taught her and Emma how to care for and load the gun. When she was done, she slipped it beneath her pillow, aware the dogs were watching her. They hadn't moved from their spot by the door.

"That's good. Stay right there," she said.

She thought of the diary and pulled the book out of its cubbyhole. Carefully, so the dogs wouldn't rush forward, she donned her nightgown, then crawled into bed. She opened the journal:

February 1775
Today my life has ended. I have learned I am with child. God help me. I do not want Balmoral's children. It will ruin my figure. No one will ever hire a fat actress—and I will return to the stage. I begged Balmoral to take me to London for some diversion, but he refuses and wishes to keep me prisoner here. I believe he correctly suspects I wish to do away with his child. How shall I rid myself of this burden? I must find a way.

September 1775
Fifteen hours of labor and I delivered a boy, an heir. I cannot bear to look upon his face. I cannot forgive him for the pain he put me through. I sent him to the

wet nurse. Balmoral preens like a peacock and has
already named his son Lachlan and seems so proud.
Of course he should be happy, 'twas not him scream-
ing in agony for hours. I should not care what the
child is called.

Regan shook her head and thumbed past a year's worth of
entries.

May 1776
Horrible, horrible news. Balmoral has gotten me
with child again. I shall die this time. I'll not go
through such pain again and have my body ripped
stem to stern. No, I'll not suffer it again. I know of a
witch who practices in the northern tip of the island.
She can purge me of my horrid fate.

Regan paused in her reading, her trembling hands gripping the sides of the journal. No one—especially Lachlan—must ever see this ugly diary. She couldn't read any
more and slammed it closed.

The next morning, a knock at the door roused Regan
from a deep sleep. She'd been dreaming she was being
smothered by the person who had warned her to leave. She
woke with a start.

All she could see was a mound of gray fur and floppy
ears in her face. She realized it was Prince's head. Every
muscle in her body tightened. She glanced to her right and
saw Charlie, big as you please, snoozing on her other side,
his long legs sprawled over her thighs and chest. They were
so heavy it felt like human limbs pressing down on her.
Now she knew who had been smothering her.

She forced herself to breathe, summoned her courage,
and said, "Get down." Her voice had been shaking and she
couldn't muster enough authority into it.

The dogs raised their heads and looked indifferent.

"Get down." She tried again, this time adding a military bark to the order.

The dogs' ears cocked. They shared a glance, then leaped off the bed.

The knock came again.

"Coming."

Regan hoped it was Lachlan. By the time she donned a dressing gown and reached the door, she was out of breath.

Gillis stood before her, holding a tray, the hand minus the three fingers wobbling slightly. "The master said to bring your breakfast up."

Regan tried to keep the disappointment from her face. "Where is he?" She glanced over and saw a chair had been placed by her door. Lachlan must have spent the night there.

"His wing, miss. He ordered me to watch you."

"Oh." Regan kept the disappointment from her voice. "Are you all right, Gillis?"

"Sometimes I get the shakes in that hand, miss. Dinna know why."

"I hope they get better."

"Thank you, miss. They always do."

Regan noticed a bruise on the side of Gillis's cheek and said, "Did you get hurt?"

"I get dizzy sometimes, too, miss."

"Oh."

Regan recalled last night when the person had grabbed her arm in the dark. If she wasn't mistaken, there had been a slight tremor in the person's hand. It couldn't be Gillis. Could it? What reason would he have to want to keep her out of the circle?

Gillis looked uncomfortable at her silence and said, "Lady Margaret is asking for you, miss. She said soon as you're done tae come tae her."

"I shall." Regan took the tray.

"Oh, I forgot. You left your drawing tablet in the master's room last eventide. I put it on the tray."

"Thank you. Will you please get rid of these monsters?" She pointed at the dogs.

Their ears dropped, and they seemed to know she was speaking about them.

"Can't, miss. The master said you should feed them."

"But you can feed them very well."

"He said you'd say that. I'll be outside." He closed the door.

The dogs eyed her and sniffed the air.

"Stay," she commanded. Feed them? They looked like they wanted to eat her.

She opened the covers on the plates. One plate contained eggs, scones, clotted cream. The other two had huge ham steaks.

The dogs perked up at the sight of their breakfast.

"Oh, very well, I guess you have to eat." She tossed the dogs their ham.

They gobbled the meat in two gulps.

Regan wanted to question Lachlan's grandmother about Lady MacGregor. After reading more of her diary, Regan wondered just how callous and selfish Lachlan's mother had been.

R*egan had breathed easier when the dogs hadn't fol-*lowed her into Lady Margaret's room. It had taken only one scathing glance from Lady Margaret and they had paused at the threshold.

Throughout the morning, Lady Margaret had kept her so busy she hadn't been able to inquire after Lady MacGregor's character, but she had managed to post the sketch she'd made of the Tender stone to her father. He would be as overjoyed and intrigued as Regan had been upon finding it.

Lady Margaret squinted down at her stitches.

"Perhaps you should use spectacles," Regan said.

"I do not need spectacles, gel. I have perfect vision. I've always had perfect vision. Spectacles, indeed." She shot Regan a baleful glance.

Regan wouldn't give Lady Margaret the argument she wanted and sat down to write a list of menus for the week.

Not one to be ignored when trying to make her annoyance known, Lady Margaret said, "Stop writing this instant."

Regan looked at her. "Yes, my lady?"

"We were not through with our conversation."

"I thought we were. I said you needed spectacles, you said you did not. What else is there to discuss?"

"Your reasons, gel. I suppose you have a whole headful of them."

"I'm certain I have none that can convince you that you need spectacles, my lady. You've made up your mind."

"Aye, I have, and no slip of a gel is going to change that." When Regan turned back to writing, Lady Margaret said, "You were hired as my companion. Converse with me, gel."

Regan smiled. The grand madam was lonely; it was the first sign she had given that she had any warmth in her soul. "I do have something on my mind."

"I knew it. What is it?" Lady Margaret asked eagerly.

"I've been wondering about Lady MacGregor's character."

"Character?" The lady harrumphed. "She had no character. There was a reason they called her the Flame, and it wasn't just because of her bright red hair. If ever a chit had a scarlet heart, she did. She was a cruel, wicked gel." Hatred gleamed in the swimming brown eyes. "I told my son to annul the marriage. Did he listen? Blind as all men are to a pretty face. She married him only for his wealth and position. She was nothing but an actress. If you ask me, she should have been the one to have been locked up, not my son. When she embroiled McAskill into a liaison, it disgusted me. The young man was half her age and Lachlan's friend. I'd had enough. I told her so the night she disappeared. She didn't like what I had to say, but we never minced words."

"Do you think she died out on the moors?"

"I couldn't say, but I was never so glad in my life as when her horse came home without her."

Gillis had mentioned he was glad when Lady MacGregor left. Now Lady Margaret. Had someone made it so the lady would never return home? "Do you think someone murdered her?" Regan asked, measuring Lady Margaret's expression closely.

"Heavens, no, gel." Lady Margaret pursed her lips at Regan. "Not only are you an insolent piece of baggage, but you have an uncontrollable imagination." There was no malice in her voice.

Was the lady beginning to warm to her? "I've been thinking. Someone has threatened me. Three people have been found drowned in the circle. And Lady MacGregor disappeared. I cannot help but wonder if they all connect in some way."

"Absurd, gel. You've been reading too much fiction. Those deaths in the circle were from stormy seas. And Lady MacGregor's horse probably threw her into a bog, giving us all some peace. Now earn your wage and read to me, gel."

Regan had left *The Lady of the Lake* on a table near the window. When she went to retrieve it, she glanced out and saw the little crofter's cottage in the distance. Lachlan was just stepping in through the door with Quin.

"Stop dawdling, gel. I've acquired another wrinkle waiting for you."

"Coming," Regan said, turning away from the window. She wondered what Quin thought of his mother. She also wanted to question him about Tyg. Lachlan had said Quin was devoted to the servant. Regan couldn't fathom Tyg being close to anyone.

Regan started to sit in the chair opposite Lady Margaret, but the lady patted a spot beside her. "Sit here, so I can hear."

As Regan opened her mouth to read, Lady Margaret interrupted her. "I know about the debacle in the village. My grandson would never have done that had he not formed an

attachment to you. I mean to put you on your guard, gel. Do
not fall in love with a MacGregor. You will regret it."

"Do you have regrets?" Regan asked.

"When my husband didn't know my name and I had to
watch him be dragged behind a locked door, yes. I grieved
for him, and me, and our life together."

Regan understood a little of why Lady Margaret seemed
so bitter. "How many years of happiness did you have, my
lady?"

"Five and thirty. My Oswald didn't go mad until his later
years, but it only takes one unbearable recollection to destroy a lifetime of contentment." Lady Margaret blinked
and her eyes glistened with something close to tears. "But I
had to watch my son's madness destroy him when he was
only forty. Spare yourself watching your husband and children go mad, gel."

"Surely a little happiness is better than none at all. I
wouldn't care if my husband went mad, if I were truly in
love with him."

"You're a naive dreamer. It is easy to say that until it
happens to you."

Regan knew she couldn't change Lady Margaret's mind.
She was an embittered lonely lady. Regan could never
make Lady Margaret understand that just one day of happiness, one day of seeing Lachlan really smile, would be
enough for Regan to endure just about anything.

The door opened and Darcy sailed inside, carrying Lady
Margaret's customary midmorning snack of lemon water
and tarts and pecan biscuits.

Regan noticed that Darcy's complexion already looked
remarkably clearer since she'd been using Emma's balm.

The intrusion snapped Lady Margaret out of her un-
guarded moment. She looked annoyed at having intimated
so much of her past and said, "Well, gel, get on with the
reading. I'd like to finish Scott today." She waved to Darcy.
"Put that on the table there and then leave."

At the lady's stentorian tone, Darcy almost upset the
teapot. China rattled as she set down the tray. Quickly she

curtseyed and scuttled from the room, shooting Regan a commiserating look.

"Impossible to get decent help here," Lady Margaret muttered, and picked up her knitting.

Regan began reading and hoped Lady Margaret fell asleep quickly. She wanted to pay a call on Quin, and see Lachlan. She couldn't wait to test Lady Margaret's assumption that Lachlan cared for her.

Lachlan followed Quin through the three-room cottage. They passed a doorway that opened into a parlor, where an Egyptian-style sofa and chair filled the room and vases of cut flowers sat on several small tables, giving the room a wholesome, homey feel. To his right a doorway led into a small bedroom, where the bed had been made in a tidy fashion. Quin had always been one for neatness.

Quin led him into the kitchen. A small table and four chairs sat near a stone hearth in which a peat fire burned. Another large bouquet of wildflowers filled the center of the table. Various pots and pans hung in an orderly fashion above a sink and counter. "You can sit by the fire, if you're wantin' tae," Quin said, grabbing a teakettle and pouring water into it from a pitcher.

"Did you see Tyg last night?" Lachlan asked.

Quin nodded. "He came by at ten tae check on me. He always does. We play cards. I like playing cards with Tyg. He lets me win. He's no' much tae look at on the outside, but he's a nice mon on the inside. I'm liking Tyg."

Lachlan didn't know if he could trust Tyg. Last night Tyg had said he hadn't left the area near the circle, but Quin had just said otherwise. "Did he stay long?"

"Nay. We talked for a minute, then he said he had tae get back and guard the circle."

Lachlan understood the bond between Quin and Tyg. It had begun when Quin's mother had shipped Lachlan off to boarding school in England. It had almost killed Lachlan to leave Quin.

Lachlan could still see the tears rolling down Quin's cheeks as he had fought Tyg to come with Lachlan. That was the first day Lachlan had felt real resentment toward his mother. His relationship with Quin had never been the same after he had left for school. While Lachlan was away, Tyg had taken his place in Quin's affections. When Lachlan returned before their father died, Quin wouldn't speak to him for several months. He still showed signs of reserve toward Lachlan for having deserted him.

"Why were you kissing Regan?" Quin asked.

"You're no' to speak of that to anyone."

"Like tae Lady Mar," Quin said, using his term for their grandmother.

"Aye."

"You like Regan?"

Lachlan frowned. "I like her."

"How? Like you like me, or like a wife?"

Lachlan rubbed his throbbing temples. "If I were going to marry, aye, I'd like her like a wife."

"You love her, Lachlan?" The kettle whistled and Quin poured the hot water in the teapot.

"I dinna."

"Looked that way tae me."

"You were no' looking properly."

"I may be slow but I can see, Lachlan. You look at her different. You love her."

"I dinna," Lachlan said, straining to keep his voice level.

Quin grinned in that simple maddening way of his. "You do, and you're no' admittin' it. You gonna marry her, huh, Lachlan?"

"Nay," he said, adding more emphasis than he wanted. How could he explain to Quin about the curse? "You're knowing we can never marry. We've been over this."

"Da married the Flame." Quin never called her Mother.

"Look what happened. Their life was never a happy one."

"She wasn't very nice. She never wanted me—but that's a'right. I never wanted her either."

"If Regan questions you aboot the night our mother disappeared, you're to say nothing."

"I know. You told me tae never speak of it. I never speak of it."

"That's good. See that you dinna."

"What if I've got the curse for both o' us? I've had it since I was born. What if that's enough? What if you dinna get it because I have it for both o' us? What aboot that, Lachlan? Then you could marry Regan."

"It's no' working that way, lad."

"I wish it did. I would be the mad one for both o' us. And you could have Regan."

"I have you; that's all I'm needing."

"You dinna look at me like you look at her. And ladies smell nice. I dinna smell nice. Neither does Lady Mar; she smells like turpentine and lavender. That's a bad combination, Lachlan. I mean like Regan. She smells nice. I want us tae keep her."

How could Lachlan make Quin understand that madmen should not take wives—if they have a conscience? "We canna. She'll have to go away one day." Lachlan felt a dark void opening in his gut when he thought of sending Regan away. But he knew one day soon it would come to pass.

"Like you did?"

"Nay, she'll no' come back like I did."

"Like the Flame then." Quin put the strainer over a cup and poured the tea in.

"Aye." Lachlan frowned and watched his brother's methodical movements as he strained the tea.

chapter 25

A n hour later the dogs trotted beside Regan as she
headed for Quin's cottage. She was almost getting used
to her three new shadows: the dogs and Gillis. He trailed
several feet behind her, while the dogs flanked her sides.
She felt safer, but having Gillis watch her every move
posed a new challenge in getting to the circle. How could
she excavate with Tyg guarding the circle and Gillis watching her? Somehow she'd have to find a way.

"Miss, are you sure you should be leaving the castle?"

"Lady Margaret's asleep. I don't see why I can't visit
with Quin a little while." She hurried past a line of purple
heather that bordered the path to Quin's cottage.

"The master may no' like you leaving the castle without
him. He gave me specific instructions."

"Really, Gillis, I don't think he'll mind. I saw him calling on Quin only an hour ago. He may still be here. How
could he object—especially since I have you and the dogs
to protect me?"

"He's no' likely tae be likin' it."

"Don't worry."

The cottage came into view. In the daylight the tiny house looked quaint, with beds of flowers providing a riot of color along its perimeter. Two ravens sat on the eaves, their vigilant eyes watching her every move.

She watched them as she walked up to the stoop and banged on the door.

No answer.

"Try around back, miss. Master Quin stays in his garden."

As Regan headed for the backyard, Quin trudged around the side of the house. He wore black tailored clothes with a beekeeper's mask over his face. He carried several jars of honey.

"Eh there, Regan. Want some?" He held a jar out to her.

She couldn't see his face clearly behind the dark netting, but she could make out his teeth gleaming in a wide smile.

"Thank you. That is very kind."

"The bees help my flowers."

"You are responsible for all these lovely flower beds?"

"Aye."

"My sister loves flowers, too. Maybe I can bring her here sometime to see yours."

"I'd like that. No one ever comes here but Lachlan and Tyg. Lachlan brings me things."

"He does? What sort of things?"

"Books, food, flowers."

"Flowers?" Regan couldn't imagine Lachlan fetching flowers for anyone.

"Aye, wild ones from the moors. Knotgrass, sheep sorrel, sea sandwort, and sea campions—sea flowers are my favorite. They've pretty petals on 'em. Lachlan dinna care tae look at the flowers, he only brings them tae me." He stepped toward her and gently placed the jar in her hands. "He's good tae me, is Lachlan. Canny he is, the best."

Regan marveled at Lachlan's love for his brother. She glanced around and asked, "Is Lachlan here?"

"Nay, said he had tae go and find you."

Disappointment swept over Regan.

Gillis piped up. "See, miss, I told you. He'll be rantin' when he canna find you."

"Please go and inform him where we are."

"But I'm no' supposed to leave you."

"I have the dogs, and Quin will protect me. You'll do that for me, won't you, Quin?" Regan also had Old Gray in her pocket, loaded.

Quin smiled and stuck out his chest. "I will. No one will be hurtin' you when I'm around."

"See." Regan addressed Gillis. "And someone should tell Lord MacGregor where I am."

"A'right." Gillis trotted back across the yard, not looking pleased, his long, polelike legs eating up the distance to the castle.

Regan waited until he was out of hearing range, then said, "Your brother tells me you are very close to Tyg. Does he bring you things, too?"

"Nay, Tyg plays cards with me, keeps me company."

"You like Tyg?"

"Aye, he's a friend." Quin pulled a face.

If he was telling the truth, Tyg must not be as unkind as he seemed. Still, someone had pushed her down the stairs, and Tyg had been the only one there.

"Come in, will you? I can make tea. I make good tea. Lachlan likes my tea."

"All right, I'd like that."

Regan was struck again by how much he favored Lachlan. Both men were darkly handsome.

"Know what my name means?" Quin asked.

"No."

"It means wise." Quin chuckled at the humor of it, then his face sobered and sadness twinkled in his expressive eyes.

"My name means nobility. Now that's irony for you."

Quin eyed her, lost.

"Never mind. I think my mother was getting back at my grandparents when she named me."

"My mother never wanted tae name me. She hated it that

I couldna read. She wasna very nice about it. She tried tae forget I was alive. There's no pictures o' me in the gallery. Lachlan wanted me tae sit for one, but I dinna want my picture in that haunted place. Bad things happen in there." He glanced toward Castle Druidhean and shivered. "I'm afraid tae be puttin' my picture in there. The ghosts will know who I am and come tae find me. Nay, I told Lachlan I'll no' have my picture in there. I ne'er go in there."

"I'm sure there's nothing to harm you." Regan recalled having been pushed down the stairs and the deep voice in the dark: *Leave this castle.* It wasn't ghosts who would harm him, but someone with flesh and bone and a beating heart.

"Lachlan is always sayin' that tae me. He gets mad 'cause I willna live there."

Regan remembered the argument between the brothers in the bailey. Quin's refusal to live in the castle must be a worry for Lachlan. Regan had hoped Lachlan had a tender spot in his heart and she had found it: Quin. It gave her hope.

"Let's go in. I'll put on the tea. I grow it myself. Make it with mint and flowers." Quin had pulled off the netting covering his face, and he tossed it aside now as he opened the door.

Regan followed him inside. The cottage was surprisingly neat, with colorful flower arrangements in every corner.

"This way." Quin led her into the kitchen. "You can sit by the fire, if you're wantin' tae," he said, grabbing a teakettle and filling it with water.

"You have a lovely little home here, Quin." Regan thought of how untidy her father used to keep his own room when he had been well enough to take care of himself and said, "Very orderly for a gentleman."

He beamed a smile at her. "I like tae keep things put away." He walked over and set the kettle on the hob. "Would you like tae see my garden?"

"May I invite my sister?"

"Aye." His mouth widened into a sheepish grin and a dimple came alive in his right cheek. Regan wondered if Lachlan would look that handsome if he really smiled. He brought out two cups and saucers from a cupboard and set them on the table. "What is your sister's name?"

"Emma."

"Emma." The name drifted from his tongue with an awe-inspired slowness. "I'll pick her some daisies. The Flame liked daisies. She wouldn't yell at me so much if I gave her daisies."

"Your mother yelled at you?"

Quin nodded sadly, and a lock of black hair fell over his forehead. "I couldna please her."

"Do you remember the night she disappeared?"

Quin's gregarious air closed down. "I dinna want tae be talkin' about that night."

"I'm sorry," she said. "I'll never speak of it again." What had really happened the night the Flame disappeared? It seemed everyone disliked Lady MacGregor, even her sons.

The front door opened and closed so loudly the windowpanes rattled in the kitchen.

"Quin." The deep bawl bounded off the walls of the little cottage.

Lachlan. He didn't sound happy. Regan tensed, hearing his boots pounding a path through the cottage.

chapter 26

❧

"In here," *Quin said, his moment of anxiety dissolving behind a smile.*

When Lachlan spotted her he ground to a halt. Regan had seen thunderclouds over the Isle of Skye look less menacing than his expression. He advanced toward her, his cane thumping on the plank floor.

"Quin was just making tea. Won't you join us?" Regan tried to sound offhand, but her voice came out ragged.

"Aye, Lachlan, I make good tea," Quin said, raising his jaw to a prouder, higher level. "Regan's staying for tea."

"Is she now?" Lachlan's harsh eyes raked her body.

"Aye, but where did I put the cream?" Quin scratched the side of his head.

"It's on the counter behind you," Regan offered, her voice cracking beneath the weight of those icy black eyes.

Quin glanced behind him and said, "Aye, there it is."

Lachlan leaned a shoulder against the doorjamb and crossed his arms over his chest, not drawing his gaze from her. "Why did you leave the castle?"

"Don't be provoked." Regan nibbled on her fingernail.

"I have the dogs and Quin to protect me. I asked Gillis to go to the castle and inform you of my whereabouts."

"From now on, you'll no' be without one of us guarding you at all times."

"Very well, but I can take care of myself."

"Nonetheless, I'll take no chances with your safety."

Regan saw his frown darken, so she changed the subject. "I have discovered Quin has a penchant for flowers. So does my sister. I believe she would be heartily jealous of Quin's gardens if she saw them."

Quin lapped up the compliment, and his cheeks blushed from it. "She's coming tae see my flowers, Lachlan."

Lachlan hardened his lips and in a tight voice asked Regan to step outside. He latched onto her arm, forced her to stand, and guided her out the door.

"Lachlan, don't take Regan away. Her tea."

"I'll be back," Regan said, unsure if she would. Regan felt Lachlan's thigh brush hers, and her skin tingled all the way down to her toes.

He slammed the door and faced her. "What are you up to now?"

"Must I always be up to something?" Regan asked, noticing the dogs sitting behind them.

"One never knows with you."

Regan felt her desire for him slipping over the edge into anger. "I just wanted Emma to see his flowers. They share a love for gardening. I see no harm in that. I'm sorry if you do."

"Quin forms attachments easily. 'Tis better he does no' meet your sister. It will hurt him when you leave the island."

She felt as if he had tied a rope to her insides and had given it a jerk. "Quin is lonely here. He has no acquaintances. What harm—"

"He has me and Tyg."

"You don't share his love of gardening, and Tyg—need I say more?" Regan snapped at him. He had unleashed something aggressive in her when he used that threat of sending her away.

"I'll not have him hurt—"

"Emma would never hurt him. Just because you have predetermined your solitary life, does not mean Quin should not go out in society and make friends."

"The trouble with you is you turn a blind eye to everything. You think you can make everything perfect, but it'll no' be that way. I've seen how cruel the villagers can be, and I'll no' let Quin be treated that way by anyone."

"Not everyone is heartless. Certainly Emma is not. You underestimate Quin. He's a kind, gentle person. Anyone who meets him cannot help but love him. Whether you want to admit it or not, it's not good for him to be sequestered here. You may want to wallow in unhappiness, but don't force Quin to do it."

"I'm no' forcing him."

"You want to believe that, but you are making him live a life as dismal as the one you've chosen."

The door swung open behind them, and Quin looked like a mauled kitten. "Please, Lachlan, dinna argue with Regan."

"We're no' arguing." Lachlan glowered at her.

"No, we are not." She glowered back.

Quin took in their dog-fight expressions and grimaced. "Please, Lachlan, I want Regan's sister tae see my garden."

Regan cut her eyes at Lachlan in a silent "I told you so."

Lachlan glanced at Quin, then at her. His mouth hardened and he resembled one of the immovable Celtic stones in the circle.

"Please," Quin begged again. "Regan says Emma likes gardening. I'd like tae have a wee bit o' time tae ask her what she grows."

The supplicating tone in his brother's voice and a little of Regan's pointed glance must have persuaded him, for Lachlan shook his head slightly as if regretting his own decision, then said, "All right. I'll arrange one visit."

"Thank you." Quin leaped out the doorway and gave his brother a bear hug.

Regan had to jump back to keep from getting stepped on. Lachlan frowned at her over Quin's shoulder as Quin pounded on his back.

Regan kept hearing Lachlan's words, *Leave the island*. Lady Margaret had seemed so sure Lachlan had affection for her. Regan wasn't certain at all. If he cared about her, he would not talk about her departure with such absolute certainty. It was as if he were already resigned to it. Did he care so little for her?

She left the brothers, the feeling of thumbscrews wrenching down in her belly.

L*achlan watched Regan cross the lawn, her strides stiff.* "You upset her, Lachlan. What did you say?" Quin put his hand on his brother's shoulder.

"Nothing but the truth. Did she ask you aboot the night the Flame disappeared?"

"Aye." Quin nodded, following Lachlan's gaze.

Lachlan thought she had. "You did no' tell her anything?" He grabbed Quin's arms.

"Nay. You said no' tae, and I didna." Quin jerked his arms free.

"Remember, it is our secret. You're never to speak of it."

"No' tae anyone."

Regan's meddling would have to be curtailed. He didn't want her dredging up the past.

He watched the sensuous motion of her swaying hips. A rock-hard throb pulled at his loins. He wanted her more than any woman he'd ever known. But he wouldn't use her to satisfy his carnal urges—he cared for her too much. His mind summoned a memory: Tyg and Gillis carting his father up to the west keep. His father screaming, struggling, swearing he'd kill them. Lachlan had felt only relief when the door had slammed shut.

That day Lachlan had sworn he'd never let anyone he

cared about witness such a thing when his own time came to be carted off to the west keep. Eventually it would come. The memory would give him the impetus he needed to send Regan away.

"I'd better follow the lass," Lachlan said.

"You'd better wait. She looks like she's needin' some time alone."

"I can't leave her alone." Lachlan hurried after her.

Quin frowned at both of them, then shook his head.

Lachlan called to Regan. *"Wait, lass."*

"Leave me alone. I'm in no humor to talk to you at the moment." She marched ahead of him, her fists swinging near her hips like hammers, her walking boots crushing heather and anything else in her path.

"What's the matter with you, lass?"

"You don't want to know, believe me."

"I do, or I would no' be asking it."

"I wish to high heaven you'd stop trying to act solicitous. It's out of character for you."

"I'm concerned. Tell me what has you so upset. If 'tis about your sister coming—"

She whipped around and jammed her fists on her hips. Her eyes blazed with blue fire. He'd never seen her look so bonny, or so tempting. In the sunlight her hair glistened like golden threads of silk. Tendrils had blown free from the tight bun at her nape and fell along the sides of her face. One strand had stuck to the side of her mouth, and he held back a desire to brush it back and place his lips there.

"It's not about my sister. And stop looking at me like that."

"Like what?"

"Like you want to kiss me."

"I do. You're a bonny lass standing right in front of me. Naturally, I'm wanting you." Lachlan couldn't keep his gaze from combing her body. Her small proud breasts were heaving in her brown dress. He remembered how they'd felt in his palms when she'd arched against him.

Abruptly she turned and continued on her way.

"Och, wait." Lachlan double-hopped to catch up to her, leaning heavily on his cane.

"I don't understand you. You want to kiss me, but you also can't wait for me to leave my position here." She blinked several times.

"I've always been honest with you, lass. I'm wanting you until I ache from it, but it must end there. I canna have you. I'll no' use you in that way." Lachlan thought he saw tears in her eyes, but she kept her face straight ahead and he couldn't be sure.

"How honorable of you, but you already have used me ill. You've made me care what happens to you." She snatched her skirt up around her ankles and broke into a full run.

Lachlan let her get ahead of him, but kept her in sight. She'd said she cared what happened to him. Damn her! He didn't want her to care. He wished he could take her in his arms and beg her to stay here, but he couldn't. He couldn't.

chapter 27

A week later the walls of the castle pressed in on Lachlan. Never in his life had Castle Druidhean felt small to
him. If he were honest with himself, it was because Regan
was in the castle, and she bloody well cared for him.

Try as he might, he couldn't get her out of his head.

Go to her, said a voice.

The voices wouldn't stop. He picked up his cane and
dashed out of his room. If he didn't leave soon, he'd find
her and . . . God knew what he'd do. Quin would help him
get his emotions under control. He hurried out of the north
wing, his cane thumping a vacant tattoo in the empty hallway.

Outside, Regan tapped on Quin's door. Gillis shifted
uneasily and said, "Master Quin might be napping."

Regan knocked again. "I hope he's not ill." For days she
hadn't been able to get Quin out of her mind. What a lonely
life he must lead.

A window opened above them and Quin leaned outside.

In the afternoon light his head and shoulders were in shadow; he looked like a marble bust sitting on the ledge. He yelled down to them. "Who is it?"

"Me," Regan said.

"Come in." Quin slammed the window shut.

"I'll walk aboot and see that it's safe," Gillis said.

"Very well."

The dogs followed Regan inside.

When she reached the kitchen, she heard a loud thump overhead. She thought Quin might have fallen. To her left she saw a door that stood ajar. It opened to a staircase. She commanded the dogs to stay, then ran up the stairs to see if Quin was all right.

The stairs opened into a small attic. Stacks of boxes in neat rows rose along the walls. Quin was bent over a trunk. When he saw her, he leaped up and hit his head on a rafter.

"Regan," he said, rubbing his brow.

"Are you all right?"

"Aye, 'tis just my noggin." He rocked from leg to leg, his face red with discomfort.

She had a feeling it wasn't from the mishap, but from her startling him. She felt a need to explain and said, "I heard a noise a moment ago and thought you'd fallen."

"I was up here."

Regan noticed his ears had turned red and a padlock dangled from his fingers. "Does that go on the trunk behind you?"

He nodded, looking like a guilty little boy who'd been caught putting a frog down a girl's back.

"Were you trying to lock your valuables back up? Can I help you?"

"All right, but you'll no' tell Lachlan aboot it."

"Why?"

"He wouldna like it that I kept this trunk."

"All right, I promise it will be our secret."

Regan stepped over to the trunk, bent beside Quin, and said, "When I lift the chains over the top, you put the lock through."

As Quin locked the chains, she noticed a gold name-plate. Engraved on it were the words *To My Darling Flame*.

"This trunk belonged to your mother." Regan spoke her thoughts aloud.

"Aye," Quin said, then he spurted out words like he was defending himself. "I'm no' supposed tae have it. Lady Mar was going tae have it burned after she cleaned the Flame's room out. I didna want tae see it burned, so I told Tyg tae bring it up here. I swore Tyg not tae tell, too."

"What is in here?"

"Clothes, mostly."

"They remind you of your mother, don't they?" Regan felt the space over her heart tighten.

"When I look at them, I dream o' a different minnie who might have liked me a little." Quin's bottom lip protruded and his chin quivered with emotion.

"She just didn't appreciate how special you are." After reading her diary, Regan was certain Lady MacGregor didn't care about anyone but herself.

"I'm no' special. I'm a bad seed."

"You are not. You are an extraordinary person in your own right. Had I a son like you, I would have considered myself blessed beyond my wildest dreams." Regan put her arms around him and hugged him. He felt stiff and unresponsive and uncomfortable with being close to others.

"I'm really bad. I think bad things."

"What kind of things?" Regan pulled back and stared at him.

"Sometimes I dinna listen tae Lachlan, or Lady Mar. Sometimes I just want tae run away from here. Sometimes I wish I'd never been born."

"You don't mean that."

"I do. Lachlan's life would have been different. He wouldna o' had tae take up for me so much. I used tae make our da mad all the time. He wanted me tae do things I couldna do—just like the Flame. Lachlan was always keeping me out o' his sight and worrying aboot me."

"I'm sure he didn't mind. He's your brother and he loves

you." Regan thought Lachlan's love for his brother was admirable. If only Lachlan could learn not to smother Quin with his affection.

A door opened below. "Quin." Lachlan's deep bellow swept up the stairs like a blast from a hunting horn.

Regan and Quin shared a glance. "You have tae help me hide the trunk."

"With what?"

"Look there." Quin pointed to a crate against the wall. "There's old blankets in it."

Regan had never moved so fast. She flew to the box, yanked out several old brown moth-eaten blankets, and tossed them to Quin. He snapped them over the trunk.

"Quin." The voice was more insistent.

"Coming," Quin called down.

"I'll come up."

"No," Quin and Regan both shouted together.

"Who's that? I'm coming up." The thud of Lachlan's footsteps sounded on the stairs.

Regan and Quin leaped in front of the trunk.

When Lachlan reached the top step and saw her, his frown deepened into a scowl. "Och. What are you doing here?" Lachlan asked, his gaze flicking over her.

"I—I just came to convince Quin to come to dinner at the castle." She turned to Quin. "Will you dine in the castle tonight?"

"Nay, I couldna go in there. Dinna ask me tae." Quin put his hands over his ears and shook his head.

"All right." Regan pulled his hands from his ears. "It doesn't have to be tonight. But just think about it. All right?"

"I will, but I'm no' changing my mind." Quin scrunched his expression into a determined mask.

Lachlan broke into the conversation. "What're you doing up here, Quin?"

"I was looking for a—a rake I lost."

"A rake?" Lachlan frowned and looked unconvinced. He

saw they were standing in front of something and covered the distance between them.

Quin stepped up to him and said, "There's no rake up here. We'd better be going down now."

"Capital idea," Regan said, closing in behind him. "We'll just go and see how well Gillis is doing securing the perimeter." Regan nudged Quin forward and took a step to go, but Lachlan's large hand clamped down on her wrist.

"Stay, lass. I'm needing a word. Go below, Quin, and wait for us."

"Aye, Lachlan. You'll no' howl at her like you did before?"

"Nay."

"Good, 'cause I'm liking her, Lachlan. She's a good friend, is Regan."

Regan wanted to grin, but looking at Lachlan's dark expression, she couldn't muster even a lip twitch.

Quin's gaze shifted to the trunk, then to Regan. He looked hesitant, his eyes saying, "Keep my secret." Then he turned and padded down the stairs.

"What were you really doing?" Lachlan asked, not loosening his grip on her wrist.

As irritated as she was with him, she felt that familiar awareness of him surge through her. "I found him up here. We were talking. Is that a crime?"

"Aye, when Quin forms attachments the way he does."

Regan tried to jerk her arm free, but his fingers were iron manacles. "Are you worried about Quin, or yourself?"

Her words were the magic key, and he unclasped her wrist. Without looking at him, she fled down the stairs, Lady Margaret's words ringing in her ears: *Do not fall in love with a MacGregor. You will regret it.*

Lachlan watched Regan disappear down the stairs. She had a way of unnerving him whenever he was near her. She shot words out of her mouth like bullets; they pierced him every time. Och! Maybe because they were so true, they hit their target with such accuracy.

His scowl deepened until his temples ached. As he turned to follow her, he saw the bottom of a brown trunk peeking out from beneath a moth-eaten blanket. In one yank, he snapped off the blanket. His mother's trunk? He bent down and pulled on the padlock.

Abruptly, he was fifteen again, standing in what used to be his mother's chamber. Gillis had packed away the last of her things. She'd been missing for a year. His grandmother insisted the room be cleaned out and remodeled. There was no sign of her left. All the drawers had been emptied, the top of her dressing table cleared of all its cosmetics and perfumes. Lachlan could not even feel her essence in the room; it, too, had been stuffed into the trunk. It was over. Yet tears had come to his eyes, burning, stinging tears. Unscrupulous and vindictive as she was, she had still been his mother.

Lachlan dropped the padlock. Quin must have intercepted the trunk after Lady Margaret had given the order to burn it. Had Regan been going through it? What did she hope to find?

He limped back to the stairs, determined not to let her out of his sight—especially when she was near Quin.

*T*he next morning Regan thought of how distant Lachlan had been last night at dinner, yet she had caught him staring at her with that same starved longing in his eyes. She had wanted him to kiss her again, but he'd kept his distance, even when he'd led her to her door and sat outside her room all night. If only she could get him to kiss her again, he might not be so eager to send her away.

She recalled Lady MacGregor's diary. She hated having to finish reading it. But there might be something in the pages that would help her discover what had really happened the night she disappeared. She had wanted to go through Lady MacGregor's trunk, but Quin seemed overprotective of it and she knew he would never let her see inside.

When she opened the board and reached in to find the diary, her fingers met only cobwebs. The book was missing, but who could have taken it?

She remembered the incident with Old Gray and glanced frantically around the room. Had someone snooped in her room and found it?

A cold draft brushed past her. Behind her the bed canopy rustled. She heard the crackle of turning pages. She wheeled around and found the diary on the pillow, opened to a page.

Gooseflesh broke out along her neck as she said, "Did you do that?" Regan realized she was talking to the castle. She grimaced, sat on the side of her bed, then picked up the journal. Its icy cover bit at her fingers and made her shiver as she rested it against her stomach and read:

June 1776
The witch's potion did nothing but make me ill. The child still grows in me. I did, however, purchase something from the old crone to stem Balmoral's sexual appetites. I put it in his drink when he's not looking. At least I didn't waste my money on that. He does not come to me at night any longer. Hopefully he never will again.

February 1777
Another son has been born. Balmoral named him Quin, though I do not suspect the child will live. He was bluish when he was born and would not take a first breath until the midwife had smacked him three times. Balmoral fades in and out of sanity. I still continue to give him the witch's brew.

Regan frowned down at the page, revolted and ill. Could whatever Lady MacGregor had given Lachlan's father have caused his madness? Lachlan believed the curse had caused his father's insanity. How could she ever convince Lachlan otherwise, without letting him read the journal? Poor Quin and Lachlan, having a mother who had been so detached from her own children that she had neither wanted them nor loved them.

A knock brought Regan's head up.

"Coming." She dropped the diary back in its hiding place, then scrambled off the bed. Was it Lachlan?

She smoothed out the wrinkles from the tobacco-brown bombazine before she opened the door.

Gillis held a tray of food out for her. "Mornin', miss. The master thought you'd be wantin' somethin' tae eat right away, seein' as how he just sent for your sister. She'll be here anon."

"So soon?"

"Aye. Master Quin refused tae eat his breakfast until she comes. He's a stubborn one. The master has a soft spot for him and let him have his way."

Regan felt a prick of jealousy. She wished Lachlan had a soft spot for her. "Thank you, Gillis," she said, taking the tray.

Gillis wore his usual dour expression, but she could see a little light of excitement in his eyes.

"Is something the matter, Gillis?"

"I'm glad we're havin' a caller, miss. It gives us all something tae look forward tae. The master ordered a large luncheon. We'll be getting out the good silver. 'Tis been a devil's season since we've used it."

Regan thought there was a hint of a smile on his face as he said, "I'll be outside if you need something." He darted out the door.

Regan opened the wardrobe and reached for the rose dress. It would please Emma. She was always harping about Regan's frumpish attire. But it wasn't Emma entirely whom Regan wished to please, but a dark, brooding, handsome Scotsman. Regan yearned to see him so overcome with desire that he lost all his iron self-control.

She usually wore her hair in a chignon. Not today. She

took great pains styling it, leaving several long curls trailing over her right shoulder and piling the rest on top of her head. Several wisps were left to straggle around her face.

When she was pleased with her coiffure, she nibbled at her tray, then hurried out to wait for Emma.

When Gillis saw her, he leaped up. His gaze swept over her. "Och! Miss, these old eyes havena seen such a bonny sight in years."

"Thank you, Gillis." Regan saw a smile tug at his mouth. "Do you think Emma will like it?" It wasn't Emma of whom she was thinking.

"Aye, but she'll no' be the only one."

"Let's go and see."

Gillis escorted Regan to the gallery.

When they neared the library, the unexpected voice Regan heard coming down the hallway caused her mouth to drop open.

"What's the matter, miss?" Gillis asked.

"Matter?" she said absently. "I'm not sure." She ran the rest of the way to the library.

chapter 28

"**B**y Jove, you have an impressive collection here, my
lord."

"You may borrow any book you like." Lachlan's deep
voice came back.

Regan hurried through the library doors. Lachlan
lounged in a chair, wearing his customary dark suit, his
long legs stretched out before him. Across from him, Emma
sat near the fire, fetching in a bright lemon and red plaid
morning dress. Beside her, his eyes radiant with life, looking the way they had when she'd discovered the bard's song
in the Whitorn Priory, was Seamus Southworth.

At the sound of her footsteps, Lachlan was the first to
glance over at her. The moment they looked at each other,
his eyes warmed.

His gaze grew so probing, so intense, Regan felt her
clothing peeling away one layer at a time. She had hoped
Lachlan would take note of her dress—not devour it while
she was wearing it.

Her father said, "There you are, my girl."

The sound of her father's voice broke the trance.

Regan glanced away from Lachlan and noticed her father holding his arms wide for her.

"Papa!" She covered the length of the room and hugged him. "What are you doing out of bed?"

"Am I to be scolded before I am greeted? Are you not happy to see your father? What a fine daughter I have here. Ringing a peal over her father's head the moment she walks into the room. I hope her nagging scolds do not offend you or Lady Margaret, my lord." A teasing smile creased her father's lips as he looked over at Lachlan.

"The lass speaks her mind, that's for certain." Lachlan seemed unable to take his eyes off Regan.

"Yes, well, my girl has never had a problem making her wishes known."

Regan glowered at both of them. "I am in the room, you know." Her gaze shifted to her father. "And I see no harm in caring about your health. Why are you out of bed? You know the doctor said bed rest." Regan used her most matriarchal tone.

"What does that old goat know?" Seamus's smile slipped from his lips. "I shall get out of bed when my constitution allows. And it happens to be very agreeable today, thank you very much. So while I had a little wind in my sails I decided to see for myself how you were getting along here, my girl."

"I'm fine, as you see."

"I must say, Castle Druidhean seems to agree with you. Let me look at you. I did not know my own daughter for a moment. Can't remember the last time I've seen you in anything other than brown and with your hair down. You did not have to dress for us, but I daresay you're looking fetching." Her father winked at her. "Does she not, Emma?"

"I've told her for an age she should wear color," Emma said, rolling her eyes at Regan. "I'm glad you finally listened to me. That rose is very becoming on you. What do you think, Lord MacGregor?" Emma addressed him with a mischievous smile.

Lachlan grumbled something unintelligible, while his hand choked the lion on the tip of his cane.

"Tell me how you've been getting on." Seamus looked expectantly toward Regan.

"Castle Druidhean is a most interesting piece of architecture, Papa. Built with the same maze of hallways and staircases as the Great Pyramid of Giza."

"I would love to explore it. Lord MacGregor was kind enough to show us his library. He said I could borrow anything I liked."

"How very kind of him. Lord MacGregor isn't as forbidding as he would have everyone believe." Regan bestowed a playful smile on Lachlan, while he continued to look at her like he wanted to pounce at any moment.

"Would you like a tour, Mr. Southworth?" Lachlan asked.

Her father's eyes widened with excitement and he motioned to the doors. "By Jove! Very much indeed."

"But are you well enough?" Regan touched her father's arm.

"When I get tired, I'll sit."

Lachlan held out his arm to Emma. "Allow me to escort you, Miss Emma."

Emma hesitated a moment, then took his arm.

Regan smiled inwardly at Lachlan's kind gesture. He could be very charming, when he wanted.

Seamus hooked his arm through Regan's and they lagged behind Lachlan and Emma. "I never thought I'd see it, but you're smitten with him, my girl."

"La! Papa, nothing could be further from the truth." Regan added too much conviction to her voice. She couldn't tell her father that Lachlan had driven her crazy with his lips and hands, touching her in places that she dared not name.

Seamus cocked a bushy gray brow at her. "I admit he doesn't seem at all daft and formidable, as I had been led to believe by gossip. He has a generous nature."

"Yes, he has."

"Do you know him well enough that we can take him into our confidence?"

"I'm not sure, Papa. I asked him if I could excavate the circle and he refused me. He believes he is protecting me from the evil there."

"Superstitious, is he? Well, one cannot be reared on an island so steeped in lore and mysticism as this one and not come under its spell. I'll not have you putting yourself in danger and suffering Lord MacGregor's wrath by going against his wishes—"

"Perhaps if I dig there and prove to him there is no need for concern, he'll allow us to excavate."

"Perhaps. Have you managed to examine the circle?"

"Not as I would have liked. But I did do a little digging and found a ring."

"Can you show it to me?"

"It's of no use to us—it's a modern piece." Regan reminded herself to question Lady Margaret about losing it.

Her father's face fell a little, then he patted her hand. "No matter, one of the drawings you sent me will help us immensely. I have been researching them. This one"—he pointed to the middle of a Celtic cross carved into one of the many stones—"is from the Etruscan alphabet in an anagrammatized form with which I'm not familiar. It took many hours of poring over old notes and research texts, but I deduced it is an anaglyph that the early Celts used to supposedly keep evil from reaching fruition."

"What of the Tender stone?" Regan's next breath hung on his answer.

"That little gem is of great import, as you must know from the stone's history you intimated with the drawing."

"What have you found?" Regan watched her father's eyes glistening with the kind of intoxication that only came with discovery.

"I believe the text is Etruscan in nature and encrypted with a form of ogham, but I need to examine the strokes of the lines closely. Your drawings were a little indistinct." His brows furrowed in worry. "That is highly unlike you not to make a clear drawing."

Regan remembered how her hand had trembled with Lachlan so close and said, "I drew it at night and the rush-light was dim."

"Uh-huh." His eyes gleamed with a skeptical light.

"Did you see enough of the drawing to speculate on its origin?"

"I believe the legend about it is true, and that it was a burial stone, perhaps used for Arthuis's grave. If that is so, perhaps it contains proof that Avalon is here on the island." Her father squeezed her arm, his expression beaming, the sallow color of skin almost gone. The only sign of his illness was his labored breathing.

"I've no doubt it is."

Down the hall, Lachlan paused with Emma and waited for Regan and her father to bring up the rear. "Are we going too fast for you, mon?" Lachlan asked her father.

"Not at all. I just find the castle fascinating."

"I'll order tea, then we'll take the tour. After, my brother is waiting to show the lasses his garden."

"Capital idea, my lord." Seamus smiled, then added in a lower tone to Regan: "Is Lord MacGregor aware of the importance of the Tender stone?"

"No."

"With Sir Harry Lucas poking his nose around the island, I would like to keep it that way and not draw unnecessary attention to the stone."

"Very prudent, Papa."

Her father shivered and Regan's brows met in worry. "Is something wrong?"

"There is a strange phenomenon in this castle. Do you sense it?" Seamus glanced around him.

"I know what you mean. It feels like it's watching you."

"Exactly. An odd sensation. It must have something to do with the architecture and the placement of the stones. Do you not think so, my girl?"

"You may not believe this, but I have proof it is possessed."

Seamus chuckled. "Stop pulling my leg, my girl."

"It's true. Things go missing or get moved around. And it speaks to me."

"You've always had a good imagination, but you've no need to entertain me with it," he said, gracing her with an indulgent grin.

"I see you'll never believe me, unless you experience it for yourself."

"Indeed." He laughed again, and Regan gave up trying to convince him.

*L*achlan walked behind Seamus Southworth and his daughters as they headed toward the Tender stone. Emma Southworth supported one of her father's arms, Regan the other. Lucky mon. Since her family's arrival, Lachlan had tried to squelch his unbidden envy.

Lachlan had never seen a normal family who loved one another so much. His own mother and father had never looked at him the way Seamus looked at Regan and Emma. No matter how much Lachlan tried to deny it, their open displays of warmth made him aware of how much he'd missed in his life.

The sassy sway of Regan's hips beneath the rose dress drew his attention. He hadn't been prepared for the bonny sight of her earlier and had almost swallowed his tongue. He tried not to look at her now, tried to look everywhere but at her, yet she drew his gaze. Och, she was bonny. The deep rose color of her dress accentuated the bright blue of her eyes. That damned dress hid very little of her slender curves. What happened to the drab gray and brown she normally wore? Had she worn this one to drive him over the edge?

And her hair. Och! Why wasn't it flattened to her head like it usually was, instead of piled up like a siren's? Sensuous curls fell over her creamy shoulder and touched the tip of her breast.

He saw himself peeling off that dress, burying his hands in her soft hair, watching it spill down over her breasts. He grew hard and couldn't drag his gaze from her bottom swishing seductively in the dress.

The longer he looked at her, the shorter the gossamer thread holding his self-control became. He could taste her lips already.

"How do you find your way through this place? It's a labyrinth of corridors and staircases." Emma spoke.

The young lass had a pleasant oval face. Mahogany curls bounced near her ears. Her young coltish body barely filled her bright plaid dress. One day she would be a bonny lass, but she could never rival her sister—especially with Regan wearing that bloody dress.

"Just like one of Mrs. Radcliffe's novels," Regan teased.

"You're not reading that rot?" Seamus tried to look chagrined, but a smile spread across his lips.

"Regan reads it, too."

"Emma." Regan tried to look indignant.

"Well, you do."

Seamus's grin widened. "Do not sound so affronted, my girl. I've known for years you both read novels. My heart is failing, not my eyes."

Seamus was the first to chuckle, then his daughters. Regan's husky laughter filled the air. Lachlan felt an overwhelming desire to take her in his arms and kiss her until he tasted some of her happiness. What would genuine happiness feel like? He was sure that watching Regan laugh was as close to it as he would ever get.

A few moments later they reached the Tender stone.

"This is it, Papa," Regan said, bending over and pointing to the embedded stone.

"Hmm! Interesting indeed." Seamus leaned over to get a better view.

"Oh, dear, you will get dizzy standing like that."

Seamus and Regan shared a scheming look, then he said,

"I do feel a little tired. Perhaps I can rest here while you all go out to the gardens."

"I'll have a servant stay with you," Lachlan said, aware Regan and her father had huddled together earlier and spoken in undertones while plotting this little ploy to study the stone. Why was it so important to them? Why wouldn't Regan trust him enough to tell him the truth? He vowed to find out later.

"Thank you, my lord," Seamus said.

"Yes, thank you." Regan turned her liquid blue eyes on him.

Those eyes could suck a man into them and doom him forever. "No need to be thanking me," he said, forcing his gaze down to the stone.

"Quin will be waiting for us," Regan said. "We'd better go meet him."

"Come to think of him, I'm wondering where he is." Lachlan drummed his fingers on the top of his cane.

Regan said, "He's certainly waiting in his cottage for us."

"I'm no' sure, lass. I thought he'd have met the carriage when it drove up with your father and sister. He's like that. Sometimes his enthusiasm turns him into a nuisance. But he's nowhere to be found."

"I'll help find your brother," Emma offered.

"I appreciate that, lass."

Regan said, "Gillis told me Quin had sent word he wouldn't eat this morning until you sent for Emma." Her brows arched in worry.

"He did. That's why I'm wondering where the lad has gone."

"We'll find him together." Regan patted Lachlan's shoulder reassuringly. "Don't worry." She slipped her arm through his with an ease and comfort of a wife.

Together. The word repeated in his mind. His fingers tightened around her arm as he guided her down the hallway behind Emma.

chapter 29

The afternoon sun threw long shadows over the crumbling fortress wall of the castle and made strange shapes dance over the ground. There wasn't a cloud in the sky. It was one of those rare clear days on the isle, when the sky looked like blue crystal. Regan breathed in deeply the scent of heather as she walked beside Emma. Lachlan followed far enough behind them to give them privacy.

Emma pulled Regan close. "Now that I've spent a little time with him, he isn't Schedoni, he's more a Count Udolpho."

"He's neither." Regan turned a chiding glance on Emma.

"Oh, Regan. You're in love with him." Emma's voice rose.

"Shhhh! He'll hear you."

"Admit it, you love him."

"I do not." Regan frowned. Did she love him? She added, "Even if I did, he doesn't love me."

Emma peeked behind them at Lachlan. "I don't know. All those dark, enigmatic looks are directed at you. I'd say he was desperately in love with you. And you'll be married within the year, and have little stripe-headed MacGregors running through this drafty old haunted castle. I'll live here and be their crotchety old aunt." Emma grinned as if the idea pleased her.

"You're talking nonsense." Regan elbowed her sister.

They both laughed.

"What's the jest, lasses?"

The deep voice sobered them.

Regan looked over her shoulder at Lachlan. He was different, more intense, if that was possible. Every muscle in his body looked taut. Strain marred his expression. He was holding back something that took all of his will. She could feel the air between them sizzle. If she had known a simple change in her appearance would get her this much of his attention, she would have worn the dress long ago.

"Oh, nothing," Regan said. "We were just speaking of flowers."

"Flowers, that's correct. The striped kind." Emma shared a top-that grin with Regan, then glanced past the wall. "Is that the cottage? I can just make out the chimney. I'll run ahead and see if I can discover your brother." She hurried up the path.

Regan frowned at her. "Please forgive her; she's still young yet and impetuous, I'm afraid."

He nodded in understanding, then asked, "You love your sister?"

"Very much. She and Papa are everything to me."

"It shows." He slipped her arm between his broad chest and muscular forearm and held her hand in a tight grip.

His thumb stroked the top of her hand. Wanton thoughts flashed in her mind: his hands touching her all over, stroking that dark secret place that had driven her mad.

"You and Quin are close." She struggled to keep the conversation going.

"Aye, but 'tis naught like what you share with your sister." He glanced ahead at the cottage, his brows forming a worry line.

"Don't worry, we'll find Quin."

"I know." His gaze settled on her lips.

"Thank you for giving my father a tour of the castle," Regan said.

"Do not thank me, lass. I could see your father enjoyed it—especially the Tender stone." He shot her a pointed look.

A pregnant pause settled between them while he waited for her to speak.

As they reached the front yard of the cottage, Regan said, "Yes. It is a rare find for an archeologist."

She couldn't look him in the eye any longer. He wanted her to tell him why her father was interested in the stone. Could she trust him? As she was about to open her mouth, she saw something move out of the corner of her eye.

Near a ravine of hazel and birch trees, Quin stepped through the cover of leaves. Regan could see someone behind him, but the person's face was hidden by the grove.

Quin ran toward them, his arms muddy up to his elbows, dirt smudges on his face. A bucket swayed at his side. Quin turned to glance back down the ravine, and Regan caught a fleeting glimpse of golden hair; then the person disappeared from sight. Had it been Eth McAskill? She couldn't be sure. Surely she was seeing things. Quin would never associate with McAskill.

Lachlan followed her gaze and said, "There's our wayward lad." He scowled at Quin.

"Yes." Regan's brows met in worry.

"Lachlan. Regan," Quin yelled, his voice carrying through the field. He ran toward them, his expression pensive.

Quin skidded to a halt beside Regan. "See what I found." He held the pail up to them. Inside were clumps of flowers.

"Where have you been?" Lachlan asked, his tone clipped.

"Looking for these." Quin pointed to the bucket.

Regan didn't want Quin to explain any further and said,

"See, Quin, I've brought my sister. She is already admiring your beautiful garden."

Quin noticed Emma kneeling and examining the daisies. He grinned and said, "That's Emma?"

"Yes."

"She likes my garden." A self-satisfied grin pulled at Quin's lips, and he shifted from one leg to the other like he couldn't hold still. "She likes my garden, Lachlan."

"Dinna be pestering the lass." Lachlan leveled a warning look at his brother.

"I willna, Lachlan. She'll be my friend. I like friends. Can she stay for dinner, Lachlan? Please let her stay for dinner. I can cook something good. Look, I found some wintercress. I could stew them up."

Regan spoke up. "I might be able to persuade her if you come into the castle and eat with her," she said, an artful undertone lacing her words.

"I dinna know." Quin hesitated, his hand tightening around the bucket handle. He shifted again, looked toward the castle, then at Emma. "I dinna like tae eat in the castle. I have no' eaten in there for a long time"

Lachlan said, "She can stay, but only if you eat in the great hall."

At that moment Emma cocked her head and glanced at them. She took Quin's measure for a moment, then waved to him. "You must be Mr. MacGregor, the missing brother. Pleased to meet you. I demand to know all your secrets for these lovely daisies."

This sealed Quin's fate and he blurted, "I'll be eatin' in the great hall." He grabbed Regan's hand and pulled her from Lachlan's grasp, the bucket bumping against his thigh. "Come on, Regan. See the flowers with us."

Regan glanced helplessly back at Lachlan.

He mouthed the words "Thank you." A glimmer of happiness flitted through the raw longing in his eyes.

He had never looked so vulnerable, nor so possessive. Could the walls around his heart be crumbling?

Before she and Quin reached Emma, Regan whispered, "Were you with Eth McAskill?"

"Nay, I wasna with anyone."

"But I saw you with someone."

"Nay, you didna." Quin shook his head adamantly.

Regan knew he wasn't being honest and said, "You know Lachlan dislikes Mr. McAskill."

"I know." Quin's lips settled into a sulk.

"McAskill's not a kind man."

"Some people on the island like him."

"Promise me, if he ever comes near you, you'll stay away from him," Regan said, growing frustration in her voice.

"I will if you're wanting me tae." Quin gazed at her with the eyes of a trusting child.

"I do."

"I will then, Regan. I'll stay away from Eth McAskill if he ever comes near me."

"Very well, I'll take you at your word." Regan wasn't sure she'd gotten through to Quin. Who had been with him? And why wouldn't Quin admit he wasn't alone?

Emma perked up and said, "I still can't tell what's in this soil."

Quin grinned. "You can taste it if you want."

Emma glowered at him. "Very amusing. That's all right. You haven't seen my herbs. My herbs are twice the size of yours. How do you like that?"

"You'll tell me your secret, won't you, Emma? Won't you?" Quin walked toward Emma, seeming to forget all about his conversation with Regan.

"If you like, you can come and taste the soil," Emma countered.

Regan listened to them argue and glanced back at Lachlan. He was staring at her as if he might whisk her off into the woods. A delicious shudder passed through her. If he kissed her again, she wouldn't mind being carried into the woods at all.

• • •

*I*n the castle, Seamus sat next to the Tender stone and glanced over at Gillis. "My good man, would you mind fetching me a dram of whiskey? That would relieve my palpitations." He held a spot over his heart.

Gillis scrutinized him with deep-set, skeptical eyes. "Are you sure you should be drinkin' it, sir?"

Seamus smiled. "Spirits are the only thing that have kept me going this long, my good man. I keep a little bottle beneath my bed at home. Please do not tell my daughters."

"Your secret's safe with me." Gillis's expression remained cryptic, while his eyes twinkled. "I'll go and get that dram."

"Good man." Seamus patted the butler's arm and received what looked like an exhale of a smile.

"Will you be a'right here alone?"

"Most definitely. I'll rest here in the chair you brought me. Take your time."

"A'right." With some hesitation, Gillis left him.

Seamus watched the tall, lanky butler's departure, his footsteps melting into the murmuring silence. When he was certain Gillis was out of sight, he bent near the Tender stone, unable to dismiss the feeling that the walls in the castle were watching his every move. He was a man of science. There must be an explanation for the phenomenon. If he had more time, he would love to explore it.

He reached out and touched the markings on the stone. They were like nothing he'd ever seen.

A draft wafted over the back of his neck, feeling like icy fingers brushing his skin. He heard a voice say:

> *One intrepid soul shall enter*
> *and find the lure of olden tinder.*
> *Goodness, truth, and love doth last*
> *bless Arthuis in Avalon's grasp.*

Seamus glanced around. A cold sweat broke out on his body. "Wh-who said that?"

There were no windows nearby. The only light came

from two torches that burned on the walls. Light flicked over the empty hallway. The air had a strange teeming feel, as if it were alive.

Seamus's profession had taken him to many strange places, but none more peculiar than this one. Walls that talked? Preposterous! Though he couldn't dismiss the poem. For some reason it seemed significant. He committed it to memory; then he realized that after the way he'd teased Regan earlier, he could never admit he'd heard the castle speak to him. Frowning, he went back to studying the stone.

T*hat evening, Lachlan looked down the length of the* table at Quin, who sat next to Emma. Lachlan thought never to see Quin in the great hall again. After the disappearance of their mother, Quin had abruptly refused to enter the castle. With good reason. Lachlan wished he could take away the horror of that night from Quin's memory, but he couldn't.

Quin had been only two and ten at the time. After that ill-fated night, Lachlan had tried to reason with his brother to come inside, but Quin had thrown tantrums and refused. Out of desperation, Lachlan had turned the cottage into a home. There Lachlan had stayed with Quin at night, until Quin grew older and wanted to sleep alone. Without Emma and Regan's influence, Quin would not have been sitting at the table now.

He glanced at Regan, watching the candlelight play along the bright golden highlights in her hair, touching the plump curve of her red lips and the delicate slender lines of her creamy neck and rounded breasts. He felt the weight of the MacGregor curse bearing down on him, making him force air into his lungs. Och, he wanted her with every fiber of his being.

As if Regan had heard his thoughts, she looked at him behind long golden lashes. She took in his expression, and her white teeth flashed in a quick half grin. She leaned past her father and spoke to his grandmother. "Does your grandson always look so fierce when there are guests at his table?" Her voice sounded light, but a little on edge.

Lady Margaret peered down her nose at Regan. "Lachlan was born with a frown on his face, gel," she said, the gray plume in her wig fluttering.

"I daresay he was, my lady," Regan said, grinning as she scrutinized him.

Seamus set his glass of wine down with a thump. "I beg to differ on that score, my girl. No one is born with a frown; the world brings out one's woes."

Lady Margaret lifted her spoon and shook it at Seamus Southworth. "Point taken. I have always believed we cannot escape our environment." Her eyes locked on Lachlan.

Lachlan felt the iron grasp of the look and knew he'd never escape Druidhean and its madness.

"You're wrong," Quin blurted, slamming his fork down on the table. "You can escape it, if you're wantin' tae."

Emma, Regan, and Seamus shifted uneasily at Quin's outburst.

"I was speaking in generals, Quin, not particulars," Lady Margaret said.

"I dinna care. You shouldna have said that."

Emma touched Quin's arm. "Your grandmother didn't mean to upset you. Look, your peas are getting cold. You don't want to eat cold peas—they are not even good when they're hot."

Quin recalled himself and relaxed.

Lachlan marveled at how a slip of a girl of fifteen could influence Quin. Lachlan always had to struggle with his brother to calm him down. The castle caused Quin's agitation tonight, which inflamed his temperament even more, and made Emma's authority over him that much more astonishing.

The tension at the table grew palpable.

Lachlan broke the silence. "Southworth, Regan spoke of your recent work in progress. We MacGregors have always supported scholarly endeavors—especially concerning our own ancestry. I'm knowing the cost of such endeavors, and if you're taking patrons, I'd like to be counted among them."

"Well, well, dashed kind of you, my lord." Seamus's eyes grew luminous with excitement.

Regan smiled at Lachlan, and he felt the contagious effects of it on his cheeks. Ever so slowly his lips parted in a grin. "We'll work out the particulars later," he said.

"That's very kind of you." Regan's eyes still glowed with a deep blue hue.

"'Twas no' kindness. I expect to make a keen profit off the sale of your books." Lachlan glanced to see if Regan had been influenced by his practicality, but she still smiled at him.

"By Jove, you shall." Seamus's voice held an unmistakable note of uncertainty.

"You're not fooling me," Regan whispered to Lachlan. "You did that out of kindness, and I'm indebted to you."

"How indebted?" he whispered back, a husky edge in his deep voice.

Regan wore a come-hither expression as she said, "You'll just have to find out."

Lachlan forced himself to look down at his plate. That bloody dress had turned her into a seductress. Would he make it through the evening without dying?

Seamus addressed Lachlan. "Lord MacGregor, you've been kindness itself with your hospitality. I would like to repay you. Did you know both my daughters have a little musical talent when they can be persuaded to use it?"

"Why did you not tell us, gel?" Lady Margaret leveled a look of reproach at Regan.

"My father is given to exaggeration when it comes to my talent."

"You play and sing very well, my girl."

"Oh, Papa." Regan's face turned the color of the rare beef on her plate.

"Well, it's true."

"Have you forgotten what Mr. Morton said?"

"Who's Mr. Morton?" Lachlan interrupted, feeling the sting of jealousy.

Seamus spoke. "A doddering old fool I hired to teach my daughters music. The man never drew a sober breath. I'm still amazed he taught them to play at all."

"What did he say?" Lady Margaret inquired, arching a curious brow.

Regan said, "He left the house screaming one day that I should find another pastime. He ranted that he'd seen a two-year-old child play better than I."

Seamus chuckled. "You showed him, did you not, my girl? When Regan wants something, she gets it. She set out to prove him wrong and she did, though I have not heard her play since we were forced to sell her mother's pianoforte." Seamus seemed to realize what he'd said. He looked despondent and stared down at his plate.

"And it's a good thing for all our ears," Regan added, touching her father's hand.

"We have a pianoforte," Lachlan said.

"Can they play, Lachlan?" Quin sat up on the edge of his seat, glancing between Emma and Regan.

"Of course." Lachlan's gaze shifted to Regan's cleavage, exposed by her low bodice. He longed to kiss a line down between her breasts. "Will you play for us, lass?" he asked her.

She stared over at Quin. "I'll play, if all of you promise not to laugh. It has been years since I've hit a note."

"Well, gel," his grandmother said, "it has been years since I've heard music in this castle—not since my daughter-in-law . . ." Her words drained away. Her gaze snapped in Lachlan's and Quin's directions, then back to Regan. "I'm sure anything you can pound out will entertain us."

Seamus Southworth's expression melted into one of amusement as he touched Regan's cheek. "I've never heard Regan's playing described as pounding, but there is always a first time. Is that not correct, my girl?" He winked at Regan and chuckled, his voice hitting the castle's suffocating atmosphere like a shot in a dense forest.

Lachlan could never remember having heard laughter in the dining hall. Meals in Castle Druidhean had always been as somber as wakes, the enjoyment snuffed out by the overwhelmingly suppressing milieu of the castle itself. He found himself imagining what it would be like to eat dinner with Regan and her family every night.

"I shall endeavor to keep my fingers from hammering the keys. You've shamed me, Papa, into letting Emma play first, for she plays much better than I."

"Aye, Emma, play for me," Quin insisted.

Emma pouted prettily. "Only if you tell me the secret for your daisies."

"You canna be expectin' me tae give it away."

"This is a shabby way to treat a fellow gardener." Emma jammed her arms over her chest.

Quin wore a beaten look, then said, "All right. Sea kelp."

Emma beamed. "Aha. I knew it. What a bounder you are, not telling me when I guessed it."

"I'm sorry. You're no' mad, are you, Emma? Say you're no' mad," Quin said, looking like a scolded little boy. "Will you play now?"

Emma bit her lip in thought, then said, "I suppose."

Quin grabbed Emma and yanked her up out of the chair. "Come on, I'll show you where the parlor is."

"No need to be a brute about it, I'm coming."

"You're no' fast enough."

"Any faster and I'd be running. . . ."

Their voices drifted away as they left the room.

Regan must have noticed the assessing look on Lady Margaret's face, for she said, "I'm sorry. Emma has never gone out in society."

Lady Margaret set down her wineglass and said, "I find her refreshing. One must admire a gel who knows how to handle my grandson. Let us hear her play." She forced a halfhearted smile at Regan, then rose and pointed to a room off from the great hall. "The parlor is this way."

Seamus rose, a little unsteady on his feet, and held out his arm to escort Lady Margaret. She took it, yet she wrapped her arm around his elbow and seemed to be the one supporting him.

Lachlan was left to face Regan.

He was struck by the tenderness he saw in her vivid blue eyes. It flowed through him with the intensity of a waterfall, enveloping him. He found himself surrendering to it.

"It appears you're stuck with me," she said, her voice filled with an underlying current.

"I should be so lucky, lass." His smile widened.

"La! But I thought I'd never see you smile at me. One would think you were trying to charm me." She stepped over to him and slipped her hand in his. "If so, do not stop." She blinked up at him from behind her golden lashes. "And thank you for sponsoring my father. I owe you more than I can ever repay."

"There are many forms of payment. Seeing you looking so bonny at my table has been one of them." Her palm singed his skin. White-hot lust surged through him. He kissed the back of her hand and let his lips move along her skin, the tiny veins beneath tantalizing the sensitive areas of his mouth.

She shivered. "I like pleasing you," she said, smiling seductively.

Pleasing him. Och, there were hundreds of ways she could please him. She could start by letting him carry her off to the north wing and ravish her until he was sated, until she wasn't driving him mad every time he was near her.

Gillis rustled dishes behind them.

Regan said, "Perhaps we should join the others." She locked her arm with his, and he let Regan guide them out of the room. She glanced over at him. "You're frowning again."

He felt her thigh brushing his leg and groaned, thumping his cane on the floor harder than he needed to. Her words, *Pleasing you*, thundered in his mind.

chapter 30

Half an hour later, Regan watched Emma's fingers pluck the last chords of Mozart's Requiem. The music floated through the room, sweet and somber. The parlor was half the size of the library, and cozier. A dark burgundy Asian carpet filled the center. The pianoforte stood in one corner, with chairs and a sofa circling it.

Her father had drifted off to sleep on the sofa next to Lady Margaret, who didn't look half as intimidating with an expression of bliss on her face.

Lachlan sat in a corner, his long legs crossed at the ankles. He downed another glass of whiskey. How many times had Gillis filled his glass tonight? He motioned Gillis over again with a flick of his finger.

When Emma had begun playing, Lachlan had actually smiled again. He had appeared the happiest Regan had seen him thus far, but as soon as he had glanced at her, the smile had faded into a pensive look. Then he had started drinking.

Emma finished with a flourish.

"That was lovely, gel," Lady Margaret said begrudgingly.

"Bloody good," Lachlan echoed.

Her father snorted, but didn't wake up. He'd had a long day and he looked exhausted. Regan wondered if he had decoded the lettering on the stone.

"Have a turn, Regan," Quin said, an eager smile on his face, while his gaze flitted between Regan and Emma. "Then Emma will play again. Her playing is fine tae the ear, 'tis. I've never heard better."

"You certainly won't hear it with my playing." Lachlan's gaze followed Regan as she sat down before the pianoforte. She let her fingers flutter over the keys and gazed at Quin. "What would you like to hear?"

"'O Once I Lov'd,'" Quin said. "Are you knowin' it?"

"I do. The first song Burns ever wrote. A lovely piece— and easy to play. Created for a keyboard bungler like me." Regan sat and began to play and sing. "O once I lov'd a bonny lass, aye and I love her still, and whilst that virtue warms my breast, I'll love my handsome Nell. Fal-lal-de-dal."

When Regan broke into the second chorus, Lachlan glanced up at her. Candlelight struck his eyes, emphasizing the need and raw desire in the onyx depths. It tugged at Regan, and she saw not a man sitting alone in a chair, but the young boy beneath, rejected, withdrawn, never loved. She felt an ache in the region over her heart as she finished the song.

For a moment there was only silence in the room. Her father woke with a start. "Capital, Emma . . . jolly good." He glanced toward the pianoforte, realized Emma was done playing, and found Regan.

Regan grinned at the bewildered expression on his face.

"Play another," Quin begged.

Lachlan polished off another three fingers of whiskey, set the goblet on a table, and said, "We're wearing out the lasses. Perhaps another time." He used his cane and stood.

"Quite right. It's late," her father said. "Should be getting home. It's been the most pleasurable day I've had in some time. Thank you, Lord MacGregor." Her father gave an unsteady bow.

"My pleasure." Lachlan turned to Gillis. "See that Tyg gets them home and make sure there's enough light to the carriage."

Gillis nodded and hurried out of the room.

Regan hugged her father good night. "Do not overtax yourself and stay in bed."

He rolled his eyes. "You're as bad as the sawbones." He pecked her on the cheek.

"Good e'en." Lachlan raised his cane in a farewell salute.

Emma waved to Quin. "Night, Quin. It was a pleasure seeing your garden."

"Maybe I'll come see yours soon."

Emma grinned at him. "I'd like that." She hugged Regan and whispered in her ear, "MacGregor keeps giving you those fierce-eyed looks. He'll probably propose tonight."

"Good night, Emma," Regan said in a scolding tone, though she felt a thrill of hope taking hold of her.

Emma winked at her. "Good night, Regan." She took her father's arm and disappeared out the doorway.

Lady Margaret turned to Quin. "Come, walk your grandmother up to her chamber."

Quin reluctantly took his grandmother's arm. "I'll take you up, but I'll no' be stayin'," he said.

"Sweet Mary! You've been out of this castle too long, using that curt tone with me, young man."

"But I dinna want—"

"I'll hear none of that, thank you. You're my grandson. You'll escort me to my room and then you'll tell me what you did today and you'll not leave out anything. Is that understood?"

Quin nodded, then frowned, possessing an uncanny resemblance to his brother. "Very well."

Regan made a move to leave, but Lachlan's deep burr stopped her. "I'm needing a word, lass, before you retire."

Lady Margaret turned, her dark copper eyes targeting

Regan with a silent warning: *Don't fall in love with him—you'll be sorry.* Aloud, she said, "Don't let him keep you overlong, gel."

Regan nodded, almost afraid to be alone with Lachlan.

"What did you want?" she asked, struggling to keep the excitement from her voice. Her stomach fluttered and her breath caught as she watched him walk toward the doors.

"I'll be collecting on that debt now."

chapter 31

L achlan closed the doors, pausing with his hand on the handle. He should send her back to the other side of the castle, to safety, away from him. But he'd waited all night to have her all to himself. He shoved the bolt home. The lock thumped through the empty parlor with a final note.

When he turned and faced her, he felt light-headed. Was it the whiskey, the lust running through his veins, or the fact he had Regan alone and at his mercy? Most likely it was all three. He grinned so wide it hurt his cheeks.

"Why are you looking at me like that?" she asked in a silky voice.

"Like what?" He let his gaze linger on the creamy flesh mounded in the low bodice of her dress.

"Like someone standing over the Rosetta stone."

"Tonight, lass, you're my Rosetta stone. Have I told you how bonny you are in this dress?" He put his hands on her shoulders and felt a shudder go through her.

"No." She returned his smile, the tiny dimple in her cheek coming to life.

"'Tis high time I did." He loved the husky sound of her voice, and let it melt over him.

"Smiling and giving me compliments?" She arched her honey-gold brows at him. "You're not acting like yourself."

He cupped her chin and made her glance up at him. "You've given me a night I'll no' be forgetting. 'Tis been a long time since I've enjoyed myself so much. Thank you."

"The pleasure was all mine." Her smile widened. "You said you wanted to collect on the debt. What can I do for you?"

"Someone bonny as you shouldna ever ask a mon that. But since you're asking, I'm wanting a song." He eyed her cleavage and watched the orange shadows from the fire flick along the rounded flesh, turning the alabaster skin a translucent amber.

He fingered the long blond curls cascading over her shoulder. The tip of one just touched the top of her left breast. He slid his hand beneath the silken strands, letting his knuckles glide along the swell of her breast.

"A song?" Her breathing quickened and she gazed up at him from behind half-closed lids.

"Aye." Just for him. He'd never had anyone play just for him. What was the harm in a song?

You're knowing what the harm is.

Damned walls, talking again. 'Course he knew. Och, he knew all too bloody well. Yet he still wanted the song. Was that too much to ask? One song in exchange for a lifetime of imprisonment here in Castle Druidhean. One bloody song!

"What would you like to hear?" she asked, her breath catching as he rolled the silky curl between his fingers.

"Anything." He saw his reflection shift in the liquid blue of her eyes, trapping him deep inside their brightness. He wanted to be trapped, to melt into her. "Just sing to me, lass," he said, his lust-filled voice sounding foreign to him.

She gulped, sat down at the pianoforte, and put her hands on the keyboard. Lachlan stood behind her as she began the first stanza of "Mary Morrison."

"O Mary, at thy window be . . ."

The shaky softness in her voice touched him to the quick. He let his fingertips glide along the puffy sleeves of her dress. When he reached the bare skin on her shoulders, the warm softness tantalized his fingers, and he trailed them up to her slender neck.

Higher, he stroked her hair, then he glided his fingers into the satiny mass. Pins rained down on the bench beside her. Flaxen curls tumbled down her back. He dove his hands into the downy threads, feeling the strands teasing his fingers.

She paused, but he said, "Keep singing."

She did his bidding, the cadence of her voice fluctuating.

An unyielding madness to submerge himself in her drove him. He bent and ran his lips along the flesh on her shoulders, all the while inching down the sleeves of her dress.

She dropped a note and said, "I don't know—"

"Go on, lass," he urged, hearing her breaths quicken, feeling her back stiffen.

She continued to sing and play, her voice thready, her fingers missing keys.

He kissed a line to her throat as he let the sleeves drop to just above her elbows. Her breathing grew so rapid her breasts quivered.

He nibbled her ear, hearing her voice vibrate inside him; then he learned the swanlike contour of her throat, pausing to feel the tiny pulse at the base.

She turned just enough to give him free rein of her neck.

The scent of her, lilacs, herbs, and her own feminine sweetness, filled his senses. He breathed her in as he let his hands slip down to caress her breasts.

Her voice quavered as she arched against him.

"Don't stop, lass." He let the swell of them fill his palms. The pain in his groin became unbearable.

Before he knew what he was about, he grabbed her waist, eased her past the bench, and stood her in front of him.

"Lachlan . . ." She glanced up at him, her eyes willing, but her expression unsure.

"Keep singing, lass."

She sang the second stanza: "C-could I the rich reward secure, the lovely Mary Morrison." Her voice cracked, off-key.

With a few deft movements, he worked open the ties on her bodice and slid his hand inside.

She faltered.

"Continue." He felt the silk of her dress brushing his skin as he opened her bodice wide.

"This is more than just a song."

"Aye, and I'll remember it to my dying day." He ran his tongue between the cleavage of her breasts, then suckled one of her nipples through the chemise.

She inhaled sharply.

"Sing, lass," he said, feeling the hard little nub of her nipple beneath the cambric.

Her whole body trembled as she fell into the third stanza. She wrapped her arms around his neck and twined her fingers into his hair.

He slid her dress down. The silk dropped past her rounded hips and pooled around her ankles. "Bonny, sweet lass." He eased the shift off her shoulders and felt the worn cambric pulling at her breasts.

He slipped her undergarments all the way off, drinking in the sight of her slender body clad only in corset, drawers, and silk stockings. Then he went for the laces of her stays.

"Lachlan . . ." she hesitated.

"It's all right." He slid one hand into her drawers.

She tensed, clamping her legs together.

"Let me in. Please." He slid his knee between her legs, parting her thighs just enough to let him slip his finger into the wet, hot folds there.

She cried out.

"Go on, lass. Sing."

"I can't."

"Please, for me. Only for me." He found the center of her pleasure, stroking her.

Her voice shaking, she spoke more than sang the next line, "O Mary, c-canst th-thou wreck his peace . . ."

With deft movements, he used his free hand and worked loose her corset. It hit the floor near her dress. Her breasts sprang free. He cupped one, letting it fill his palms, rubbing her nipple between his thumb and fingers. It hardened instantly for him.

She slumped against him and clung to his neck.

He kissed her, cutting off the last notes she squeaked, savoring the curves of her lips. He slid down her drawers, feeling the creamy texture of her thighs brushing his hands.

"That was lovely. A gift I'll no' forget," he said against her mouth.

He let his gaze roam over her thick honey gold hair falling down over her full proud breasts, the rosy hardened nipples peeking through a swirl of curls, the slender waist, the flaring of her hips and sandy-blonde triangle between her thighs. Firelight danced along her skin, turning it pale umber, siren's umber. She still wore her shoes, stockings, and garters, and the erotic sight of her made him burn with wanting.

She brought her arms up and covered her breasts, her cheeks glowing bright red.

"Let me see you." He gently eased her arms down at her side. "You're so bonny it hurts my eyes to look upon you."

"Do I please you, Lachlan?" she asked, her voice hesitant.

"You're perfect." He couldn't stand the sweet torture any longer. He eased her down on the rug.

She went willingly.

His gaze moved over her feminine curves, so beautiful, radiant. If he didn't feel all of her against him soon, he knew he'd spill his seed. He pulled off his boots and ripped at his frock coat, cravat, and shirt, tossing them over his shoulder to drop and settle over her garments.

As he worked the buttons of his breeches, he felt her eyes on him.

She watched him, her gaze curious, assessing, roaming over the contours of his chest, making his blood boil for her. "You're extraordinary," she said.

"I'm only a mon, lass," he said, feeling her scrutiny inflame his desire. He slipped off his breeches; his fully aroused manhood sprung free.

Her eyes widened.

"Dinna be afraid."

"I—I know what male anatomy should look like, but aren't you rather large?"

"'Tis my Scottish blood. It runs thick in areas." He grinned and came down on her.

The moment their naked bodies contacted, his grin faded. He groaned at the feeling of his weight settling into her heat. With all the hunger brewing inside him, he took her lips, even as he parted her thighs and slid inside her. He felt her hot moist flesh expanding for him, taking him deeper and deeper.

He kept his gaze locked on her, watching her eyes turn a misty blue as her face contorted with desire. When he reached her maidenhead, he paused.

You're taking a virgin, the castle voice came to him.

"Bloody hell," he moaned, and drove into her.

She stiffened.

"Are you all right, lass?" His voice was ragged as he forced his hips not to move.

"Yes, it's all right."

She said it so matter-of-factly that Lachlan grinned. He kissed her and began to move within her, slowly at first, then faster.

She cried out, and Lachlan took her cries into his mouth as he pushed harder, touching her womb again and again. She was singing for him, but in a different way. Her seductive body was her voice, and as she met his thrusts and cried out his name over and over again, she serenaded every deep empty hollow within him. He gave himself over to her melody, and when he was filled with it until he thought he would explode, they both cried out, and he spilled his seed.

Lachlan let his weight settle back down on top of her and felt her trembling. He kissed her gently on the lips, then he saw tears welling in her eyes. "What's the matter?" he asked, brushing back a strand of hair from her cheek.

"I never dreamed lovemaking could be so intimate. I feel like we are one, like I can trust you with my life."

"Always," Lachlan said.

"I need to confess something, something very important. Vow you will never speak of it to anyone."

"I'll keep your secrets." Lachlan looked deep into her eyes, and they were open and tender, and he could see feelings there that he didn't deserve.

"The night we met, I was searching for clues to the whereabouts of Avalon."

"You believe something in the circle will lead you to it?"

"Yes. A bard's song led us to the circle. I'm sure there are clues buried there that will help us find Avalon. It means everything to me to find it for my father. You saw how happy he was today. I've never seen him so animated. It's given him a reason to live." A tear streamed down her face.

"I'm glad you told me, lass." Lachlan pulled her close and kissed the tears away, tasting the salty wetness.

"He'll get better now, when we find Avalon." She snuggled against his chest, laying her ear over his heart.

"Can you be sure of that?"

"Of course," Regan said with certainty. "I lost Mama to typhus. Papa survived for a reason. I know he'll get well."

He should be honest with her and tell her that for her own safety he couldn't let her anywhere near the circle. But he couldn't break her heart. Not now, when she was so optimistically innocent and believed that it would make her father well. Happiness in life was rare, he had learned. For the moment he would not destroy hers.

Her hand trailed down his hip, then she sat up on her elbow and traced the scar that ran along his outer thigh down to his knee. "How did this happen?"

Lachlan hesitated as the disturbing memory came back to him. "My father was determined Quin should learn to ride. Quin was afraid of horses, always has been. One night, in a mad rage, my father forced him into the saddle. Quin tried to scramble down." Lachlan paused, then spoke more to himself. "I remember begging him to let Quin down. Quin was bawling. Instead, my father struck the horse with a riding crop. It reared. Quin fell off. I was holding the reins, and both hooves came down and crushed my leg. A few weeks later my father was locked away."

"I'm so sorry." She bent and pressed her lips to the scar.

Lachlan felt a surge of emotions crushing a place inside his chest. No one had ever shown him such compassion. "Come here, lass." He pulled her back up onto his chest, cradled her tightly to his body, and buried his face in her hair, breathing her inside him.

When he held her, the past, steeped in all its darkness, drifted far from him and couldn't touch him; there was only Regan's closeness filling him. He wished he could stay in her arms forever, but he knew eventually he'd break her heart by denying her access to the circle and forcing her to leave the castle. He would not ever let her watch the madness take him. He cherished her too much to let that happen.

He cupped her chin and brought her mouth up to his again, then all thoughts of letting her go were lost in the taste of her.

chapter 32

❧

Regan opened her eyes and stretched like a lazy cat, painfully aware of the soreness between her legs. She reached over and felt for Lachlan. Cold sheets met her hand. One eye cracked open, and she recognized the boxy walls, the green brocade curtains, the slightly bowed board beneath the one window: her chamber. Her clothes were draped across the foot of the bed, her stays and drawers slinking over the edge in a carnal pose.

A shiver went through Regan as she recalled their making love a second time, and Lachlan carrying her back to her bed. He hadn't left her, but crawled in with her. They'd fallen asleep holding each other.

Lachlan had been so loving and attentive last night, not a hint of the remote, withdrawn man she knew he could be. The side of him that needed love and tenderness had stepped to the fore, and Regan was drawn to that part of him like she'd never been drawn to anything in her life. She smelled his scent, coupled with the musky scent of their lovemaking, still on her and savored it.

In the whole time they were together, he had never once

said the words she longed to hear, "I love you." Yet she'd felt them in the tender way he'd caressed and kissed every inch of her body. Deep down she feared he might never say those words, and all she'd have were the few stolen moments they shared while they made love. In her heart she knew that wouldn't be enough to sustain her. She wanted him desperately.

Someone pelted the door.

When she threw on her dressing gown and opened the door, she saw Gillis, his deep-set eyes directed at her in a knowing, disconcerting way.

"The master is wantin' you tae walk with him, miss," he said, wearing an odd, perceptive expression.

"I see." He must know they had made love. If he knew, all the staff must know—including Lady Margaret.

Gillis's transparent skin stretched around his mouth in a hint of a grin.

He eyed her for so long, Regan asked, "Is there something else?"

"Naught, miss." Two round splotches formed on his cheeks. "Just wanting tae tell you I've ne'er seen the master so happy as he was last night. Thank you, miss."

"It was nice to see him smile." Regan thought of the smile she'd seen when they were alone in bed.

"The master said he'd meet you out in the bailey. I'm tae take you down, miss."

"I'll be ready in a moment."

Would Lachlan declare his love for her? Was that why he wanted her to walk with him? She prayed it was.

On his way to the bailey, Lachlan strode into the gallery. The onerous hush in the castle absorbed his uneven footsteps. He stroked the baby rabbit in his arms. The silken feel of its fur reminded him of Regan's hair. Last night, he had experienced his first taste of true happiness. Until meeting her, he had been resigned to his desolate life here. Now he felt an uneasy restlessness growing in him. He didn't want to think of the inevitability of her leaving. The moments of rapture with her were fleeting. But he would live for the moment and take what little joy Regan had given him. It would have to sustain him.

Lachlan heard someone approaching, and his heart thumped with anticipation at seeing Regan again. But Lady Margaret appeared instead, dressed all in black.

They stood at opposite ends of the gallery, confronting each other like two duelers. By the look of haughty reproach on her face, Lachlan surmised she knew all about last night.

"Well, what do you plan to do with the gel now that you've used her?"

"I'll no' discuss her with you." Lachlan held the rabbit in his hands and stroked the top of its head.

"Listen to me, young man. I like the gel. It will be cruel of you to take her for a mistress."

"You like the lass? Och, that's unusual."

"You can avoid my question, but let me tell you this. Last night I spoke with Southworth about her lineage. Her grandfather is Lord Clarington, a baron. She could still make a good match, but *not* if you continue to keep her in your bed. Give the gel a handsome dowry and send her to London to find a husband."

"Naught has changed." Lachlan did not want to let Regan go, but more than that he didn't want her to see him go insane and turn into his father and grandfather.

"You must let the gel go." With that, Lady Margaret whipped past him, her back board stiff.

Lachlan felt his brows draw together so tightly his head throbbed. He strode down the hall, his chest hurting, his footsteps smothered by the dense air within the castle.

R*egan found Lachlan standing beneath one of the yews,* clutching the young rabbit in his hands.

At the sight of him, she felt an inner longing that made her heart race. He wore a kilt and a white shirt. The wind whipped his hair around his face. A day's growth of stubble darkened his chin and cheeks. His black eyes were haggard, and stress lines crossed his brow. An aura of remoteness emanated from him like heavy vapor. The old Lachlan was back.

"What's wrong?" she said, unable to keep the fear from her voice.

"Nothing, lass. Walk out with me to set the rabbit free."

Regan took his arm. Her gray gown swirled around his legs as they left the bailey. "Please, tell me what is wrong."

"No questions, lass. Just walk with me."

He really was alarming her now. Where was the tender man who had lain with her, held her, and whispered he wanted her—the man she loved?

He guided her toward the same wooded ravine where she thought she had seen Quin speaking to McAskill. This prompted her to ask, "Where is Quin?"

"With Tyg."

"They must spend a lot of time together."

"Aye."

At the edge of the wood, he paused beside a thick elm. "Here's as good as any." He stared down at the tiny rabbit and spoke more to himself. "All things have to be let go sooner or later."

The severe resolve in his voice made Regan grimace at his profile.

He leaned his cane against the tree trunk, then scooped the rabbit from the crook of his arm. After bending down, he opened his hands.

The rabbit sat there in his large palms for a moment, sides heaving, nostrils flared, then felt the pull of the untamed wood around it. In one leap the animal left his hands and hit the leaves. He watched it hop away into the underbrush, a dismal expression on his face.

"Will it be all right?" Regan asked.

"Aye, better than being in a cage," he said, standing.

"Why are you being so distant, Lachlan?" She touched

his shoulder. "You're frightening me. Please, what is wrong?"

His gaze slowly caressed her face, her lips, then he crushed her in a breath-stopping embrace.

chapter 33

Regan wanted to drown in the feeling of his strong arms around her. He held her head next to his heart, and she listened to the steady beat, breathing deeply of his woodsy masculine scent. She glanced up at him and whispered, "Don't keep me out, Lachlan. Let me in."

"I'll no' let you into the misery of Castle Druidhean. I'll no' see you burdened with it."

She recalled the last entries she'd read in Lady MacGregor's journal. No wonder he thought there was misery here. "Together, we'll make it go away," she whispered, pressing against him, feeling his erection prodding the apex of her thighs.

"You canna, lass." His lips found hers, urgent and drugging.

She melted in his arms, her knees growing weak. She leaned against his powerful body. As his lips slid over hers, the coarse stubble on his face brushed her tender skin and caused her to shudder.

"Och! I'm needing you again, lass," he said, his voice

rough with lust. His hands went to her breasts, stroking sweeping hot waves into her belly.

"Oh, Lachlan," she murmured, while she smoothed her hands over the hard ridges of his chest.

His body tensed from his barely reined desire.

Knowing he wanted her so much set her blood on fire for him. Her hands grew clumsy as she plucked at the buttons on his shirt.

He caught the frenzy and pulled on the strings of her bodice.

For a moment, they tore at each other's clothes. The last piece of clothing to go was his kilt. Regan enjoyed unbuckling the belt and watching the woolen folds drop from his body and pool onto the ground.

Regan drank in the sight of his powerful thighs with the scar on one leg, the thrusting manhood, the ripples along his flat stomach, the black hair covering his chest. "You're beautiful."

"And you should no' be devouring a man with your siren eyes." In one deft motion, he spread his tartan on the ground between two trees.

"I cannot help it if I want you," she said, running her hands over his broad shoulders and feeling him shiver.

"Come here." His hungry gaze moved over her as he laid her on the kilt. The wool was still warm from his body and she nestled down into the fabric. She slid her arms around his neck and eagerly drew him on top of her.

When their naked bodies met and the hard contours of his body molded against her soft curves, desire flowed in her like liquid sugar.

He kissed a line down her throat and paused at the base, and she felt the heat of his lips brand her skin. Lower still, he trailed his tongue down between her breasts, then over to take a nipple in his mouth.

She moaned and arched, pressing his mouth closer to her breast.

He suckled, and her nipple hardened against his tongue. He gave the other breast equal attention, then kissed a path down her belly, her lower abdomen, all the while easing open her thighs with his knee.

When his head dipped lower, Regan grabbed his shoulders. "What are you about?"

"You'll ken soon enough." He spread her legs wide.

She could see him looking at her, the hunger in his eyes darkening and glazing as if it'd been brushed with oil. Even as she blushed, her breathing grew irregular with anticipation. "I don't think—"

"Shhh!" He bent, separating the soft velvet folds, then his mouth touched her, and his tongue, and all of Regan's protests faded. Her hips began to move of their own accord. As he stroked the nub of her pleasure, she felt every sense in her body chorusing, then she was crying out his name.

He rose and kissed her.

Regan tasted her own dewy essence and felt the burning ache for him deep in her belly.

He raised her hips and drove into her, again and again, as if he wanted to find a way inside her soul. They cried out together, their voices dulled by the forest sounds.

He covered her and groaned, then laid his head on her chest. "Och! I'm no' wanting to let you go," he whispered against the swell of her breasts.

She felt an agonizing pressure clamp over her heart. Let her go for the moment? Or forever? God, she wanted to believe he'd eventually propose, but she could feel him holding back a part of himself from her. The feeling melted away when they were in each other's arms, but evidence of it lurked in the hidden shadows of his eyes.

"We don't have to leave yet. We'll not be missed." She struggled to keep her voice even as she felt the sweat of their bodies sliding and blending together.

"We have a little while," he said, stroking her hair.

Regan shivered, but it wasn't from the cold. "Hold me, Lachlan."

He slipped his arms around her waist, rolled them over, and pulled her on top of him. He wrapped the kilt around them and held her tightly to him.

Regan snuggled next to his chest, feeling the rough hair there brushing her cheek. If they could only stay this way. For a moment she couldn't hear the beat of his heart. She slid down until she found it. Steady and strong. She committed the rhythm to memory, for she had a horrible intuition that they would never be this close again. She tried to ignore it, but the feeling clung to her.

T wo hours later Lachlan escorted Regan back to her room, then ordered Gillis to guard her. As she watched Lachlan walk away, she felt him slipping back into that bleak, dark place where he felt comfortable and safe. Could she reel him back? She wouldn't give up without a fight.

Lachlan had left her at the door with a kiss. The feeling that they would never be together still loomed over her. Perhaps if she managed to dig in the circle, it might convince him that curses did not exist. Perhaps he wouldn't be so quick to believe he was going to go mad. She'd have to circumvent Gillis again, but she was determined to dig there and prove to Lachlan his superstitions were unfounded.

She opened her trunk. The lantern was still there, but she would have to find the shovel she had dropped when Tyg found her in the circle—if he hadn't found it first. Later tonight she would try to sneak past Gillis.

She spotted the ring she had found and slid it on her finger. The emerald and diamonds winked at her. She had plenty of time before dark, so she decided to question Lady Margaret about the ring.

Regan slipped the ring into her palm and headed for Lady Margaret's room.

The lady held court on the sofa. A crocheted shawl stretched over her legs. She didn't glance up from her needlepoint and waved to a spot next to her. "Sit, gel."

Regan did as she was bidden.

"Despite my efforts you've fallen in love with my grandson." She made a *tsk-tsk* sound in the roof of her mouth and shook her head.

Regan felt a blush travel down to her neck. That wasn't all she'd done; she was certain the clever lady knew that as well.

"Don't say I didn't warn you, gel. Lachlan is dead set against marriage."

"He could change his mind."

Lady Margaret pursed her wrinkled mouth at Regan. "You are obviously unaware of the MacGregor stubbornness." She jabbed the needle into the center of a half-sewn orange blossom. The stitches were irregular from her poor vision and the petals looked like splatters of paint. "My husband once didn't speak to me for six months."

"Why?"

"A wager. My son bet him he couldn't speak to me without arguing—we had some wonderful arguments, mind. He had quite a temper. Well, the only way he could keep the bet was to not speak to me at all."

"What did you do?"

The first real smile she'd seen on Lady Margaret slowly touched her mouth. "Do? I spoke to him, then I answered for him. Let me tell you that provoked him. Finally he relented. The wager was for a year."

Regan laughed. Lady Margaret chuckled, a rusty heaving noise as if her vocal cords hadn't struck such notes in a long time.

"What did your son win?"

"He won my husband's favorite jumper. My son never let him forget it either. Always using the stallion when there was a hunt."

"You sound as if you had been happy," Regan said, searching for a little reassurance.

"By turns, I suppose."

"I could be happy with Lachlan."

Her golden eyes held Regan's with a severeness that made Regan shudder. "But for how long? That is what you must ask yourself. Believe me, gel, if you know what's good for you, spare yourself heartache and leave this island. Forget my grandson."

"I cannot." Regan spoke with desperate firmness.

"You must. There is darkness here that you do not understand."

"Don't tell me you believe in the curse also."

"There is evil within the hearts of all men, and Castle Druidhean has a way of manifesting it." Lady Margaret's countenance turned caustic and resolute.

"I do not believe this castle is evil at all."

"If you'd lived here as long as I, you would be a believer."

Regan couldn't leave Lachlan until he ordered her to. She drew a deep breath and forbade herself to tremble. Her fingers closed over the ring and she felt it digging in her palm; then she recalled why she had come here. She leaned over and placed the ring in Lady Margaret's hand and said, "Would you look at this and tell me if it belongs to you?"

The lady squinted down at it, then the blood drained from her face. "Where did you find this?"

"Near the shore," Regan lied.

A sour emotion flashed in Lady Margaret's features.

At her silence, Regan asked, "Is it your ring?"

Lady Margaret shook her head. Her hand began trembling as she handed the ring back to Regan. "Here, gel, get this out of my sight."

Regan slipped it into her pocket. "Who does it belong to?"

"It looks like a ring The Flame used to wear."

chapter 34

R egan's jaw fell open for several seconds, then she said,
  "Are you certain?"

"It's very similar, but I cannot be sure. Forget you found
it." Lady Margaret narrowed a warning glance Regan's
way.

"Was she wearing it the night she disappeared?"

"I have no idea." Lady Margaret rubbed her right temple. "Leave me. I've a sudden ache in my head."

Could Regan believe her? She stared at the ring. Recognition dawned on her. She'd seen it before somewhere. As
she left the room, the answer came to her.

She hurried past Gillis, who had been waiting for her
outside Lady Margaret's door.

"Where you goin', miss?"

"To the gallery." Regan picked up her pace.

O nce Regan reached the long corridor, she paused before Lady MacGregor's portrait. After having read the
woman's diary, Regan couldn't believe how angelic the

lady's face was on the outside, but how nefarious she had been on the inside. She was a good actress indeed.

Regan's gaze shifted lower on the canvas. Lady Mac-Gregor's hands rested across her lap, placed in a position so that the ring was clearly visible. The artist had painted the huge emerald and diamonds with the same acute highlight as he'd put in her eyes. Somehow the artist had glimpsed into the lady's soul.

The unavoidable truth nagged at Regan. There was a reason the ring had been buried in the circle, and she was determined to discover it.

Gillis paused next to her, out of breath. "What is the matter, miss?"

Regan didn't want anyone to know she'd found the ring. Not yet anyway. "Do you think Lady MacGregor was lost out on the moors?"

"You wantin' the truth, miss?"

Regan nodded.

"No."

"Then you think she was murdered?"

"I'm knowing she was."

"How?"

"I know Tyg did it."

"Did you see him?"

"Might as well have. He always argued with her. She was cruel tae Quin, berating him for things he couldna control—she was cruel that way. The night she disappeared Quin had tipped over his soup. He had always been nervous eating at table with her—but she forced him. She screamed at him and started tae strike him, but Tyg stood up tae her and forbade her tae hit the boy. There was threats o' firing him thrown about, but she backed down. I believe she was afraid o' him."

"Then what happened?"

"Later, I remember, I couldn't sleep. I heard something outside my window. It was hot that night; I'd left my window cracked. When I looked out I saw Tyg carrying something large over his shoulder. I couldn't be sure what it was, it was dark."

"Why didn't you tell the magistrate?"

"I couldna be certain, miss. And tae tell you the truth, having her gone was like a blessing. She was no' a nice person. And, too, there was Quin. We all have a soft spot for the lad, and he's devoted tae Tyg—creeshie wonner that he is."

"I see. But you have approached Tyg on it?"

"Aye, and he's never said he was guilty one way or t'other. He just gets riled when I mention it."

Could she believe Gillis? She wasn't certain. He didn't like Lady MacGregor either. Regan pointed to the ring in the portrait. "Did she always wear that?"

"Aye."

"Was she wearing it the night she disappeared?" She had asked Lady Margaret the same question but didn't trust her answer.

"Dinna know, miss. Ne'er thought tae look at her hands that night." Gillis rubbed his chin in thought. "Why you ask, miss?"

"Just curious." Regan tried to disguise the untruth in her voice.

Regan wanted to believe Lady MacGregor might have lost the ring before she had ridden out on the moors and that there wasn't a murderer on the loose. But all the signs pointed in the opposite direction. Now she wished she had never found the ring.

The rest of the day Regan kept her suspicions to herself. She spent her time with Lady Margaret, putting compresses to her head and reading to her. Regan wanted to see Lachlan, but at noon he had ridden away from the castle like a goblin was following him. She hoped Lady Margaret was wrong about Lachlan not changing his mind about marriage. They could face the truth of his mother's disappearance together.

It was getting dark. She needed to reach the circle, but she had to wait for Gillis to relieve himself before she could make her escape. Sooner or later he'd have to go.

She left Lady Margaret and headed for her own room. The moment she closed the door, an icy breeze met her. Pages fluttered. The journal lay on the nightstand by the bed.

A chill prickled the hairs along her neck as she picked up the diary. Her eyes moved over the page that was open:

January 1788
There is no hope for that slow-witted Quin. He cannot read. His governess assures me she's taken a hard hand with him, but he refuses to pronounce the letters. I would like to send him to an asylum, but his grandmother—witch that she is—actually threatened my life if I sent Quin away. Balmoral is so insane, he could not care less what I do with his children. I despise that woman and his son. My life here is dreadful.

February 1788
I thought at least Lachlan had promise, but today he hid his brother from me when I wanted to send him to the schoolroom. I was forced to punish both of them. Lachlan sees himself as Quin's protector, and it causes nothing but dissension in the house. I'm sending Lachlan off to school, whether Lady M approves or not.

March 1788
Lachlan left today. Quin howled for a full eight hours. Perhaps now he'll sit down and learn his lessons. Also I tried to discharge that horrid Tyg today, for disobeying me, but he actually threatened me and said if I tried to have him fired, he'd tell Lady Margaret that I had been giving her son a potion all these years to keep him from my bed. How I hate the man!

April 1788
Quin stays in the schoolroom, brooding for Lachlan,
and will not respond at all. I am resigned he'll never
learn anything. I cannot believe he is half my son.

The sorrow she felt for Quin was like an iron weight inside her. She couldn't begin to imagine the emotional abuse
he must have suffered from his mother without Lachlan to
protect him. The brothers must have hated her. Tyg was
blackmailing her. And Lady Margaret had threatened to kill
her. Gillis had held back information from the authorities
about Tyg's part in her disappearance—if Regan could believe his story.

Regan pulled out the ring. An eerie sensation crawled up
her fingers. She quickly stuffed it back in her pocket. There
was something macabre about holding it while she read the
diary. She couldn't read any longer and dropped the journal
back into the hidey-hole beneath the window.

She heard Gillis's chair bump against the wall as he
stood. He'd be gone only long enough to relieve himself.
She had to hurry. She grabbed the lantern from the trunk,
then peeked out the door.

No Gillis, but the dogs lifted their heads to look at her.

She had saved a piece of ham from her lunch tray and
lured the dogs into her room with it. They no longer frightened her as much as they used to, and she gingerly patted
their heads, then tossed them each a piece of ham.

As soon as they were inside, gobbling, she eased the
door closed, hearing the hinges creak. Rushlights flicked
along the empty hallway. She paused long enough to light
the lantern, then hurried toward the staircase.

Lachlan spurred Phoebus along the edge of the waves,
bent low over his neck. Spray from the horse's hooves
splashed on his legs, on his face, and he didn't care. He'd
ridden so long his hair, shirt, and breeches were soaked.
Tonight was as close to madness as he had come in his life.

His thirty-fifth birthday was in a fortnight. He had to send Regan away. Soon.

Storm clouds rolled on the darkening horizon. Gusts whipped past his face, the moisture stinging his skin. The wind swished past his ears and whispered, "You must do it now."

All day he had stayed away from Regan, because he had ached to be near her. He wanted her to look at him in that tender way she did when they made love. He wanted her to hold him again and keep holding him.

The last time they'd made love, he'd seen the tears in her eyes. She wanted a commitment; he loved her too much to keep her near him.

Anguish tore at his gut, foamed up into his chest, and spiraled up into his throat and over his lips. His cry echoed off the cliffs of the island and out into the sea. Then he spurred Phoebus toward Castle Druidhean.

chapter 35

❧

Regan heard a strange deep bellow off in the distance. The sound rumbled through the air, drowning out the crashing of waves below her. She froze near the stones. What was that? It sounded like a wounded wolf, or a Celtic war god going into battle.

An icy wind blew in from the sea and whipped her dress around her legs. The copious smell of a rising storm rode the drafts. Thick damp mist entered her lungs as she stepped inside the circle.

She thought of Morgan and Arthur. Morgan would have carried Arthuis's body to his funeral pyre, perhaps here among the stones. She could see the tears in the priestess Morgan's eyes, feel her pain as she said good-bye to his spirit. She would have poured his ashes in an urn and buried it in the fortress in which they had loved and laughed and probably raised their children. She would have marked the grave with the Tender stone, and, like a scene right out of *Romeo and Juliet*, taken her own life. Morgan would have wanted Avalon to remain a secret, a place where the two lovers could be in peace for all eternity.

By the time Regan luckily found the shovel and set down the lantern, a feeling of sadness weighed on her. Discovering Avalon had seemed so important. For the sake of her father's health, it still was. Yet not once had the plight of Arthuis and his Druid mistress entered her mind. Somehow having experienced love in Lachlan's arms brought it home to her. She was nothing more than an intruder into the sacred lives of two lovers.

Lightning cracked overhead and several raindrops pelted her head and shoulders. An image of the ring flashed in her mind. If there was such a thing as curses, then this circle was under a hex. Keeping one eye on the tall megaliths, she set down the lantern.

Light flicked over each stone. The depressions in the uneven surfaces resembled disapproving faces. She ignored them and began digging where she'd found the ring. Clouds thickened overhead and drizzle steeped the air.

Frantic now to be done before the storm struck or someone found her, she drove the blade in rhythmic motion. Breaking more earth. Digging until her shoulders ached and her arms felt heavy. One foot of earth. Two.

Thunk. Regan hit something hollow and brittle. Her hands trembling, she laid the shovel down. She carefully scooped away the soil, feeling it crumble in her hands. Something slender, knobby, and long met her fingertips. Regan had been an archeologist long enough to know what the phalanges of the human skeleton felt like.

In fixed horror, she eased the hand out of the ground. Remnants of lace from the sleeve of a dress still clung to the corpse's wrist. No doubt, this was Lady MacGregor's. Her ring must fallen off when she was buried here.

A gust of wind blew through the circle and knocked the lantern over. It rolled several feet and crashed into one of the rocks. Glass shattered. The flame died. Total darkness engulfed her.

An eerie feeling pricked her senses. Someone was behind her. She turned and saw a tall dark figure standing near a stone. The person's face was hidden, until lightning flashed.

Tyg.

She panicked and blurted, "Your secret is found out."

He stepped toward her, grabbed her arms, and jerked her up. "Too bad I'm late."

"You buried her here, didn't you?" Regan felt his hands digging into her arms like claws.

"You've been snooping aboot, hey? If you know what's good for you, you'll go on aboot your business and no' remember the night." He shook his fist at her.

"Did you kill her?"

He hesitated, immediately on his guard. His expression hid something. "If I did, she deserved killin'. She was a bitch, plain and simple. She ruined everyone's life around her, including her sons'."

Regan wasn't absolutely sure he'd killed her, but she knew who did. "Who killed her?"

"I'll be taking the truth tae me grave." He glared back at her with his one good eye.

"You might be there sooner than you think, if you're charged with this murder." Regan stepped back. Her spine hit one of the stones and she grimaced.

"Tyg! What the bloody hell are you up to, mon?"

At Lachlan's deep bellow, Tyg dropped his hands. "Naethin'."

"Get back to the castle and wait for me."

With a harsh glare, Tyg stomped off.

Lightning struck again, flaring across Lachlan's face. The white streak at his temple seemed to glow in the charged air. He dismounted, his expression so ruthless and grim Regan was afraid to approach him.

"Why did you leave your room?" Lachlan asked, his tone abrupt. "Where is Gillis?"

"It isn't his fault. I waited until he relieved himself and slipped away."

"You shouldna have done that. You could have been hurt." Lachlan was drenched. Regan could smell salty seawater on him. He must have ridden along the beach. His hair stuck out at odd angles. The scowl on his face shadowed his eyes, until they were almost hidden by his brows. "What are you doing out here?"

"Digging."

"Go back to the castle."

"Wait! Listen to me." She couldn't think of a delicate way to tell him, so she said, "I found your mother's body."

A glimmer of surprise flashed in his eyes, then they turned as dark as midnight. "Where?" he said, dismal relief in his voice.

"Here." She pointed to the center of the circle. "That is why Tyg was threatening me. He knew the body was buried here and didn't want anyone to know."

He stared at her for the longest time, seemingly lost in a memory.

Regan felt raindrops spatter her face as she asked, "What do you know about that night?"

"I'll no' discuss it," he said, his voice laced with a warning. "Go back to the castle. I'll be along directly."

"Do not push me away." Regan felt the sickening spread of despair. Why wouldn't he be honest with her?

"I said go, lass," he growled as he stepped inside the circle. He picked up the shovel, then began re-covering the body.

Rain fell harder and harder until it came down in sheets and pelted her so she couldn't breathe. She decided to confront him later and dashed for the castle.

Twenty feet away, three young boys lay on their bellies, hidden beneath a black slicker and the cover of a hawthorn bush. Bully peeked past a corner and gazed at the MacGregor as he threw shovelfuls of dirt back over the hole. The dirt was quickly turning to mud in the rain and dropped from the shovel in large splats.

He kept his voice low, bent near Runt's brother, and said, "Aye, I double dare you tae go in the circle now."

"I could if I wanna. I ain't afraid o' Mad MacGregor, or curses, or anything."

"Then go over," Bully said, nudging the older boy with his elbow. "See if he willna bury you, too."

Runt piped up. "I tol' you we shouldna ha'e come here."

Bully said, "Think we should go for the magistrate. Might mean a ha'penny for us all."

"Aye, it might at that." Runt's brother nodded.

All three boys looked at each other in agreement, then they slithered back down the cliff toward the beach.

chapter 36

Changed into dry clothes, Regan thought of Lachlan. He had appeared surprised to learn Lady MacGregor's body was in the circle, but why didn't he want to call the authorities? Was he protecting Tyg? Or someone else?

The wind blew open the window she had left cracked and rain poured in. She ran to close it, and when she turned, she stared down at the hiding place where she'd put the diary. Could something in there point to the murderer?

She opened the board over the ledge. She hadn't expected the diary to be there, the castle playing one of its games. Perhaps the castle knew now was not the time for games, for she found the diary next to Old Gray, where she had put them.

She opened it and read:

May 1788
My only respite from this wretched existence is when
I walk along the beach. There is an ancient circle of
stones there where sound does not enter. It mesmerizes

*me. I think I shall plant a flower bed there and make
it my own special place. Perhaps entertain my lovers
there, when the mood strikes me.*

"Or die there," Regan said ruefully. She skipped ahead:

*November 1789
Things are looking up. Thank goodness, Balmoral is
wasting away on his deathbed. I'll finally be free of
him at long last. How I wish to be rid of all of them.*

*August 1790
Today, Balmoral finally died. He was so pale his skin
looked the color of my white stockings. I cannot find
one tear for him, only elation at his passing. Free-
dom! I want to wallow in it. Go anywhere my fancy
takes me.*

*September 1790
Lachlan brought a friend home some years his senior. He's a fine young man, Eth McAskill, and
handsome in a brutish, immature sort of way. I believe I shall enjoy seeing him about. He stares at me
with hungry eyes. How that sends thrills through me
to know I can still captivate much younger admirers. Ha! I was always a head-turner. The Flame still
burns.*

*December 1790
Life is looking up. Eth and I meet in the circle, and
what love we make. He has a boy's ardor. Oh, something interesting. I was planting flowers in our Circle
of Eden when my spade hit the top of a lead box. I
cannot wait to break the lock on it and see what is inside. At first I thought it might be Eth playing love
games, but I'm sure it's ancient. There are strange
writings on the sides and top. I believe there are more
boxes buried beneath it. . . .*

Could the box have contained the clues to Avalon's whereabouts? Regan felt sick as she realized that had been the final entry in the journal.

The words were squeezed on the last page and ended abruptly. Where was the other journal? Why wasn't it in the hiding place where she found this one?

And what had Lady MacGregor done with the box? Regan had failed her father. A lifetime of work destroyed. Her father wouldn't get better now. She couldn't swallow past the strangling sensation in her throat, or blink away the building tears in her eyes.

A knock brought her gaze to the door. Regan was glad for the interruption. When she opened the door, Gillis stood there, his hand raised to knock again.

"You've got tae come, miss." He wrung his hands, rubbing the three nubs on his left hand. "Somethin' terrible's happened."

"What?"

"The magistrate is in the library, with Eth McAskill." Gillis spit out the last name.

"Oh, no." Regan's fingers tightened around the diary as fear clawed at her insides. What did Lachlan know about the murder? "I'll be there in a moment."

She closed the door and stuffed the journal back into its hiding place. With the edge of a book, she pounded the nails in the slat and secured the board beneath the window.

"No one must ever read the hurtful things Lady Mac-Gregor has written in this diary. Do you hear? Keep it safe."

The castle didn't answer her.

Talking to wood and stone again. She was losing her mind.

She felt her heart hammering her ribs as she left the room.

Another boom of thunder rattled the windowpanes.

L achlan stepped into the library, his damp hair clinging to the sides of his head. He'd changed clothes, but hadn't had time to towel off his hair before Gillis informed him that the magistrate was here.

Lachlan faced the magistrate, Angus Dunwoody, a man as broad as a bull, with the bloodthirsty instincts of a hunting hound. Lachlan had faced Dunwoody once before, twenty years ago. He had tried to intimidate Lachlan into admitting his mother had been murdered. Lachlan had maintained his silence, much to Dunwoody's chagrin.

Dunwoody wasn't quite as large or as fierce as Lachlan remembered. Lachlan had grown taller than Dunwoody and had to look down on him. Enthusiasm shone in Dunwoody's expression; it was clear he was eager to finally prove Lady MacGregor had been murdered.

Behind Dunwoody stood two men with shovels draped over their shoulders. They wore slickers that still dripped with rain. They kept their eyes averted from Lachlan, but Eth McAskill glared directly at him. His white teeth glistened in a scheming smile.

"To what are we owing this visit?" Lachlan asked Dunwoody, his tone curt.

"Look here, MacGregor." Dunwoody thrust out his square jaw. "We'll have tae be searching your property."

Thunder roared outside and shook the windows in the room. The men looked at the windows like they were alive, then backed away from them.

"On what grounds?" Lachlan asked.

"We've gotten word there's a body buried out near the shore—"

"Who said this?"

"Lads from the village."

Lachlan's gaze shifted to McAskill. "It was you, wasn't it?"

He smiled. "Nay, laddie, no' me."

Dunwoody said, "He's here 'cause he was drinkin' in the tavern when the lads reported tae me."

Lachlan said, "I demand to speak to them."

"You're in no position tae be makin' demands." Dunwoody's tone was smug. "We're goin' tae have tae be diggin' the body up. Just wantin' tae let you know."

At that moment, Lady Margaret sailed through the library doors. "What demned bit of nonsense is this?" Lady Margaret covered the length of the room, cowing the men with a queenly look of contempt. "Angus Dunwoody, explain yourself this instant."

"Well, my lady—"

Eth stepped forward and faced her. "A body was found. And I'm thinking the both o' you know whose it is."

"I know nothing of the sort. This is obviously a ploy by you to disparage this family. It's no secret you've hated my grandson since you had that sordid affair with his mother. How dare you come here with such an accusation? If there is a body there, how do we know you didn't bury it there?"

"That's a damn lie." McAskill's face inflated with anger. "MacGregor killed his own mother and buried her there."

"That's enough. You'll be savin' those remarks for the inquest." Dunwoody motioned to the men. "By, lads, get around there and start the diggin'." He turned to Lachlan. "I'd like everyone in the household assembled for questionin'."

"Aye." Lachlan locked gazes with McAskill. In a way, fate had brought them to this juncture. Lachlan was glad it was finally over. But he couldn't stop the desire to wrap his hands around McAskill's throat.

McAskill's eyes widened slightly, hinting he'd read Lachlan's thoughts, then he turned and followed the other men, wearing a self-satisfied grin.

"Who brought them?" Regan paused behind Lachlan, out of breath. Her damp hair hung in a braid down her back.

He didn't want her dragged into all of this. "Dunwoody said some lads from the village," he said.

"I always suspected they'd eventually find her body," Lady Margaret said in a dry, sublime tone. "Such a shame it had to be now." She turned and glided past Regan through the doors.

Regan's eyes searched his. The liquid blue in them glistened like two pieces of stained glass. "You have to tell them who did it," she said.

"Stay out of it." He headed toward the door.

"Who are you protecting?"

"This is none of your concern."

"It is. We can see this through together."

"Nay, lass. 'Tis part of the evil here at Druidhean, and I'll no' have you in the middle of it."

"But I want to help you."

"You canna."

"If you care for me, you'll trust me enough to tell me the truth about that night so we can resolve this and get on with our lives."

"We have no life tae get on with." His voice softened slightly.

"Look me in the eye and tell me you have no feelings for me." She searched his face, tormented. Tears glazed her eyes.

"I dinna care for you," he said, his voice harsh. He couldn't bear to see the heartache in her face, but he couldn't turn away. If he did, he might lose his resolve and beg her to stay.

"You don't mean that."

"I told you I had no feelings. Did you no' ken it?" He gripped his cane, feeling the lion head bite into his palm.

She held her stomach, her whole body trembling. She swallowed hard. "I wanted to believe otherwise. I can see I've been a naive fool," she said, bitter anguish tainting her words. "I'll be leaving Castle Druidhean tonight." She wheeled around and ran out of the room.

Lachlan took a step to run after her, but froze in midstride. Why prolong the misery? She must leave. He felt his heart tearing from his chest. He hated hurting her. Worse, he hated the thought of never seeing her again. And surely he wouldn't, now that he might hang for murder. A bottomless ache gnawed at his gut as he stepped out into the hall.

The cavernous interior of the castle lapped up his footsteps until another blast of thunder covered them completely.

chapter 37

Regan cried so hard she could barely make it to the great hall. Lachlan didn't love her. She could never forget the bladelike and uncaring gleam in his eyes when he'd told her so. How could she have been so naive to hope that he might care for her?

Someone touched her shoulder.

Regan blinked away enough tears to see Quin's worried expression. He patted her back and asked, "What's wrong, Regan?"

"Nothing." She lost control and collapsed against him, sobs racking her body.

"Dinna cry, Regan," he said helplessly. "Please. I'm no' likin' it when you cry."

Quin sounded so upset, Regan forced herself to check her emotions.

He handed her a handkerchief. "Take this."

She blew her nose. "I'm sorry, Quin," she said. After a moment, she blinked at him in surprise. "You're inside the castle?"

"Aye, Tyg told me the magistrate had come. Why were you crying?" He looked at her in that guileless way of his.

"I have to leave."

"Nay, you canna. Tyg told me the magistrate's here." Quin worried his lower lip.

"Yes."

"They willna take Lachlan away, will they?"

"I don't know." Regan was certain Lachlan didn't murder his mother, but he probably knew who did and would protect that person with his life. Regan recalled something and said, "Do you want to help Lachlan?"

"Aye, I do. Lachlan's canny, he is. I'll no' let the magistrate take him away."

"What makes you think the magistrate will take him away?"

Quin's face contorted with emotion. He looked almost wild as he blurted, "They will, I'm knowing. I canna let them take Lachlan. Do no' let them take him."

"We shall not let them." Regan thought of Lady Mac-Gregor's trunk. It held the last of her belongings. "Do you mind if I look in your mother's trunk?"

"Why?"

"It might help Lachlan."

"Come on, I'll show you it." Quin grabbed her hand and yanked her through the hall.

A *pregnant silence choked the air in the library and refused to let go.* Regan felt the tension in the air straining against every sense in her skin. The tick of the mantel clock sounded like the steady thump of a bass drum. Outside, the rumblings of the storm had moved north. Only an occasional roll of thunder penetrated the walls of Castle Druidhean.

Regan glanced around the room. Quin and Tyg sat together on the sofa. Quin fidgeted with a small rock, while Tyg watched him with a troubled expression. In a chair by the fire, Lady Margaret squinted down at her needlework.

A slight tremor in her hands made her jabs at the canvas unsteady. Darcy bustled around the room, pouring tea.

Lachlan hadn't once looked in Regan's direction. He sat in the wing chair opposite Lady Margaret, his legs crossed at the ankles. He clutched his cane in a white-knuckled grasp and watched the firelight dancing along the tips of his black boots.

The thump of footsteps brought all their faces toward the door.

Mr. Dunwoody appeared, his slicker still dripping rain. McAskill stood beside him. The two men with them stood guard at the door. Gillis slipped past them into the library, scowling.

Dunwoody tramped down the room's center, muddy wet footprints following in his wake. "Well, well, glad tae see you've all gathered like I asked."

Lachlan leaped up and razored a glance at McAskill. "Leave my home," he said in a soft deadly voice.

"Dinna fash yourself, my lord," Dunwoody said. "I've asked him tae join us. For a moment you'll be putting your differences aside."

McAskill paused near the doors, sporting that self-assured grin, then his eyes met Quin's. The grin faded.

Regan watched the exchange as Dunwoody paused before the fire. He slipped off his slicker and turned to warm his backside. "A mess out there, but we found the remains."

Darcy hustled over to him. "Tea, sir," she offered.

"A lifesaver, lass." Dunwoody took the proffered cup.

When Darcy turned, her gaze met McAskill's and held longer than it should.

Lady Margaret glanced up from her sewing. "Are you sure it's my daughter-in-law's body?"

"Aye, my lady. Her stays were no' yet deteriorated. Her initials were carved into the ivory. 'Tis a good thing she was meticulous that way."

"She was meticulous, all right," Lady Margaret said with a heavy dose of sarcasm; then she went back to bludgeoning the canvas with the needle.

"Now all that's left is tae determine the murderer." Dunwoody glanced at each person in the room.

When his gaze landed on Quin, he jumped up and yelled, "I did it, I did it." Tears gleamed in his dark eyes.

"You didna, lad." Tyg grabbed his arm and pulled him down.

McAskill shouted, "Lachlan MacGregor did it. The lad's lyin'."

"He's correct, it was me," Lachlan said, his voice quiet, yet filled with cold resignation.

Regan felt as if Lachlan had driven his heel into her stomach. She wanted to scream at him to take it back, but she held her tongue.

Gillis walked toward Lachlan and stopped near his side, his dour face tortured.

Dunwoody waved his hand. "Jesus, Joseph, and Mary! I'll be hearing from you first," he said, pointing at Quin.

Quin shifted on his feet. "Tyg knows I did it. He saw me with blood on my hands. Tell them, Tyg. Tell them, you helped me bury the body."

Tyg eyed Quin and rubbed the stubble on his chin until he left long red marks there.

"Well?" Dunwoody waited.

"I'm no' tellin' you naethin'."

"You'll hang for being an accomplice."

"Then I'll bloody hang."

"I'm tellin' you I did it," Lachlan said. "Quin's lying."

"Stop it, Lachlan," Quin said. "You're just trying tae take up for me. Let me tell the truth."

"You've no need tae say anything, lad." Tyg pulled on Quin's arm protectively.

"Leave me alone." Quin jerked away. "I want tae tell the truth. I've been living with this for years. 'Tis time the truth should come out."

Dunwoody piped up. "Aye, lad, you're right. You"—he pointed at Lachlan—"we'll hear from in due time." To Tyg, he said, "And you'll keep your mouth shut, or I'll have you bound and gagged."

Tyg glowered at Dunwoody with his good eye.

Dunwoody frowned at Quin. "Tell us what happened, lad."

Quin took a deep breath and rolled the rock around in his palm as he spoke. "I'm no' sure how I killed her—"

"What?" Dunwoody's brow creased, resembling a bloodhound's.

"'Tis true. You've got tae believe me. I don't remember how I got there, but I found myself in her room with blood on my hands. I wanted tae tell you when it happened, but Tyg told me not tae say anything. Didn't you, Tyg? Didn't you?"

Tyg wouldn't answer, only shook his head and shot Quin a rueful look.

"What happened tae yer minnie, lad?"

"When I woke up, she was lying near the fireplace—a big gash on her head. Bleeding, 'twas." The memory made Quin grimace and tears flowed freely down his cheeks. "I must have pushed her. I must have! That's why I would never come back in here. For a long time, no' 'til Regan and Emma came."

"Nay." Lachlan strode toward Quin. "You didn't kill her. Don't you remember? We were arguing. I pushed her—"

"You're lying!" Quin bellowed. "You weren't even there. You didn't even know where Tyg and I buried the body. I couldna go in the circle, but Tyg did."

"Quin—"

"Shut up, Lachlan! Shut up!" Quin put his hands over his ears. "Let me take the blame."

"I told you tae be quiet," Dunwoody bawled at Lachlan.

Lady Margaret threw her needlework on the cushion and said, "You cannot address my grandson in that manner."

Regan raised her voice and said, "Please, may I speak, Mr. Dunwoody? I believe I can shed some light on this."

chapter 38

"Glad someone can. Go ahead, lass. And no' a word outta the rest o' you."

"You see," Regan began, "during my employment here, I was pushed down the stairs by someone. And on another occasion someone tried to frighten me away. Someone in the house didn't want me here, and I believe I know why. I also believe this person is involved in the murder of Lady MacGregor."

Darcy dropped a cup. Porcelain shattered. A piece landed near Regan's foot. She bent and picked it up. Every eye in the room was on Darcy, save Regan's. She was watching McAskill. For the first time, Regan noticed how closely he scrutinized Darcy.

"Out with it, lass," Dunwoody said.

Regan held the jagged piece of porcelain between her thumb and first finger and glanced at Darcy.

"Hech! It weren't me." Darcy began backing away from Regan, her footsteps grinding in the broken pottery.

"It was you who pushed me down the stairs." Regan stepped toward her. "I thought it was Tyg, but it wasn't."

"You're wrong," Darcy said.

Tyg leaped up and pointed at Darcy. "The miss is right. After the accident, I saw this one here enter the stairwell from the opposite direction o' Lady Margaret's room. And when she said she'd been in there 'fore the accident, I didn't think much o' it, 'til now."

"I have further proof," Regan said. "You came and told me about the Tender stone because you knew I'd be interested in it. Then you followed me and tried to frighten me away, *after* you unloaded my pistol to make sure I wouldn't use it on you."

"Nay," Darcy said, shaking her head adamantly. "You're wrong."

"I wish I were. I kept wondering who could have entered my room undetected, then I realized it had to have been you." Darcy tried to speak, but Regan stopped her. "There is more proof." She turned to Quin. "It's imperative you tell the truth. I saw you with someone the day you first met Emma. Remember? I questioned you, and you said you were not with anyone, but you were. Was it Mr. McAskill?"

"Aye." Quin stared guiltily down at the rock in his hand, avoiding Lachlan's stunned expression.

McAskill's gaze shifted toward the door, his superior expression gone. Real fear glistened in his eyes.

"What were you doing with him?"

"He gives me things."

"What kinds of things?" Regan saw the anger in Lachlan's face as he eyed Quin in disbelief.

"Flowers . . . for my garden."

"And when he gives you these things, does he ask you for something?" Regan asked.

Quin blinked at her in thought, then nodded. "He kept asking if I had a diary that belonged tae the Flame. I told him I didna have it. I didna trust him." Quin wrinkled his nose at McAskill. "I gave it tae you, Regan."

McAskill snarled at Quin. "He's lying."

"Quiet." Dunwoody shook a finger at McAskill. "Another outburst and you'll be gagged."

Regan shot McAskill an indignant look, then saw Dunwoody's bewildered appearance. She addressed Quin. "Tell Mr. Dunwoody where you found the diary."

"When Tyg took the body out, he told me tae clean up the blood as best I could. I did. Every bit. I was cleaning the spot near the fireplace, and I saw an edge o' the diary poking out o' the flue. I pulled it out. I didna know what it was, 'cause I can't read. She always told me I was stupid and would ne'er learn. I wanted tae learn so I'd know, but I hav'na. So I kept it and locked it in her trunk."

Dunwoody's brows rose. "A trunk?"

"Aye, I saved her trunk from being burned and locked it in there."

Regan asked, "And Mr. McAskill assumed you had it?"

"That's why he pretended tae be my friend, ain't it? He thought I was simpleminded and I would give it tae him. Well, I showed him." Quin leveled a scornful look at McAskill.

He glowered back at Quin.

"The diary is still safely locked away," Regan said.

Quin nodded.

"What does the book have tae do with it?" Dunwoody asked.

"It shows motive," Regan said. "I read its contents."

Dunwoody looked confused. "But Quin pushed her."

"No, I believe Mr. McAskill knew Lady MacGregor kept a diary, and he also knew she had written that he was aware of a certain treasure she had found. McAskill wanted that treasure for himself, so he went that night to dispose of Lady MacGregor and find her diary. She obviously knew he wanted it and wouldn't tell him where she had hidden it. He lost his temper and struck her with something, then left her body. Quin probably heard the commotion and went to the room and found her—but too late. Quin must have blacked out when he saw the blood. When he woke, he didn't remember what happened."

"What about Lord MacGregor's confession?" Dunwoody asked.

Regan's gaze swept Lachlan. It hurt her to look at him, so she turned back to Dunwoody. "Lord MacGregor was protecting Quin. He must have seen something that led him to believe his brother had murdered their mother, but he never inquired after the particulars. It was a bad business."

Dunwoody turned to Lachlan. "That true?"

"I heard footsteps outside my door. I opened it and saw Quin run to his room. There was blood on his nightshirt. I went in, helped him change, and burned it. I never asked him what happened." Lachlan cast Regan a bleak, dark look.

"And you said naught?" Dunwoody asked, his tone one of censure.

"He's my brother. What would you have done?" Lachlan's scowl wiped away the condemning look on Dunwoody's face.

Regan glanced at Lady Margaret. "And you knew, too."

Lady Margaret nodded. "Tyg told me all. I instructed him to remain silent." She glowered at the magistrate as if daring him to question her actions.

Dunwoody frowned and said to Regan, "I still dinna see what the journal has tae do with the whole business."

"It will show Lady MacGregor told Mr. McAskill about the artifacts."

"That's a lie," McAskill growled.

Dunwoody ignored his outburst. "If my memory serves, your da was naethin' but a crofter. You came into your wealth twenty years ago, more or less. I'm sure it'll be easy enough tae be finding out how you came by it." He turned to Regan. "How do you know this?"

"I found her first journal. In there it points out she made love to Mr. McAskill in the circle, where an ancient box was buried. In the second diary she states she found golden artifacts in the box and entrusted the selling of them to Mr. McAskill. She wrote of her fears that he was lying to her about the price he'd received for the items. She must have threatened to have him arrested for his greed. Mr. McAskill didn't want to be exposed and go to jail, so he killed her. It all fits together."

"I'll be needin' both diaries."

"I'm sorry, I burned the first."

Dunwoody glowered at her and said, "You shouldna have done that."

"I'm sorry. There were sensitive personal entries better left unread. If you need me to testify, I shall. You may have the second one. Quin will get it for you."

"You still have no proof that I killed her," McAskill said, sounding smug while his expression implied something else entirely.

Regan turned back to Darcy, who had backed up against the wall. "You're our proof."

"I'm no'," Darcy said.

Now that Regan examined Darcy closely, she appeared much older than Regan had first thought, maybe in her twenties. "My guess is you're Mr. McAskill's mistress."

Darcy gulped hard. "Aye, but I did no' kill anyone. He killed her, not me—"

McAskill said, "Shut up, you drab hizzy."

Darcy fired a look back at him. "He told me he killed her." She faced Regan. "I'm sorry, miss. He asked me tae come work here so I could find the diary. Then he wanted tae frighten you away so you wouldna go near the circle and asked me tae do it. I was daft tae have ever listened tae him."

Regan saw the confused look on Dunwoody's face and explained. "Mr. McAskill somehow knew that my father was looking for Avalon on this island. He also pretended to be interested in me—I'm quite certain to keep an eye on me so I wouldn't find the whereabouts of Avalon and all its treasures. My guess is that he hasn't found it himself, and when he ran out of artifacts to sell, he thought he'd sold the one artifact that could tell him where the rest of the treasure of Avalon was located." Regan narrowed her gaze at McAskill. "What you do not know is that all the treasures that belonged to Arthur would have been buried in that circle along with his ashes. There is no more treasure; Avalon itself is the treasure."

Lady Margaret addressed Regan. "How did you know these two were plotting all this, gel?" She pointed at Darcy and McAskill.

"I didn't until I saw them together in this room."

"Smart, gel." Lady Margaret smiled at Regan, a genuine warmth curving up both sides of her mouth.

Mr. Dunwoody grabbed Darcy's arm, then eyed the men at the door, while he motioned to McAskill. "Take him away."

McAskill leaped back from them and pulled out a pistol. "Don't move." He waved it at the people in the room, then pointed it at Lachlan. "You die first."

chapter 39

Regan instinctively pulled Old Gray out of her pocket, aimed, and fired.

McAskill screamed and dropped the gun, then clutched his hand.

Dunwoody's men grabbed the murderer by his arms, threw him to the ground, and tied his wrists. Blood oozed from his fingers where the bullet had grazed his skin.

He raised his head off the floor and glared at Regan. "Wee bitch. I should have drowned you when I had the chance."

"I'm sure you've done a lot of things you regret, Mr. McAskill."

"I'll get you for this!" McAskill bellowed as they hoisted him to his feet.

One of the men, a burly, dark-haired man, grabbed Darcy. "Come on, you."

"I didna do naethin'."

"Tell it tae the judge."

They dragged Darcy and McAskill from the room,

McAskill fighting the ropes. "I'm a wealthy mon. I'll have you all in jail. Let me go!"

The murderous rage in his eyes made Regan shiver. Why hadn't she seen through him when she had first met him? She gulped and glanced down at the smoking gun in her hand.

Dunwoody slapped Regan on the back. "By, you're a canny lass."

Regan was glad she'd brought Old Gray with her; it never hurt to anticipate the worst—especially when dealing with a murderer.

She noticed Lachlan wouldn't look at her, only glowered at the gun. He didn't seem happy she'd saved his life. Well, they were even now. He'd saved her from drowning, and she had saved him from McAskill's bullet. There was nothing left owed him—save a good heartache. One day she hoped he'd fall in love and suffer the worst arrows Cupid could muster. Yes, one day he would know the kind of pain she was feeling.

Dunwoody asked, "Where'd you learn to use that, lass?"

"My father taught me." Regan stuffed the gun back in her pocket and remembered something. "Oh, about the three dead men found in the circle. You might want to question Mr. McAskill about them. I have a theory that they may have learned of the artifacts and Mr. McAskill disposed of them."

"By, I'll do it. And here we thought it was the Druid curse all these years."

"There's no curse, Mr. Dunwoody. Curses only exist in the minds of men."

"You're wrong, Miss Southworth. I've lived here all my life, and I've seen many a peculiar thing on this isle."

"No doubt you have. Since coming here I have, too." Regan glanced around the castle. It was like saying goodbye to an old friend. "But I still don't believe they came from curses. However, I do believe structures such as this one"—Regan motioned around the room—"can survive so long that they take on a character all their own. I believe the spirit of Skye rests here in the castle."

"Spirit?" Mr. Dunwoody glanced around, his superstitious propensity on the alert.

Regan shook her head. "Pay me no mind, I'm a bit rattled. Could I impose on you for a ride home, sir?"

Lachlan stepped near her. "I'll take you home."

"I rather you didn't," she said, forcing her voice not to crack.

"How can I thank you—"

"You needn't." Regan couldn't bear to look at the aloof expression in Lachlan's eyes and she turned away.

Quin grabbed her arm. "You canna leave us, Regan."

She swallowed to get rid of the thickness creeping into her voice. She hugged him and said, "I have to."

"Can I still come and visit Emma's garden? Can I?"

"Yes. Anytime."

"Dinna let her go, Lachlan."

"She has to." Lachlan's voice held steely resolve.

She felt each word stab her.

Lady Margaret walked over and took Regan's hand. "'Tis been a pleasure meeting you, gel." Lower, in her ear, "This way is better."

For whom? Regan felt her heart cracking just a little more as she hugged Lady Margaret. Lady Margaret's frail bones belied the hard invincible facade she hid behind, and Regan realized just how slight and fragile the elderly woman was. "I'll miss you," Regan said.

"Don't go getting all maudlin, gel." Lady Margaret's voice had a hitch in it as she returned the embrace.

Regan stepped back and waved to Quin and Gillis. "Good-bye." Even Tyg waved good-bye to her.

Regan followed Dunwoody toward the door. It took every ounce of inner strength not to look back at Lachlan.

"Wait."

At the sound of his voice, Regan wheeled around. Had he finally realized he loved her? Would he ask her to stay?

She watched him pull something out of his pocket as he stepped near her. His expression hadn't softened.

"I found this." He held out her mother's comb.

Regan's heart fell. "Thank you," she said, barely able to speak as she reached for the proffered item. He held the comb with two fingers so he wouldn't touch her hand. The gesture wounded Regan again.

Fighting back tears, she turned and quit the room. He didn't love her. She had to put him behind her now. Why, then, did it feel like her heart was being torn into tiny pieces?

A s soon as Regan left the library, Quin turned to Lachlan and said, "Why didn't you stop her? Why?"

"You dinna understand."

"I understand. I'm no' as daft as you think—"

"I didna say you were daft."

"You might well have." Quin jammed his hands down in his pockets. "I may be daft but I'm knowin' she's the light in our darkness. I'm knowin' she saved me. I thought I'd killed the Flame. You dinna know what it's like tae be lifted from such a burden. 'Cause of her, I'll no' have tae carry around the guilt. She's freed me. She can free you, too, Lachlan. You dinna have tae let the curse pull you down."

"It's in our blood; you dinna understand," Lachlan said, gripping the cane until his hand trembled.

"Is it? I'm beginin' tae believe like she does, there's no curse." Quin stomped out of the room like a recalcitrant child.

"Better see tae him." Tyg frowned at Lachlan and followed Quin out.

Lady Margaret faced Lachlan. "I must say, I'm proud of you for doing the proper thing—it just doesn't feel very proper at the moment, does it?" She didn't wait for a reply and left the room, her skirts swishing in the silence.

Gillis opened his mouth, but Lachlan caught him. "Dinna say a word."

Gillis frowned and left Lachlan alone.

The castle's onerous hush engulfed him. Oddly, the ancient structure sounded completely still. No whisperings. No blowing cold drafts. Utter silence. For the first time in his life, he heard nothing inside the walls. The quietness pressed in on him, caught him somehow, held him in its grasp. He found it hard to take in air.

He'd done the correct thing, sending her away. Curse or no curse, he'd seen his grandfather and father go insane. He'd seen the demented things of which a madman was capable. He glanced down at his leg and the cane in his hand. He wouldn't force Regan to go through what he had been through no matter how much he loved her. Never.

He hurled his cane as hard as he could.

It hit a row of books and clattered to the floor.

Lachlan limped from the room, a feeling of loneliness opening a gnawing cavity inside him, the tomblike silence in the castle suffocating him.

The storm had given way to clear sky. The moon peeped down at Regan from a blanket of stars. The clean scent of the sea and a rising fog hovered in the air. She breathed it in, struggling to check her emotions.

She hadn't cried at the castle, or along the way home. It had been the hardest thing she'd ever had to do, pretending not to care. Lachlan hadn't even thought enough of her to say good-bye. He'd only returned her mother's comb. If she had needed convincing he cared nothing for her, his indifference proved it once and for all. A stake was being driven slowly through her chest, one inch at a time. The pain steadily radiated through her body, her stomach, her neck. A knot the size of a ball of yarn had lodged in her throat.

Mr. Dunwoody's little cart rattled along the road, sloshing through mud puddles. Regan felt each bump jarring the lump in her throat, making it grow.

"You've been a wee bit quiet, lass."

"Please do not address me that way," Regan said, reminded of Lachlan.

"Fient, I'm sorry." Dunwoody looked bewildered.

"Regan will do," she managed to add.

"You needn't fash yourself about bringing a murderer tae justice. You did the proper thing."

"You think I'm concerned about Mr. McAskill?" Regan might have laughed if there was a laugh left in her. All she could do was grimace and keep the tears at bay. "I assure you, proving his guilt has been the crowning moment of my life. Because of his greed, he destroyed my chances of ever giving my father his lifelong dream—or a will to live. . . ." Regan's words choked off. How would she ever be able to tell her father that Avalon had slipped through their grasp forever?

An awkward silence settled between them. Dunwoody shifted uncomfortably on his seat, an outward sign that he hadn't much experience in consoling young ladies on such delicate matters.

Regan was glad when the cart slowed and he turned up the lane to Finn Cottage.

"You've company, Miss Southworth," Dunwoody said, staring ahead of them.

Regan glanced up the drive. Light beamed from every room in the cottage. She sucked in her breath. Had something happened to her father?

"Damn me, that's a chaise and four, ain't it?" Dunwoody squinted ahead of them and rose slightly off the seat to see up the hill.

Regan stretched her neck, too. Two running lanterns on the side of a traveling coach blinked at her. The men in red livery held the reins to four gray horses.

"Looks like the king's come a callin'," Mr. Dunwoody said. "Who but Crazy George would drive such a warly trap as that on the isle? Outsiders for sure."

"I must see who it is." Regan hefted up her skirt.

"We'll be there anon."

"Your pony is going too slow, sir." Regan leaped out of the cart.

"Wait a minute!" Dunwoody yelled at her, managing to pull back on the reins in time for her to reach the ground without being run over.

"Forgive me for being rude, sir," Regan called over her shoulder as she ran. "Please leave my trunk at the door. Thank you for bringing me home."

Was her father all right? And who did that carriage belong to? She forced her legs to pump faster and left Mr. Dunwoody far behind her.

chapter 40

❧

Regan burst through the door, expecting the worst. Voices drifted down the hall from her father's room. She recognized the sound of Emma and Seamus speaking. But there was a third voice she couldn't identify.

Regan let out the breath she'd been holding. Her father was all right and by the sound of it, receiving strange callers. Tension eased from her body as she strolled down the hall. At the sound of Regan's footsteps, the voices subsided.

"Who's there?" her father asked.

"Me, Papa."

"Regan? Come here, my girl."

In four strides Regan stood in the doorway of his chamber. Her father sat on the sofa, Emma beside him. An elderly distinguished-looking woman, who appeared close to sixty, with graying dark hair, sat opposite them. She wore a burgundy silk gown in the latest fashion with puffy sleeves. An ermine stole wrapped her shoulders. Diamond earbobs the size of walnuts dangled from her ears. Rings of rubies, diamonds, and sapphires lit up every one of her fingers. Her wealth and consequence filled the room in a garish way, and she looked very much out of place in their humble little cottage.

When the lady glanced up at her, Regan felt her heart stop for an instant. Her mother's eyes were looking back at her. They were the same perfect almond shape, the same long lashes, the same glistening dark color. It had been years since she had seen those eyes; she could never forget them. Since the night her mother had died, memories of them had haunted her—along with her own guilt.

With an unsteady hand, Seamus motioned toward the visitor. "Meet Lady Clarington." His smile was gracious, but the tension never left his lips.

Regan's jaw gaped open. Her eyes widened. For a moment all she could do was stare into those dark depths so much like her mother's.

"Pleased to finally meet you, my dear." The woman rose and offered her hand, the expensive silk of her gown rustling in the silence.

Regan stared at the manicured nails, the fortune in jewels on the fingers, the smile on the lady's attractive yet aged face. Was the smile genuine? Why was she here? Regan's gaze shifted to Emma. Her sister seemed very interested in the paisley pattern on a pillow. Regan swallowed hard and took the hand, surprised at the sturdy squeeze she received.

"So you are Regan, the older, a beauty. You have your father's coloring."

The lady spoke in the same prim cultured tones as her mother had. Regan had forgotten that one aspect about her mother, her voice. She had remembered what it felt like to be hugged by her slender arms, her sweet rose scent, but the cadence of her voice had been lost to Regan until now. There were times in Regan's life when she would have given her soul to hear it one more time, yet now, coming from this stranger who had disowned her own daughter and her grandchildren . . .

Regan withdrew her hand and said, "Please excuse me, I'd like a word with Emma." Regan walked over and grabbed her sister's hand.

Emma tried to pull away, but Regan wrenched her fingers in a viselike grip. "Leave me alone!" Emma cried.

Lady Clarington stepped between them. "Please, your sister did not bring me here."

Emma pulled free of Regan's grasp and hid behind Lady Clarington. "Excuse me, madam, but why are you here?" Regan asked, struggling to keep the pain of seeing this woman from tearing her apart. First Lachlan had destroyed her, then McAskill had snatched her chances of ever finding Avalon. Now this.

Seamus spoke up. "She's here to make amends, Regan. Perhaps you will hear her out."

"Did she hear out our mother?" Regan couldn't keep the years of bitterness from her voice.

"That was your grandfather's doing. He forbade me to have contact with my own daughter." Lady Clarington's eyes glazed over with tears. "I wanted to see her."

"You didn't even come to her funeral."

"I did." Tears slipped down the lady's cheeks. "I was off from the proceedings. I wore a black veil. I saw you and Emma. You were so small then." Her lip trembled as she spoke. "It was my first glimpse of you. I wanted to meet you, but I was afraid of how you would receive me. And, too, I knew I would suffer my husband's wrath. He could be horribly cruel. When I got Emma's letter, I grew hopeful."

"You do not know how I needed a grandmother when our mother died." Regan thought of the night she'd lost her mother. Her father and Emma had been sick, too. There were nights when she dreaded they would all die. She had no one to comfort her, to hold her, to help unburden her soul.

"I'm so sorry. I should have come to you. Can you ever forgive me?" Lady Clarington opened her arms to Regan.

She held back as long as she could, then she stepped into the circle of her grandmother's arms for the first time in her life.

She felt the lady's arms go around her, and years of bitterness drained from her. Then she was hugging her back, feeling Lady Clarington's warm tears on her cheeks. In her childhood she had imagined what it would feel like to have grandparents. It felt almost dreamlike to finally touch one. They hugged for a long time, but not long enough to make up for all the time they'd lost.

"We'll have to do a lot of catching up," Lady Clarington said, wiping at Regan's eyes with a handkerchief.

"Yes," Regan said.

"How does their grandfather feel about all of this?" Seamus asked.

"He recently passed away," Lady Clarington said. "That's why I'm here. I was hoping to convince you to come to London with me for a visit. My house is so very large and lonely."

"Can we, Papa?" Emma's eyes lit up with hope.

Seamus hesitated for a moment. His brows pursed in thought, then he said, "I think that's a capital idea."

"Oh, how wonderful. We can introduce Regan and Emma to society. I know they will be the two prettiest girls there." Lady Clarington's eyes glowed with pride as they swept her granddaughters.

"But, Papa, we cannot leave you," Regan said.

"Oh, the invitation was for all of you." Lady Clarington smiled at Seamus.

Seamus hesitated a moment, then said, "I cannot see how we can refuse."

Regan thought of leaving the Isle of Skye. What was here to hold her? Nothing. Not Lachlan. He wouldn't care if she left. Not Avalon.

At the thought of losing it, she grimaced and asked, "May I please speak to Father alone?"

Lady Clarington turned to Emma. "Come, child. You can tell me where I can find an inn."

"Oh, no," Emma said. "You'll stay here with us, in my room. I'm sure our accommodations are nothing as grand as you're used to—"

"Nonsense. They'll be fine." They walked out, arm in arm, continuing to chatter.

Emma looked happier than Regan had ever seen her.

Regan waited until their voices died away and asked, "How do you *really* feel about this?"

"It will be a good opportunity for you and Emma. Lady Clarington can give you all the things I never could."

"Oh, Papa, do not ever think we could love her more than you." Regan crossed the room and kissed her father on his forehead.

He patted her hand and wore a cheerless smile. "I know that, my girl, but she'll be here for you if something should happen—"

"Don't say that." Regan had held on to her composure as long as she could. It crumbled. The knot in her throat swelled until tears blurred her vision.

"What is wrong, my girl?"

"I'm so sorry, Papa. I tried my best, but I failed you." Regan swallowed hard.

"What are you talking about?"

"I—I tried to find Avalon, but th-that's lost to us. I thought it would m-make you well. It's all my fault you're sick." Regan spoke past her sobs.

"Your fault?" He pulled her close and held her while the tears flowed. "What are you talking about, my girl?"

"I brought the typhus home to everyone."

"You?"

"Y-yes." Regan took the handkerchief her father offered and buried her face in it. "I went to see Tommy Swenson. He had borrowed one of my books on Egyptian architecture. His mother told me he was ill and she wouldn't let me in to see him. I crawled up the downspout to his room. I spoke to him and took the book back. I'm sure that's how we all came down with typhus."

"You're wrong, my girl. Many of my students had it long before then. There was an epidemic. You're not responsible for bringing it home. Have you thought that all this time?"

Regan nodded and hiccuped.

"I'm so sorry," Seamus said, hugging her tighter.

"I haven't told you the worst yet."

"I cannot think of anything worse than believing you'd given your family typhus."

"It is quite as horrible," Regan said, dreading what she must say. "The artifacts that were buried in the circle were looted long ago."

"I'm beginning to believe I'm not meant to find it, my girl," he said wistfully. "Your and Emma's happiness means more to me than finding Avalon. I've come to realize nothing is more precious to me than my girls." He tipped her face up and searched her eyes.

"But the fame and recognition you would have had, the papers you could have written, the lectures you could have given on your work. It would have made you feel well again."

"My word! Is that the reason you've helped me look for it all these years?"

Regan nodded.

"Dear God! Had I known it was guilt driving you—"

"Please, Papa, I was interested in your work."

"What a fool we've both been." Seamus shook his head. "Avalon is not an elixir for longevity, my girl. Do not ever think it is."

"But—"

"No, that's your guilt talking. You listen to me. You had nothing to do with my getting that fever, and finding Avalon will not make me live longer. For so long you have cared for me and Emma. We have depended on you for everything. You've been my assistant, housekeeper, and nurse. To Emma, you were a mother, sister, and friend. There wasn't anything you hadn't learned to surmount for us. Your shoulders have always been wide and you never complained. Dear God! I have abused you by letting you carry all the burden—"

"But—"

Seamus raised his hand, stilling her. "Hear me out. I

know why you've done this. Guilt. It's time you stopped trying to be a martyr. It's high time you learned that you cannot change things that are beyond your control. You cannot go around believing you can make everything perfect or bear everyone's responsibilities. If you do, life will wear you down."

"I know that now," she said, her voice cracking. She felt the weight that she'd carried around for most of her life slowly lift from her chest. Still, thoughts of Lachlan pressed down on her.

He looked into her eyes and said, "Something else has happened that's upset you. What is it?"

"Lachlan happened, Papa."

"I see."

"No, you don't." Regan blew her nose in the handkerchief.

"I believe I do. You've fallen in love with him, and he doesn't return your affections."

"How did you know?"

"One has only to look at that pretty face of yours to see it."

"Oh, Papa. What shall I do?" Regan laid her head on his shoulder and wiped the tears from her cheeks.

"Nothing, my girl. He'll realize what he's lost. And if he doesn't, he's unworthy of you." Seamus's brows knitted as he patted Regan's shoulder.

"He made it plain he cares nothing for me," Regan said, hardly able to get out the words.

Seamus hugged her, his expression filled with a father's remorse and uncertainty.

All Regan could think about was living without ever kissing Lachlan again, or feeling him hold her, or having him look at her with those devouring black eyes. Her sobs began again in earnest.

chapter 41

𝒮❦

A fortnight had passed since Regan's departure. The silence in the great hall wrapped around everything like the vines of poison nettles. Lady Margaret wondered if her pulse could be heard in the room as loudly as she heard it in her own ears. She glanced down the table. Quin hadn't looked up from his plate. He'd worn the same hangdog expression since the gel had left, eating hardly enough to keep a bird alive.

Lachlan, on the other hand, ate his normal proportion, yet his movements were methodical, lifeless, like an automaton. His coal black eyes had never looked so vacant or detached, as if his soul had left his body and only a shell remained. His demeanor had never disturbed Margaret as it did now. He had shut everyone out.

Even when her son and husband had gone mad, they had had some semblance of life in their eyes; Lachlan had none. She thought of Regan. The gel reminded her of herself fifty years ago when she'd met Oswald. She had never loved anyone as much as him. How he had made her laugh. Once he told her, in that rolling brogue of his, "My heart beats only for the sight of your beauty, bearing, and bosom, lass—maybe no' in that order." He had winked at her in that bold roguish fashion that was his.

Oh, he knew just what to say to solicit her affections. At the memory, she grinned and pushed a piece of toast around the plate with a knife. It hadn't mattered that his bloodline had been tainted by madness; Margaret had been determined to wed him. She had battled the reluctance of her parents by going directly to King George and asking him to give Oswald a title. Against her parents' wishes, he had, and after meeting Oswald gave his blessing, too. She would have braved anything to have him. She remembered telling Regan, "Believe me, gel, if you know what's good for you, spare yourself heartache and leave this island. Forget my grandson."

She knew exactly what Lachlan was feeling at the moment. It had been so long since she'd closed off her feelings. After Oswald and Balmoral died, she didn't want to remember. She had alienated her own grandsons and everyone around her. But Regan had brought back all the memories, good and bad. And before Margaret knew it, she had felt affection for the gel that she hadn't wanted to feel.

Margaret knew now she would not have given up her time with Oswald for anything. How could she have discouraged the gel that way? How could she have not forced Lachlan to marry her?

Footsteps sounded behind them and Tyg entered the room, carrying a small package. "For you, my lady. 'Tis from Finn Cottage." She took the parcel.

Quin's head came up. "Is it from Regan and Emma?"

Lachlan did not glance up, only threw the dogs a piece of mutton.

His indifference worried Margaret as she tore open the package. She found two letters inside, one addressed to Lachlan. "There's a letter here for you, Lachlan, from Regan." She placed the envelope in front of him.

He stared at it for a moment, then picked up the newspaper and buried his face behind it.

"Read it aloud, Lachlan," Quin said. "Will you, will you?"

"Later," Lachlan grumbled.

Quin turned to Margaret. "Please, read yours. Please."

"Very well." She broke the seal. "Let me see." She squinted down at the blurry letters and held the paper as far away as her arm would allow.

> *Dear Lady Margaret*
> *I hope you will use the enclosed little gift. I regret to inform you we are giving up Finn Cottage and moving to London with Lady Clarington, our grandmother, a very fine lady. I must say I'm looking forward to London and all its diversions. I did so enjoy working for you.*
> *Emma also wanted to give Quin a little gift. She sends her felicitations and says she'll write Quin when we get settled in London. Please give Quin my love.*
>
> > *Best regards,*
> > *Regan*

Silence engulfed the room. Margaret glanced at Lachlan. He still held the paper in front of his face. He hadn't touched the letter Regan sent him.

"Why are they leavin' the isle?" Quin asked, his tone woeful.

"That's obvious. Lady Clarington means to introduce them to society and find them husbands."

The paper snapped loudly.

Margaret smiled inwardly. Lachlan had heard her.

"I dinna want them tae leave tae find husbands." Quin ran to her side, anxiety marring his expression. "Open the box."

Inside she found a small ball of linen tied with a ribbon. "It says here they are seeds from Emma's garden."

Quin's eyes registered a blink of excitement, but it never

touched his face as he took the seeds. "I want tae see her before she leaves."

"I'm sure they have already gone." Lady Margaret found a placating tone that she hadn't used since Oswald died. "The letter was dated two days ago."

"Please, they might still be there. I never got tae see Emma's garden. I wanna say good-bye." Quin's fists tightened at his sides, his fingers crushing the small ball of seeds.

Lachlan lowered the paper and turned his emotionless eyes on Tyg. The irritation in his voice came through as he said, "Take him."

Quin frowned at Lachlan, but seemed appeased. "Really! Let's go now, Tyg. Now!"

"Come, Master Quin." Tyg motioned him out of the room.

They left the hall, their footsteps thumping in the silence.

Lady Margaret glanced down into the box and found a pair of spectacles in a blue velvet case. They were gold-rimmed, with small rectangular-shaped magnifying lenses. Her eyes teared as she gazed down at them. The two times she remembered crying were at Balmoral's and Oswald's deathbeds. She quickly pulled her handkerchief out of her sleeve and dabbed at her eyes before her grandson noticed.

She stood and leveled a gaze at Lachlan. "Aren't you going to open her letter?"

"Had no' planned to." He glanced at it next to his plate.

"Because of your fear, you're going to let that gel go?"

"I thought you approved." He frowned at her.

She hesitated and gathered herself. Her arrogance had kept her from ever saying what she must now admit to her grandson. After a moment, she swallowed her pride and said, "I was damned wrong. I'm entitled to be wrong once in my life. And if you love that gel, you'll know that every minute is more precious with her in it."

"I'll no' have her watch me go mad."

"I watched your grandfather and father go mad, but that

does not mean that I loved them any less, or that I would take back the years I spent with them. It made me cherish the time I had with them even more. I'd forgotten they were the happiest years of my life. I had many remarkable years with your grandfather, not a one of them would I take back. And you could be so fortunate. That gel loves you. You have a chance to be happy. Do not let her get away. If you do, you'll regret it the rest of your life. It was wrong of me to tell you otherwise. I was thinking about me, not you. I forgot the joy." With that Lady Margaret picked up her spectacles and headed for the door.

Lachlan watched her plop the eyeglasses on her nose as she quit the room. He had never seen his grandmother, who was stiff as shoe leather and who had never showed an ounce of humility, humble herself as she'd just done. There had actually been compassion in her eyes as she had spoken of Regan. He didn't think his grandmother could change so completely, but Regan had a way of casting spells over people.

He glanced at the letter as if it were a snake ready to strike. His hand slipped into his pocket and reached for her comb. But he remembered he'd given it back to her. He withdrew his hand and realized it was trembling—his whole body was trembling.

He had all but convinced himself he could live without Regan. That was before he knew she was leaving the island to find a husband. If she'd stayed on the island, he could have stood it. Every now and then he could have ridden past the cottage and caught a glimpse of her. It would have been enough.

He reached for the letter and tore it open. The check he'd mailed to her fluttered down and landed in his plate.

MacGregor,
I'm returning your ten thousand pounds. Papa no longer needs a benefactor. My grandmother has kindly stepped into that position. I prefer it this way.

*I shall no longer feel obliged to you, and there will be
no need for further communication between us.*

                              Good-bye forever,
                              Regan

Lachlan reread the words "there will be no need for further communication between us. Good-bye forever."

"Och! Have I lost her forever?" Lachlan spoke aloud.

The dogs looked at him as if to say, "It would be well-
deserved if you did."

He thought of kissing her and holding her, the way she'd
looked at him in that soft, loving way. What a fool he'd
been to give her up. He tossed the letter into the fire,
grabbed up his cane, and hurried out of the room.

chapter 42

Lachlan galloped *Phoebus* along the drive to Finn Cottage. Behind him, Tyg and Quin rode in the carriage. He had no idea what he would say to her, but he knew he'd have to win her back, tell her how much he loved her. Surely she hadn't meant those things in her letter.

The anticipation of holding her, kissing her, seeing his reflection in those periwinkle blue eyes again made his heart pound. The letter she'd sent had been postmarked two days ago, but he could still hope. He leaped off *Phoebus*'s back before the animal stomped to a halt near the front stoop; then he ran to the door and knocked.

No answer.

Louder, again.

After a moment a sick feeling squeezed his chest as he tried the door.

The door squeaked open.

He stepped inside. The hollow sound of emptiness echoed through the house.

"Hellooo." He walked through the rooms and found the

furniture covered by sheets. The pressure in his chest grew almost unbearable.

"Lachlan?" Quin called.

Lachlan stepped out of the empty room. "They're gone."

"I wanted tae see Emma and Regan," Quin said, his excitement deflating.

"Too late for that," Tyg said, patting Quin's shoulder. "By the looks o' things, they've been gone a day or two. They've left the island."

"Nay, it's no' tae late, is it, Lachlan?"

Lachlan nodded, unable to breathe for the stabbing sensation in his chest

Puffy white clouds dimpled the sky. The shoreline of Skye faded in and out behind a white mist. Regan breathed deep of the sea air and felt the sway of the ferry. Her father and Lady Clarington sat in the carriage, talking and looking out the windows, while the driver and two coachmen held the horses still and chatted. Emma stood several feet away, also staring off at the island.

Regan leaned over the railing, trying to get a better view. Despite telling herself she cared nothing for Lachlan, she kept looking for him to suddenly appear and prevent her from leaving. Wishful thinking.

A cold breeze brushed her neck. It felt like his fingertips on her skin, and a shiver went down her spine. She knew she'd never see him again. When tears stung her eyes, Regan marveled. She hadn't thought she had any tears left. She wiped them away.

Emma turned and saw her and stepped over to her.

"Do not think of him," Emma said. "Toward the end, I thought him nothing like Schedoni, but I was wrong. He's a scoundrel for treating you the way he did." She slipped her hand in Regan's.

"I'm beginning to believe he's no more scoundrel than any other gentleman."

"Especially Mr. McAskill. Do you think they'll hang him?"

"Most likely." Regan frowned at the scandal his trial had brought. It had caused such a sensation that it had been moved to Edinburgh. Every newspaper in Scotland and England seemed to have followed the story, expounding on the artifacts and Avalon. It hadn't taken Sir Harry Lucas long to take up residence on the isle again. Soon archeologists from all over the world would be looking for the artifacts. At least her father's theory would be proven.

At Regan's silence, Emma said, "Do not worry, you'll forget all about him when we get to London. Grandmama says we'll go to Almacks, and routs, and the theater. Are you still angry with me for writing her?"

"How could I be?" She glanced back at the window where Lady Clarington sat. She waved and grinned at Regan.

Regan forced a smile. "Without your meddling, we wouldn't have a grandmother. It's like finding a piece of Mama again."

"I do not remember much about her," Emma said with a wistful note.

"You were too little to remember. She was very much like Lady Clarington, the same eyes and mannerisms. No, Em, you gave us a real gift. I shouldn't have let my bitterness keep us apart."

"Papa seems to have forgiven her." Emma glanced at the carriage, where Seamus and Lady Clarington sat talking.

"Yes. I believe he sees Mama in her, too." She watched her father smile as he listened intently to Lady Clarington. Regan had been worried about him making the trip, but this adventure seemed to give him a new twinkle in his eye.

After a moment of silence, Emma glanced back at the island and said, "I'll miss my garden and Quin. Do you think he can come visit us?"

"I do not see why not, if his brother does not come with him."

"Oh, believe me, I shall write Lady Margaret and make

it plain only she and Quin are invited. She turned out not to
be a dragon after all."

"One need only know how to get on with her." Regan remembered how Lady Margaret had gone from a crusty, ill-
tempered ogre to a genuinely kind person. She'd never
forget hugging the lady when she'd left Castle Druidhean.
It surprised her how much she had wanted to stay with
Lady Margaret and how much she would miss her.

"Just think, Regan. We'll be in London in a fortnight.
Won't it be lovely?" Emma squeezed Regan's hand.

Regan nodded despite the familiar suffocating feeling in
her throat and the tears building in her eyes.

chapter 43

F our days later Regan stared up at the ceiling of the inn
and listened to Emma snore next to her. Near Glen
Garry, they had finally found an inn large enough to ac-
commodate all of them. Despite boasting clean sheets and
the best haggis in Scotland, the walls were paper thin.

For hours, it seemed, Regan had listened to the honey-
mooning couple next door; the moaning, the crying, the
headboard bumping the wall. It didn't take much imagination to know what they were doing, and in spite of having
put Lachlan out of her mind forever, she found herself
thinking of his lean powerful body and the way it felt on top
of her.

At the thought of their lovemaking, a sheen of sweat
drenched her body. Until hearing the couple, she hadn't
thought of what she would do if she was with child.

Tears stung her eyes again as she rolled on her side. She
wiped them away, chiding herself for having turned into a
waterpot since leaving the island. Would the tears ever
stop?

She closed her eyes and tried to sleep, but an image of Lachlan's brooding countenance formed in her mind. . . .

A commotion belowstairs brought her eyes open.

"Here, you canna go up there!"

Regan recognized the landlord's voice.

Loud footsteps thumped down the hall, then . . .

Bang, bang, bang.

"Regan!"

Lachlan's deep brogue brought her straight up in bed. What was he doing here, yelling in the middle of the night?

"Regan!" She heard several doors open.

The couple in the adjacent room screamed.

"Sorry," Lachlan murmured, then the door slammed shut.

Emma sat up and rubbed her eyes. "What's all that noise?"

"By the sound of it, we're about to find out." Regan yanked the covers up around her for support.

The door swung open. Lachlan stood in the doorway, chest heaving, holding a candle up into the room so he could peer inside. In the light she could see deep shadows beneath his eyes, the days' worth of dark stubble on his face. His black clothes were wrinkled and mud spattered. She'd never seen him looking so haggard, or so handsome. His dark intensity filled the small room. A fierce wildness charged his eyes.

Her heart quickened at the sight of him. All the pain she'd felt at their last parting rushed back. Emotion pressed against her until she thought she would burst.

When his dark eyes lit upon her, he whispered, "Regan." The word mixed with relief and anxiety.

Regan turned to Emma, who had her mouth open in shock. "Kindly tell Lord MacGregor that we have nothing to say to each other and to leave my room forthwith."

Emma said, "She says she has nothing—"

"I heard what she said, lass." He entered, slammed the door, and locked it.

Bang, bang, bang.

"Regan, are you all right?" Lady Clarington called behind the door. "Open this door immediately."

"Go back to bed. Regan's all right," Lachlan said.

"Who said that? Is there a man in there?"

"By Jove, that's Lord MacGregor with her." Her father's muffled voice sounded behind the door. "Come, Lady Clarington, they'll be all right. Let me escort you back to bed."

"He's a Scottish savage," Lady Clarington said.

"Yes, but an amorous one." Seamus chuckled, then said, "Quin, there you are. Are you here with your brother?"

"Aye. Did he find her?"

"He did."

"Is Emma here?"

"Yes, in there. Come, you look tired and hungry. We'll go down and see what we can find in the kitchen."

Their voices drifted off.

Inside the room, Emma glowered at Lachlan. "You brought Quin on this fool's journey? Upon my word, you have some nerve. Regan wants nothing to do with you. She doesn't want to see you. I cannot blame her after the roughshod way you treated her."

"I need her to hear me out." He turned to Regan. "Lass, please."

"Tell him if he doesn't leave this room this instant, I will." Regan twisted the sheets in her fists.

Emma frowned over at Regan. "You can't leave me in here with him. I'm in my nightclothes."

"Lass, through fair or foul means I'm speaking to you." Lachlan stepped over to the side of the bed.

"Tell MacGregor that I'll not stand for his ultimatums."

His voice sounded tortured as he said, "Och, lass, 'tis no ultimatum, wanting to tell you I love you."

The three words softened some of the pain in Regan's heart. She glanced at him. His eyes were liquid with longing and hope. She'd never seen his expression so pliant with abject supplication.

Emma frowned. "She wants to know if you mean it."

"Em, I can speak for myself," Regan said, unable to

draw her eyes from Lachlan. She thought never to see him look at her with such boundless depth of feeling. It made her long to touch him.

"Very well, I know when I'm not wanted," Emma whispered to Regan, then hurried out the door.

"Did you mean what you just said?" Regan searched his eyes.

"Aye, lass. Would I have driven like a madmon to get here to tell you if I were no' meaning it?"

"You do look a little mad."

"Mad for you. I'm no' knowing how much time I have left, but I'm wanting to spend it with you, lass. Wed me. I canna live without you."

"It took you long enough to figure that out." She opened her arms to him. "Yes, I'll marry you. You're the only man I could ever marry."

He sat beside her and crushed her in his arms, kissing her until she was filled with him. She felt his coarse beard brushing her soft skin, and something wet against her cheeks. She pulled back to see tears streaming down his face.

"You're my gift, lass, and I've had few of those. I love you so much I feel like my ribs are being drawn out of me. Dinna ever leave me."

"Never. We'll never be parted again." His lips found hers, and she felt his tears meld with her own. The Isle of Skye had given her a gift much more precious than Avalon: the master of Castle Druidhean.

chapter 44

*I*t seemed everyone on the island came to celebrate with the happy couple. Rumors floated about the room that the wedding had released the castle of its curse. It was a known fact that there had never been a wedding inside Castle Druidhean since it had been built more than six hundred years ago; the lairds had not allowed it. Lachlan wouldn't have allowed it if his new bride had not insisted.

Regan had her arms entwined around Lachlan as they watched their guests dancing a reel. He had not scowled once since she'd agreed to marry him. In fact, he had tiny lines around his mouth from smiling so much. He was so handsome, decked out in a green and red kilt, a green velvet coat, and sporran. His black hair curled around his collar. Those two stray pieces of hair hung along his temples, one curling near the white streak in his hair. There was a wicked sexual intensity about him that took her breath away. He looked every bit the Scottish lord—her Scottish lord.

Emma and Quin skipped by.

"Oops. Sorry," Quin said, after he stepped on Emma's toes.

She made a face and said, "Quin, let me lead."

"I am."

"You're not."

Lachlan leaned over to Regan and said, "She's fightin' a losin' battle there. Quin's never danced in his life."

"If anyone can teach him, Emma can." Regan saw Lady Margaret sitting with Lady Clarington and a group of dowagers. Lady Margaret had taken to wearing her glasses and had actually smiled at Regan's grandmother many times.

Lady Margaret must have felt Regan's eyes on her, for she grinned and waved.

Regan waved back. "Your grandmother seems in good spirits."

"Now that you're back. I wouldna have been able to live with her if I had no' brought you back."

"My dear husband, now I know the real reason you married me." Regan grinned at him and saw Gillis and Tyg passing around tarts, oatcakes, pork pies, and brandy wafers. They hadn't, for once, had a cross word with each other, which was a miracle in itself.

The dogs sat near the fireplace, tails wagging, sitting like sentinels over the whole celebration. Regan swore they were smiling.

She searched the room. "Have you seen Papa?"

"He said he was wanting to have a look at the Tender stone."

"I'll just go and check on him."

"Dinna be long." He bent and kissed her, the hunger in his eyes making her shiver.

"I won't," she said, giving him a sultry grin.

"You keep looking at me like that, lass, and I'll be carrying you off to bed right now."

"Behave. We have guests." She squeezed his hand.

"To bloody hell with the guests," he murmured, his gaze lingering over every inch of her body. "We haven't made love since the time in the woods. I'm a dying mon here. I haven't seen you for a month, with Lady Clarington carting you off to God knows where to pick out wedding clothes, but you'll no' be needing clothes when I'm done with you." He kissed the back of her hand, letting his tongue slide along her skin.

Regan shivered, feeling that hot ache in the pit of her belly. "Behave, or I might lose my resolve." She shook her finger at him. "Only a few more hours."

He groaned. "Och, dinna say it." He sucked on the tip of her finger.

Regan melted, even as she smiled at him, a big, bright smile resplendent with all the love she felt. "I'll just go and check on Papa."

He looked forlorn and finally turned her hand loose. "All right, you've got ten minutes."

"Thank you, my lord." She shot him a saucy look, gathered up the train of her white gown, and slipped out of the room. Her heart didn't stop pumping madly until she was in the gallery.

Surprisingly the castle was silent now, no drafts, no whispers. It was like losing an old friend. Had the ancient edifice really spoken to her?

It didn't take her long to find the Tender stone and her father. He sat near it, his eyes bright with discovery, a piece of paper in his hand.

"Papa, what are you doing?"

"I've finally deciphered the writing on this stone."

"How long have you been working on this?"

"Up until you came home from the castle so forlorn. Then we decided to move to London, and—"

"Why didn't you say something?"

"It didn't seem all that important what with your heart broken."

"What does it say?" Regan said, her curiosity piqued.

He read from the paper he had translated the writing on, "One intrepid soul shall enter and find the lure of olden tinder. Goodness, truth, and love doth last only in Avalon's grasp. The circle times three, will tell upon thee. Beware Morgan's curse doth prevail, only marriage vows can set it free, and love reign for eternity."

Regan's jaw dropped open. "It doesn't mean what I think it does?"

Seamus nodded. "Indeed. Morgan, the high priestess, must have put a curse on the foundation of Avalon."

"You do not believe in curses."

"If you'd asked me that before I stepped into this castle, I could have answered unequivocally no, but now I'm not so sure."

"So you think the poem is correct."

"Circles of three, my girl. Therein lies the truth. I've checked the foundation of this old place. It's built on three mounds. I'd say Castle Druidhean was erected smack on top of Avalon. After Morgan and Arthur died, this stone must have somehow been looted to another part of the island and brought back when the first Laird MacGregor built here."

"What about the treasure in the circle?" Regan pursed her brows.

"Morgan was smart. Purely a ruse on her part to keep the real Avalon hidden."

"What shall we do?" Regan glanced at her father. He didn't look as delighted as he should.

"We'll let Avalon sleep in peace. Only you and I will know that it exists."

"But your research—"

"A vainglorious endeavor that means nothing to me now. As long as I can see you and Emma happy, my girl, that is all I need of this life." Her father pecked her on the cheek.

"What of Sir Harry Lucas?"

"I'll make sure Lord MacGregor keeps him out and the secret hidden." He wore a self-satisfied grin that stretched from cheek to cheek.

Footsteps made them glance up. Lachlan strode toward them, his kilt fluttering around his knees. When she saw the loving, possessive look in his eyes, the one that she treasured, it made her smile at him.

"So what archeological prizes have you discovered?" Lachlan slipped his arm around Regan's waist and pulled her close.

"None," her father said before she could speak. He glanced around at the walls. "I believe this castle is your treasure, my boy."

"So it is, now that I've found the mistress of it." Lachlan feathered a kiss over Regan's lips.

Love forever and be happy.

Regan pulled back and looked into Lachlan's tender eyes. "Did you say something?"

"Did you?" he asked.

They glanced at Seamus.

He shrugged. "Don't look at me."

All three glanced around at the walls, then they grinned at each other.

Epilogue

Seven years later, Lachlan strode into the dining hall, the sound of laughter making him grin. His three sons, Angus, Royce, and Seamus, sat at the table. Regan was at one end, her head buried behind old issues of the *Times*. The boys were firing globs of eggs at their uncle Quin and giggling when one hit its mark.

Prince and Charlie gobbled what fell to the floor.

Angus fired a well-placed shot at Quin's forehead. "Ah, you've killed me." Quin acted like he was dead and fell out of his chair.

Lachlan smiled inwardly. He knew he should correct his sons and their unruly uncle, but the sound of their jolly voices was a balm to his soul. No doubt he was spoiling them, but he wanted his sons to know what it felt like to be happy and loved.

Seamus, a towheaded two-year-old who had Regan's eyes and determination, was trying to throw his eggs but they kept slipping through his fingers. He was the apple of his grandfather's eye. Any hour of the day he could be found on Mr. Southworth's lap, though the elder Seamus rarely ate with them in the morning; the boys could get a little bumptious—especially with Quin's encouragement.

At three and a half, Royce, the middle child, was the stable one, the conscience of the three. Royce had an introspective, withdrawn quality that couldn't always be teased out of him by his brothers, father, or uncle. He was devoted to Lady Margaret and made the grandame's eyes tear up when he read to her.

Angus, five, was dubbed the instigator of all trouble and master of ceremonies. He could talk his brothers into anything. Of all the boys, Angus was the one Lachlan feared for the most. One day he would try to rule the world.

Angus and Royce resembled Lachlan to a T, with dark hair, black eyes. All three of his sons had the white stripe in their hair.

Regan heard his footsteps and lowered the paper. The sight of his bonny wife smiling at him in that tender and attentive way caused a familiar ache in his chest. He always felt that ache when he looked at her and realized what a lucky man he was.

He bent and kissed her. "Morning."

"It is, isn't it?" Her eyes had a steamy gleam.

He knew she was remembering their lovemaking only hours ago. "Never better." Lachlan didn't hear the boys any longer. He only heard Regan's breath close to his ear.

Quin leaped up. "Come on, race you tae the gallery." He ran out of the room.

"Unfair, Uncle Quin." Angus bounded behind him. "You're bigger." He ran after his uncle, screaming, "Unfair, unfair."

"Down. Go! Go!" Seamus shrieked, glancing toward the door Quin and Angus had left through.

"Wait," Regan cried.

Before Regan or Lachlan could reach him, Royce blurted, "I'll help him." He grabbed Seamus's hand while he crawled down from the heavy oak chair.

Lachlan could see a lot of himself in Royce. Lachlan had always protected Quin in the same way.

The boys ducked beneath the table, as was their custom, then flew out of the room, Seamus dragging his blanket behind Royce and calling, "Wai', wai'."

"Your sons are whirling dervishes." Regan shook her head, grinning.

"My sons? They're half yours. And I wouldna have them any other way." Lachlan kissed her, feeling her soft mouth against his. He knew he would never get enough of his wife. Already he wanted to carry her back to bed.

"Later," she said, reading his mind. "I forgot to tell you Emma will be here next week."

"Tired of London?"

"I believe she misses Quin."

Emma spent half the year in London and the other half on Skye. She had many beaus, but refused to settle upon any of them. Lachlan suspected her devotion to and friendship with Quin kept her from making up her mind. "He'll be thrilled to see her," Lachlan said.

Regan noticed his mother's diary under his arm, and her eyes widened in shock. "Where did you find that?"

"The workmen remodeling Royce's room found it."

"Have you read it?" she asked, searching his eyes for signs of strain.

"All I'm caring to."

"I should have destroyed it."

"You told Dunwoody you had, but you didna. Why?"

"If you recall, I left rather quickly. I was so upset I forgot about burning it." Regan kept watching him with worry in her expression. "Did reading it bring back horrible memories for you?"

"Nay, lass. Now that I have you, the curse of the past can no longer touch me." He kissed her, then he tossed the diary into the fire and wrapped his arms around Regan's waist.

She nuzzled her head against his neck, and together they watched the last traces of pain from his life go up in smoke.

Irish Eyes

From the fiery passion of the Middle Ages, to the
magical charm of Celtic legends, to the timeless allure
of modern Ireland, these brand-new romances will surely
steal your heart away.

❏ **Irish Hope** by Donna Fletcher   0-515-13043-5

❏ **The Irish Devil** by Donna Fletcher   0-515-12749-3

❏ **To Marry an Irish Rogue** by Lisa Hendrix   0-515-12786-8

❏ **Daughter of Ireland** by Sonja Massie   0-515-12835-X

❏ **Irish Moonlight** by Kate Freiman   0-515-12927-5

❏ **Love's Labyrinth** by Anne Kelleher   0-515-12973-9

❏ **Rose in the Mist** by Ana Seymour   0-515-13254-3

❏ **The Irish Bride** by Lynn Bailey   0-515-13014-1

❏ **The Black Swan** by Ana Seymour   0-515-12973-9

❏ **The Highwayman** by Anne Kelleher   0-515-13114-8

TO ORDER CALL:

1-800-788-6262

(Ad #B104)